PRAISE FOR MAGGIE ROBINSON

Just Make Believe
The Third Lady Adelaide Mystery

"Full of secrets to unearth, alter egos, and multiple murders for readers to mull over. Maggie Robinson strikes the right chord between cozy mystery fun and malevolence and murder."

—*Fresh Fiction*

"If you enjoy fast-paced, cozy mysteries with vibrant characters, well-placed humor, and twists and turns that keep you guessing, all set within the madcap 1920s, look no further than Maggie Robinson's Lady Adelaide Mysteries."

—*Romance Dish*

Who's Sorry Now?
The Second Lady Adelaide Mystery

"Rupert's back! And Lady Adelaide still wants to kill him—only he's already dead. If you like a clever mystery, a handsome ghost, and the far-from-bereaved widow who can't find the elusive killer without Rupert's help, *Who's Sorry Now?* is just your cup of English murder."

—Charles Todd, author of the Inspector Ian Rutledge mysteries and the Bess Crawford mysteries

"Readers will enjoy the lively exchanges between Addie, a thoroughly appealing narrator, and her two admirers, exasperating Rupert and smitten Devenand. Fans of witty, romance-infused paranormal historicals will have fun."

—*Publishers Weekly*

Nobody's Sweetheart Now
The First Lady Adelaide Mystery

"A lively debut filled with local color, red herrings, both sprightly and spritely characters, a smidgen of social commentary, and a climactic surprise."

—*Kirkus Reviews*

"Set in England in 1924, this promising series launch…is… frothy fun."

—*Publishers Weekly*

"*Nobody's Sweetheart Now* is a clever, charming mystery that perfectly captures 1920s society. Bored debutantes and rich bankers mingle in Lady Addie's world, which is sure to appeal to fans of Ashley Weaver or Rhys Bowen. Likable characters, a well-paced plot and an intriguing detective make *Nobody's Sweetheart Now* an excellent first entry in this delightful mystery series."

—*Shelf Awareness*

Also by Maggie Robinson

The Lady Adelaide Mysteries
Nobody's Sweetheart Now
Who's Sorry Now?
Just Make Believe

Cotswold Confidential Series
Schooling the Viscount
Seducing Mr. Sykes
Redeeming Lord Ryder

Ladies Unlaced Series
In the Arms of the Heiress
In the Heart of the Highlander
The Reluctant Governess
The Unsuitable Secretary

London List Series
Lord Gray's List
Captain Durant's Countess
Lady Anne's Lover

Courtesan Court Series
Mistress by Mistake
Mistress by Midnight
Mistress by Marriage
Master of Sin
Lords of Passion (anthology)
Improper Gentlemen (anthology)

Novellas
Just One Taste
All through the Night
Once Upon a Christmas

FAREWELL BLUES

FAREWELL BLUES

A LADY ADELAIDE
~ MYSTERY ~

MAGGIE ROBINSON

Poisoned Pen
PRESS

Published by Poisoned Pen Press, an imprint of Sourcebooks
P.O. Box 4410, Naperville, Illinois 60567-4410
(630) 961-3900
sourcebooks.com

Library of Congress Cataloging-in-Publication Data

Names: Robinson, Maggie, author.
Title: Farewell blues : a Lady Adelaide mystery / Maggie Robinson.
Description: Naperville, Illinois : Poisoned Pen Press, [2021] | Series:
   Lady adelaide mysteries ; book 4
Identifiers: LCCN 2020056425 (print) | LCCN 2020056426
   (ebook) | (trade paperback) | (epub)
Subjects: GSAFD: Mystery fiction.
Classification: LCC PS3618.O3326 F37 2021 (print) | LCC PS3618.O3326
   (ebook) | DDC 813/.6--dc23
LC record available at https://lccn.loc.gov/2020056425
LC ebook record available at https://lccn.loc.gov/2020056426

Printed and bound in the United States of America.
SB 10 9 8 7 6 5 4 3 2 1

Sadness just makes me sigh,
I've come to say goodbye,
Altho' I go, I've got those farewell blues.
Those farewell blues make me yearn,
That parting kiss seems to burn.
Farewell, dearie, Someday I will return.
Dreaming of you is sweet,
Someday again we'll meet.

— **"FAREWELL BLUES," WRITTEN BY PAUL MARES,**
LEON RAPPOLO, ELMER SCHOEBEL, 1922

CAST OF CHARACTERS

MOUNT STREET, LONDON
Lady Adelaide Compton (Addie)
Major Rupert Compton, ghost
Lady Cecilia Merrill (Cee), Addie's sister
Beckett, Addie's maid
Constance, Lady Broughton, the Dowager Marchioness
Ian Merrill, Marquess of Broughton, Addie's distant
    half-cousin
Daniel, evening porter
Mike, day porter

RUFFORD HOUSE, MADDOX STREET
Alistair Moreton, 6th Duke of Rufford, the late Duke
    Edmund's son
Elaine Moreton, Duchess of Rufford, Alistair's wife
Lady Gloria Moreton, their older daughter
Mr. Brendan Hickey, her suitor
Stephen Moreton, Marquess of Vere, their son
Lady Grace Moreton, their younger daughter
Lady Penelope von Mayr, Edmund's daughter

Carola von Mayr, her daughter
Johannes von Mayr, her son
Graf Franz von Mayr, Penelope's estranged husband
William, a footman
The volatile French chef
The Southern Belle
Dorothée Baptiste, hostess
Bettie (Elizabeth) Jones, singer
Bobbie (Roberta) Jones, singer
Walt Carter, trombone player

SCOTLAND YARD
Detective Inspector Devenand Hunter
Sergeant Bob Wells
Detective Inspector Phillip Barnes
Joe Lombard, reporter for *The Daily Star*
Bill Neal, driver

Chapter One

Mount Street, London
A Monday morning towards the end of June 1925

Mama was in gaol. Four words Lady Adelaide Compton never expected to string together. In fact, at the moment she could barely think or speak at all.

But the ghost of her dead husband, Rupert, was making up for Addie's baffled brain and syllabic silence. He stormed about the bedroom of her London pied-à-terre, tying and untying his maroon foulard tie in frustration.

Addie had buried him in that tie in just short of a year and a half ago, and she had agonized over which one to choose—her late husband had been something of a clotheshorse, and she was spoilt for choice. She never expected to see the tie again (or Rupert, for that matter) once his coffin was ensconced in the Compton family crypt in Gloucestershire, and she was rather bored with it now. It was taking Rupert a veritable eternity to winkle his way into Heaven, even after performing several good deeds as reparation for his wicked ways on Earth.

"I ask you, Addie, what have I done to deserve this?" he said, not waiting for an answer, for he probably knew exactly what she'd tell him, and at great length, too. "It's not my fault things ended the way they did on Saturday. I was so close to Heaven, sooo close. I could hear the trumpets and practically taste the clouds. Apricot custard with a dash of almond extract, by the way, in case you're interested. Though I imagine yours might taste different. I understand Heaven is an individualized experience, but at this rate I'll never find out! It's so unfair! I solved your last case, didn't I? Well, most of it. You would have been rid of me forever if your bloo—uh, blessed mother did not go and shoot the Duke of Rufford."

This stirred Addie to speech. "She didn't. She couldn't have."

Rupert collapsed on her bed. "Well, I suppose not, if I've been summoned to your side again. Damn it, Addie! I know I was a cad when I was alive, but you must give me some credit for improving! Can't you put in a good word somehow?"

"To whom would I speak?" asked Addie, genuinely curious. She said her bedtime prayers just like anybody else. *Someone* should have picked up the fact by now that she wished to be rid of her husband for good.

"I only wish I knew. The hierarchy is still a bit of a puzzle to me." He tucked all her pillows under his head, and Addie worried about hair oil residue on her silk pillowcases. How could she explain that to her maid, Beckett? Addie had lived like a nun for years now, and her one attempt to change that status had ended in humiliation.

"I'll never be perfect," Rupert continued. Addie knew an egregious understatement when she heard one. "Do you know what those rugmaker chappies do in Arabia? They deliberately make a mistake in the patterns because only Allah is without flaw."

Addie filed that nugget away. Despite the best efforts of her teachers at Cheltenham Ladies' College, she had resisted becoming a bluestocking upon graduation at seventeen—and after—as her mother had always told her men didn't like women who were smarter than they were.

And now look where Mama was!

Addie hoped Mr. Hunter could get her out as soon as possible. Imagining Mama behind bars was completely beyond her. Lady Broughton had been the properest of people for fifty-two years. Addie thought even as a child her mother knew precisely what to do under all circumstances. Instead of a primer, she'd probably learned to read with a Debrett's. As a toddler, she might have known the order of precedence at a dinner party. Which fork to use. How to address a duke, which must have come in handy now that Mama was all grown up and having an affair with one.

Addie picked up her own Debrett's and searched the *Rs*. Rufford. There were inches of titles, political appointments, and clubs for the man. Along with several far-flung properties, the principal family seat was so far up in Northumberland it was practically in Scotland, and he lived in Maddox Street when in Town.

She had never met him, had never even heard of him until her sister, Cecilia, arrived in her pin curls and pajamas at Compton Chase yesterday morning to tell her their mother had been arrested. It was true that Mama was a fair shot, even though she was so nearsighted, but then the duke must have been quite close at hand.

It was galling to think her mother was having more success with a man than she was. But then, success was moot if the object of her mother's affection was dead.

"Tell me what you know about the crime," Addie said to Rupert. According to Cee, Mama was found—wearing only a bloodstained peignoir—in a suite at the Ritz, standing over the body of the dead duke. To make matters worse, she held a pistol.

Her very own, with the Broughton coat of arms engraved on the handle. Addie's father gifted it to her mother on their twenty-fifth wedding anniversary, which showed great confidence that he didn't expect her to shoot him. One thing led to another, and Lady Broughton and her gun were carted away by the police.

Rupert sat up and sniffed. "Why do you presume I have any of the pertinent facts? It's not as if I had much preparation. I've gone straight from the frying pan into the fire."

"Do you know anything at all about Rufford, then?" If Rupert was here, he must make himself useful somehow.

"I did meet him a few times. He was a good thirty years older than I, so that would make him somewhere in his sixties. He is—was—a widower twice over, with a child from each union. I knew his daughter, Penny, better than his son, Alistair, and no, before you ask, I did not know her in the Biblical sense. She's got a face like—well, I won't insult her; she's a good egg. The poor thing must be mourning—she was very fond of her papa. Not so fond of her older brother, or his wife, Elaine, who's an established beauty, and rather a bitch, if I may say so without getting struck by lightning."

Addie found Penny on the page. "'Daughters living—Penelope Ariadne. m. Graf Franz von Mayr.' A German?" she asked. That must have made the family's Christmas dinners interesting during the war years.

"Austrian. You mustn't mix the two countries up—they may speak the same language, but that's as far as it goes. National pride on both sides, too much of it, to be frank. Penny and Franz are separated, and the children are here with her. They're hardly children anymore, though—they must be eighteen at least."

"'Sons living—Alistair James Moreton, Marquess of Vere.' He's the sixth duke now, I suppose." She didn't know him, either, or his wife. "Was Rufford, uh, nice?"

"Who, Alistair? Wangled out of the war like a treasonous weasel. He's a complete prat."

"No, no. His father." The man must have attracted Addie's mother in some significant way—she'd been true to the memory of her late husband for five years. Addie was convinced that before this secret affair, her mother had never even kissed another man except for Herbert Merrill, Marquess of Broughton. She'd married at eighteen, and Addie arrived soon after, her sister, Cee, six years after that. Alas, there was no son to carry on the marquessate, and Addie's distant cousin, Ian, succeeded to the title.

Rupert shrugged. "He was all right. He was a duke. You know the type. Dictatorial. Dismissive of the hoi polloi. Thought his own sh—*uh*, excrement was not odoriferous. I'm surprised he gave me the time of day."

That sounded nothing like Addie's father. He'd been a genial sportsman who got along with just about every living creature, especially his dogs and horses.

"I wonder how long they'd been seeing each other," Addie ruminated. "She never breathed a word."

"Well, she wouldn't, would she? This is your mother we're talking about. Her standards are impossibly high, and you've been terrified of her all your life. She wasn't about to admit she was off on a dirty weekend."

More like a dirty week. Addie's mother left the Dower House last Monday and had not been heard from since.

"I wonder what's keeping Mr. Hunter." He, Mama's solicitor, Mr. Stockwell, and a criminal defense barrister engaged for the purpose were negotiating her freedom right this very minute.

"Red tape. Forms in quadruplicate. Perhaps he'll have to leave a kidney behind for collateral."

"Don't joke, Rupert."

"Who says I'm joking? The Metropolitan Police Force will not want to look as though they're playing favorites. If your mother was not a marchioness, there'd be no hope of getting her out of the pokey. As it is—" Rupert shrugged.

"As it is what?"

"Don't bite my head off, but I don't believe you can count on your favorite detective for her release. There might be sinister forces at work."

This was not at all what Addie wanted to hear, especially the "favorite detective" part. "What do you mean? She's already been there a whole day and night!"

"Vere—Rufford now—is an ugly customer. But he knows everyone, and is a particular friend of the Prince of Wales. Don't get your hopes up."

"Why haven't I heard of these people?" Addie asked, beyond frustrated. "It's not as if dukes grow on trees as they do in romance novels."

"You've been out of the country, buried in the country, and before that, there was a war on. Before *that*, you were a virginal innocent, a veritable child. Penny's a bit older than you are, and she went off to Vienna as a very young bride—she didn't even have a debut. It was quite a scandal at the time; Franz basically kidnapped her, though she went quite willingly. He's a handsome devil, quite tall, piercing blue eyes, blond curls, just the sort who looks good in a uniform and even better out of it. You were probably still at school when he lured her away."

Addie had no recollection of such an event, and Debrett's would certainly not be forthcoming about it. "Weren't her parents upset? I thought you said she was close to her father." Addie would never have dared to defy the Marquess and Marchioness of Broughton in that fashion.

"Her mother was dead. And you know what they say—lust conquers all," Rupert said. If anyone knew that, he would.

Though sometimes it didn't last, which was apparently the case with Penelope Ariadne.

"I take it her marriage is troubled."

"Isn't everyone's?" sighed Rupert. "I believe Franz is in Town trying to patch things up. But that's really all I can tell you of the Moreton family. I've been out of the social set lately, as you well know."

Bah. What was the point of a spiritual guide when the spirit couldn't guide? Addie didn't see how Rupert could help them at all. But he *was* here. And he'd been proven to be obliging in the past, sneaking around undetected, eavesdropping, gathering information, and stopping murderers in their tracks. If he could find the duke's real killer, she might even kiss him again before she sent him on his way to redemption.

Chapter Two

The commissioner had been adamant. Constance Merrill, Lady Broughton, was going nowhere until she arrived shackled before a judge in a courtroom for her trial, and no matter how many fancy solicitors and barristers turned up banging on her bars, that was that.

She'd been caught red-handed at the Ritz holding the murder weapon, her exalted family's monogrammed device engraved onto the butt. There was the victim's blood on the hem of her nightgown, to boot. What more could a jury ask for?

True, she'd said immediately that she didn't shoot the duke but was trying to empty the chamber of bullets to prevent further catastrophe, but that's what they all said. What was a bit of perjury compared to murder? Dev didn't relish explaining all this to Lady Adelaide Compton, so he sent the lawyers on ahead to Mount Street while he hid in his office at the Yard and pored over the report.

Everything was straightforward.

And grim.

Sunday morning, a room service waiter had stumbled onto the scene—literally, as he'd tipped the cart and spilled its contents when he saw the dowager marchioness armed, and possibly still dangerous, standing by the body in the sitting room. The poor fellow had instructions to deliver breakfast at eight o'clock. When there was no reply to his discreet knock, he used a passkey to enter. His panicked shouts alerted two chambermaids gossiping in the hall, who called the house detective, who called the Metropolitan Police Force.

When Dev's colleagues arrived, they met a soggy sea of coffee and cream, crushed strawberries, croissants, and embossed butter pats to step over. Lady Broughton was seated on a sofa, the house detective training his own pistol on her. The hotel doctor and the assistant manager were also present, presumably representing the interests of the Ritz and its late guest.

Apart from her original claim of innocence to the waiter, Lady Broughton refused to comment further. It was too bad this excellent self-preservation instinct had not prevented her from picking up the gun. *Her* gun.

It looked very bad for her.

Her lawyers were unsuccessful in quashing the story. Today's morning papers were already having the time of their lives competing for lurid headlines. DUKE DEAD, MARCHIONESS MURDERESS? RITZ RENDEZVOUS ENDS RUFFORD. TOFF TOPPED, MISTRESS STOPPED. The mildest was: SOCIETY SCANDAL OF THE SEASON. More like the decade, maybe the century, Dev thought. It wasn't every day a duke got gunned down in his Italian paisley pajamas.

When he had spoken with Lady Broughton last night in her cell, she'd been pale but composed. Even in an ugly gray prison-issued dress, with her fair curly hair scraped back, she exuded elegance. Dev had found her extremely formidable in their previous encounter last summer, and he continued to do so despite the current circumstances.

Shocking him to his socks, she told him she entrusted him with her life and was willing to engage him privately to find the proof of her innocence, sparing no expense. If he was agreeable, she had instructed her solicitor to advance him an absolutely outrageous sum to assist him with his inquiries. Dev had swallowed hard, and she took his silence as consent.

According to her, she was awakened by what must have been the shot. Thinking it was a car's engine backfiring outside in the street, she drifted back to sleep, untroubled by the fact that Rufford was no longer beside her. He liked to rise early and read *The Times* from cover to cover. The newspaper was placed outside their door every morning around six, and had been strewn across the suite's dining table when she awoke. She noticed the disordered paper before she saw the dead duke, who had been lying facedown on the fitted carpet. It was unlike him to be so cavalier with the finance section.

Lady Broughton turned him over immediately and *just* stopped herself from fainting. The gun was near his left hand. *Her* gun.

She'd looked at Dev with some defiance at these words. Why shouldn't she have one? One never knew nowadays. Look at all the troublesome people her older daughter had encountered lately.

Dev rather thought she might be including him in this mangy lot.

One needed to be prepared for any twentieth-century eventuality, she continued. And it was a sentimental gift from her late husband, who always sought to protect her. She usually carried it in her purse, although she could not recollect the exact time she'd seen it nestled between her monogrammed handkerchief and her reading spectacles, which she never wore on principle unless she was signing a legal document.

Her vanity was probably her only fault.

She presumed the gun had been in her bag—why would it

not be? Lady Broughton had not left the suite except to get her hair done at the hotel's hairdresser every morning, and usually did not bring her handbag down with her. The duke kept several engagements during their stay, business meetings and such, but mostly they'd been alone in the privacy of their rooms.

Dev noted she blushed at this confession.

Her first thought was that Edmund had killed himself, although it seemed highly out of character. In her experience during their "friendship"—Dev heard the quotation marks—the man was not one to feel melancholy. He was straightforward and rather old-school, with standards that might be a trifle severe for the decadent decade they were living through but were a welcome relief to her. As far as she knew, he had unexceptional relations with his family, all of them living under one roof most of the year in a Northumberland castle.

However, one of his grandsons troubled him to a degree. The boy was seeing an unsuitable woman, but that's as much as Lady Broughton knew—the duke never explained or complained except when it came to politics, and then he became a bit of a bore, though she disliked speaking ill of the dead. She had no interest in government, although she did exercise her recently acquired right to vote, for all the good it did.

Dev explained it was impossible for him to quit his job, but he would do everything in his power to see that her case was handled fairly. The trouble was, it wasn't *his* case. He'd been allowed to borrow the file from Detective Inspector Phillip Barnes's desk only as a courtesy.

In Phil's opinion, Constance, Lady Broughton, was as guilty as sin, and he'd investigated at least thrice as many murders as Dev in his long career. He was close to retirement age, and now could expect to go out with a bang with the *Society Scandal of the Season*. He warned Dev not to interfere, and it would be tricky indeed to get at the kind of information he needed to clear Lady Adelaide's mother without stepping on departmental toes.

Dev copied the limited information into his notebook. The only fingerprints on the gun belonged to the dowager marchioness. The bullet retrieved during the autopsy matched those Lady Broughton had removed. The duke was definitely dead and couldn't assist with the inquiries.

Dev had no alternative. He'd have to send Lady Adelaide into harm's way again to get to the truth. She could gain entry into to the duke's circle, where he could not. It would be beyond awkward ingratiating herself with his family and friends, but if anyone could do it, she could. They could work out a line of questioning which wouldn't appear too obvious.

He hoped.

In his spare time, he'd discreetly explore other possibilities. Trouble was, he had no spare time.

Perhaps he should ask for a leave of absence. Lord knows, he'd taken no vacation in years, not even after he was shot in March.

Well, shot wasn't quite accurate—there had been very little blood, just a massive bruise on his chest that took a month to heal. But this weekend had taken a physical—as well as mental—toll on him. Apart from what he suspected was a dislocated shoulder, he wondered if he broke a rib when he fell off his horse on Saturday.

Fell wasn't quite accurate, either—he'd been shot at again in pursuit of a murderer and tumbled like a trick rider in an American rodeo show.

Keeping company with Lady Adelaide was proving to be injurious to his health.

Dev wasn't one to complain, either; his father was a shining example as to how one should conduct oneself at Scotland Yard. His work ethic had been ferocious, and was hard to live up to. But perhaps Dev should ask for time off to mend properly.

Who could imagine he'd be grateful to dodge bullets?

He would turn in the report on the Fernald case to his superiors today and apply for some respite. Let them think he was going away for a little while. As long as he kept his head down, there was every chance no one in the Yard would notice his interference, although he was hard to miss in the city's sea of white faces. His Indian heritage would always announce him.

Two hours later, after a quick visit to the department quack, he had a taped-up torso, an arm in a sling, and his request for medical leave approved. Dev now had an entire two weeks to discover what happened between the Duke of Rufford and the Dowager Marchioness of Broughton, as long as he continued to ice his shoulder regularly and not fall off any more horses.

This much he knew already: at some time between six and eight o'clock in the morning, the duke died. Possibly during their week at the Ritz, someone removed Lady Broughton's gun from her handbag, maybe even the duke himself. She might think the man was not suicidal, but who really knew the inner thoughts of anyone?

Though how the man wiped his prints off the gun once he shot himself gave Dev serious pause. Perhaps in the picking up of the gun, Lady Broughton somehow obliterated them. There was plenty of room for error in the lab, but Dev knew he couldn't ask for the weapon to be retested. He was without his usual resources and recourses.

His sergeant, Bob Wells, stuck his head in the open doorway. "What's this I hear about you breaking your shoulder?"

News traveled fast. "Not broken, just not quite where it should be. Now, to be sure, a rib *is* broken. Maybe two. I'm going to take a couple of weeks off to get back to fighting form. Hold down the fort for me, would you?"

"I'll try. What about Lady Adelaide?"

Dev closed the file in front of him. He was late returning it and didn't want his head bitten off by old Phil. "What about her?"

Bob colored as he was wont to do when he was about to broach something delicate. Poor sap, his wife must know his every thought. "That's her mother's case file, isn't it?"

"It is indeed, and I'd appreciate it if you could return it to Detective Inspector Barnes."

"What are you going to do about it?"

Dev looked at him, hoping he projected innocence. "I? Why, nothing. I'm going on holiday."

Chapter Three

Mount Street

Addie's tea tasted bitter, but she didn't even bother to reprimand Beckett. Bitter tea was the very least of her worries. Cee had switched to a stiff gin and tonic after one sip—actually two gin and tonics, bolted down far too quickly—and had gone to lie down in the guest room with a cold wet washcloth across her forehead.

Cee was taking Mama's incarceration badly. The gossipy newspapers which she usually relished splashed the family name on their front pages, unsubstantiated conjectures littering paragraph after paragraph, *just* skirting the libel laws. Even Rupert was resurrected in print, his wartime heroics padding what was the basically dull Broughton history up to now. Addie tossed the papers in the trash. These articles were not to be placed in her scrapbook.

Cee hadn't said as much, but her marital prospects were now doomed. No wonder she was prostrate in bed. Who would want to marry a murderess's daughter? Not that Mama had actually killed anyone, of that Addie was sure. But Mr. Stockwell and his associate, Lord Barry (Lord Barry the barrister, amusing under other circumstances), had been unable to pull strings to get her released, and a scandalous trial was guaranteed unless Devenand Hunter could solve the crime.

Addie had expected the detective inspector to accompany the legal team on their earlier visit but was disappointed. She'd taken some pains with her toilette, although that felt foolish. Mama was in gaol, after all. Who cared if her lipstick matched her embroidered voile dress? (It did, a raspberry pink.) She certainly could not leave the flat—newspapermen were camped outside in the street despite the porter's every effort to expel them.

Earlier, Addie had locked the windows and closed the drapes in case an enterprising journalist decided to climb up the building's facade or trained a lens from below. Now she was forced to turn on the electric lights even if daylight would last for several more hours.

It was a shame she was missing a lazy summer evening in the country; she could do with a spot of quiet and relaxation after recent events at Fernald Hall. Poisonings and fatal falls were exhausting. But she mustn't complain. *She* was still alive, and her mother needed her.

Taking the picked-over tea tray into the white-tiled kitchen, Addie found Beckett sitting in front of a fan and reading a movie magazine. The kitchen windows and shades were closed, too, making the small room stuffy.

The maid jumped up, her starched cap askew. "I was just about to fetch that, Lady A," she said, obviously fibbing. The film industry was near and dear to Beckett's heart, and very little could deter her from reading about upcoming productions or seeing the latest offering at the cinema.

The vultures on the street might stop her, though, unless she snuck out. Resourceful Beckett was perfectly capable of climbing the back-garden brick wall or down a drainpipe to freedom if it meant she could sit in the dark with her idols.

"It's all right, Beckett. Cleaning up will give me something to distract me." And wonder where Inspector Hunter was.

Satisfied that she was not needed, Beckett returned to her article. Addie's mother thought Beckett was too brazen by half, and Addie suspected she was right. Which of her friends would do the washing up while their servants lolled at the table reading Hollywood rubbish? But Beckett was loyal, honest to a fault, and great fun.

Addie wrapped the sandwiches in a damp towel, put the left-over biscuits back into their tin, and filled the dishpan with hot water and washing powder. She eschewed Beckett's rubber gloves and sank her fingers into the sudsy water, manicure be damned.

It was times like this that made her feel adrift—she had no occupation to divert her. Apart from Beckett's occasional harmless insubordination, Addie was very well cared for from the moment she woke up to the time she removed her mascara with Pond's Cold Cream. Breakfast was served. Beds were made. Baths were drawn, towels warmed. Addie's couture clothes were cleaned, pressed, and discreetly scented, and her shoes polished to brilliance. Under Beckett's expert hands, her obstreperous curly hair was brushed into some semblance of civilization several times daily. Dinner was served, pillows were fluffed, and coverlets turned down. All she needed to do was allow herself to be still and get treated like a doll.

It was all wrong somehow.

But as her old friend Lucas Waring had recently pointed out, she certainly couldn't get a *job*. She'd be robbing someone who truly needed it. Addie's assets were more than she could ever spend in this lifetime, despite her generosity to worthy charities. Her father settled an enormous amount upon her at her marriage, and she was the recipient of bountiful bequests from a great-aunt and godfather. Rupert had been delighted to help her spend it, but even he couldn't run through it, no matter how many automobiles he acquired or mistresses he maintained.

She never considered donating to women prisoners before, but after her brief visit to Mama last evening, she found the conditions appalling. Poor Mama! How could she possibly stay in that ghastly place until a trial? The whole building smelled of cabbage, despair, and desperation. Addie's mother was a most fastidious woman who might resort to murder if it could free her from her grim and grimy little cell.

Well, there was no logic in that thought. Clearly Addie was losing her mind.

Dishes done, she left Beckett staring into the icebox contemplating what to serve the Merrill sisters for supper. With the press outside, there was no chance to visit the shops. Beckett ordered the bare minimum this morning to be delivered in hopes that the family would soon return to Gloucestershire. Addie doubted Cee would be hungry; she knew she wasn't. One of Fitz's dry dog biscuits would suit as well as anything.

Fitz wouldn't need them—he was at Compton Chase under the watchful eye of the gardener, Jack Robertson, probably chasing butterflies and the stray cat that made its home in the converted stables. Addie wondered if she should name the feline or whether it would move on to a better, dogless situation. She was generally fond of animals, though after recent events, horses made her a touch nervous. Her stables now housed Rupert's car collection, seven gleaming mechanical beasts.

Or perhaps six. The Rolls was pretty badly damaged in her latest misadventure. Its problems were nothing compared to her mother's, however.

"You simply don't respect my cars, do you? Look how they've facilitated your investigations, you ungrateful girl."

Addie sat down abruptly on a sofa. Her ghostly husband joined her, and Addie tucked a protective flame-stitch pillow between them. "You are reading my mind again, Rupert. You know I don't like it, but then when have you ever obeyed my wishes?"

"Tut tut. It was *you* who was meant to honor and obey, as I recall."

Fat chance of that ever again. *Obey* was a four-letter word as far as Addie was concerned. "Ancient history. Why are you here? Don't you have some detecting to do?" She kept her voice down in case Cee woke up or Beckett decided to dust something in the drawing room, admittedly a doubtful undertaking at this point in the day.

"You can't very well expect me to infiltrate a women's prison. It wouldn't be seemly. Even *I* have some standards."

"Of course not! Mama has no answers anyhow—if she did, she would not ask for Detective Inspector Hunter's assistance."

"About that—she's going to get it. The fellow has a dislocated something-or-other and is on a little sabbatical, so he can snoop about. He has a sling and looks rather dashing, if I must say so."

Rupert was the snooper. And Inspector Hunter was generally dashing, sling or no sling, Addie thought ruefully. "You've been to Scotland Yard?" Nothing was too outrageous for him. Even the police were not safe from his predations.

"Briefly. Looked over the report, too, left about where anyone with eyes could see it. Careless of them, but convenient for me. Cut and dried, according to the old copper in charge of the case. Your poor mama—she doesn't have a friend there. The man's a secret Bolshevik. Off with her head, toffs to the tumbrel. *Vive la révolution* and all that rubbish. I'm off to Maddox Street for the cocktail hour. Maybe someone will let something slip."

Under normal circumstances, the idea of Rupert invading a house in mourning would disgust her. But needs must. She had plans to visit herself tomorrow. It was too bad she didn't drink much, for she'd need some Dutch courage to confront the duke's family. Although in her case, if she imbibed, she'd only fall asleep before the fun began. Addie really did not have a head for alcohol.

"Don't do anything awful."

"What, do you expect me to rattle my chains and moan convincingly over the martinis? I'm too evolved for that nonsense."

Rupert was attempting to be a changed man. Rather too late for their marriage, but good for solving crimes.

Better late than never.

Chapter Four

Monday evening, Maddox Street

Rupert felt distinctly audacious. He slipped in through the kitchen when the French chef tossed away his cigarette and grudgingly let a fidgety, fluffy, yapping dog out the tradesmen's door to do its business. For an instant the little animal stopped in its tracks mid-bark, somehow alert to Rupert's alien presence, but it had a mission. It soon continued up the steps to the tidy fenced garden and lifted its leg on a red rosebush. A male, then, and, like his wife's pet, not one hundred percent susceptible to ghosts, thank goodness. Nor was the chef. With his own accented bark, he turned to the assembled people in the kitchen and made his Gallic will known.

Rupert could have simply popped up in the drawing room, but it was always amusing to wiggle through barriers and get the true lay of the land. One could learn a lot from the private spaces in a household. Servants were always particularly useful in revealing the peccadilloes of their so-called betters.

The kitchen was a hotbed of activity, and devilishly hot to boot. Several damp-browed maids were busy whipping, pounding, and stuffing things at a wide pine table. If the family was too devastated by the duke's death to eat, it would not be for lack of effort on the kitchen staff's part.

An array of rigidly graduated copper pots gleamed on the shelves behind them. He tiptoed by the chef, who smelled of tobacco, garlic, and sweat. Rupert was transported back to wartime country villages where he was feted by the locals for his aerial exploits. A lot of wine and willing women were involved in those evenings, but there was no point in wasting time reminiscing. The sooner he could help Addie and his mother-in-law, the better off they'd all be.

He never gave serious thought to the Afterlife when he was alive and carousing his way across the Continent. Death was his constant companion in the air and on the ground, and no amount of philosophizing could make sense of any of it, or change his future.

As more and more of his comrades were lost, he became a bit fatalistic. But to his surprise, Rupert survived and thrived, only to encounter that obdurate Cotswold stone wall one icy night in peacetime. With him in the irretrievably crumpled Hispano Suiza was his French mistress, who certainly had not smelled of garlic and sweat. She did enjoy a postcoital Sobranie, however.

He'd been a rotten husband, so his demise was no doubt warranted. Addie had been a brick putting up with him for as long as she had, though towards the end he became expert at ducking airborne objects. To be fair, the poor girl wasn't a saint and was totally justified in her irritation. The Fellow Upstairs was now teaching him the Lesson of All Lessons, making him regret every minute spent in other women's beds.

Once, he had had a perfectly good wife he failed to appreciate, a full life, a handsome inherited estate from his dear old granny, eight magnificent cars—

Such delicious speed. Rupert missed driving. Flying, too. He'd never felt so alive. When he *was* alive. Now he was in this hellish limbo, a secret errand boy for Scotland Yard who would never get credit for his sleuthing. It was unfair, but then, so were a great many things. He wouldn't snivel—it was time to get busy.

He followed a footman carrying a tray of nibbles up a set of carpeted stairs. Rupert had been in enough grand houses to note that even in the servants' area, no expense had been spared in the last century. No bare painted floors or plain whitewashed walls here—this corridor would impress the fussiest fan of craftsmanship. Rufford—or probably one of his wives—had raided the family coffers for ornate William Morris wallpapers and golden oak handrails. A total waste of money, in Rupert's opinion, but then he preferred engines to embellishments.

He heard the family before he saw them. Several people in the room were shouting, and he nearly crashed into the footman's back as the fellow stopped short of entering. A servant in a good household was never expected to knock, but in this case a hammer might be required to quash the ruckus within.

"You'll do it if you know what's good for you, boy! No son of mine will behave in such a disgraceful manner!"

Hmm. Probably insufferable Alistair, lording it about, now that he was head of the household. Rupert knew the new duke could teach a class on achieving the pinnacle of disgrace if he were so inclined. Whatever his son was up to wouldn't hold a candle to his father's youthful and current middle-aged exploits.

"That's just it, Father. I'm not a boy. And you can't tell me who to love!" There was a squeak to the voice, belying the words. What was his name? It began with an *S*. Or a soft *C*. Sebastian? Cyrus? Rupert paid very little attention to children, although all of Alistair's heirs were well out of the nursery. He'd prepared himself before arriving at Maddox Street by reading Addie's Debrett's, but his memory, like so much of post-life, was failing him.

"Give it a rest. You barely have sufficient whiskers to shave."

This from a scornful, slightly accented female voice. Rupert's hand went involuntarily to the place where his mustache should be. Addie didn't like it anymore, if she ever had, so he'd gotten rid of it.

"Love! Are you completely mad? You wouldn't know love if it bit you on the arse! I am serious, Stephen. I won't have it, do you hear?" Alistair bellowed. "We have enough on our plate with your bloody grandfather shot dead by some floozy at the Ritz."

Floozy! Lady Broughton would faint if she heard herself described in such a fashion. It was a good thing his mother-in-law wasn't here, or Alistair would be the beneficiary of her wickedly sharp tongue.

Or, even better, she might shoot *him*.

"If the newspaper people catch wind of your idiocy with this… this *female*, we'll be laughingstocks. The family can only bear so much. First Gloria, now you. Think of your mother!"

There was a soft murmur of protest. Elaine. Everything about her was deceptively soft, Rupert recalled—soft auburn curls, soft brown eyes, soft white skin, soft plush lips, and a very soft and substantial bosom, which was now out of fashion. Rupert could not approve of the craze of binding one's breasts and chopping off one's hair to resemble an adolescent boy, but no one asked him for his opinion anymore. Even Addie had succumbed—not to the binding part, but much to his dismay, she'd cut her lovely golden hair.

Elaine was older than Rupert, but that hadn't stopped them from engaging in an affair before the war. Her beauty was initially dazzling, but Rupert soon discovered it wasn't even skin deep. No wonder her husband sought extensive comfort elsewhere.

The pair of them deserved each other.

Focus, Rupe, old boy, focus. He was missing something.

"Please, Alistair. Surely we can talk of something else before dinner. Fighting won't bring back Papa."

Ah, someone who was truly soft, and softhearted. Penny.

"Who wants the old fool back? Having a dalliance at his age. It's disgusting."

So much for filial feeling. Rupert would bet his last shilling that Alistair would continue his Lothario ways when he was sixty-five, as well, if he could still perform. He sidled around the uncertain red-faced footman and entered the drawing room.

It, too, was decorated in Arts and Crafts glory, stained-glass lamps and textured pillows littered about. The family sat in a circle on uncomfortable-looking brown wood furniture, quite at odds with the elegant Georgian facade of the house. A repeating painted stencil with the family's coat of arms ran along the crown molding, as if they might forget who they were without a visual reminder.

Dark-haired Alistair hadn't changed much—his pale gray eyes a little too close together, his lips thin and currently sneering. Some might call him handsome, but Rupert was not among them.

"Alistair! Have some respect!"

As usual, Penny looked as if she'd gotten dressed in the dark, which did not help her plainness. Her brother got what looks there were in the family, where she was a pallid copy of him, with a heavier, more masculine jaw. Black did not suit her, and she was wearing a lot of it between stockings, shoes, dress, shawl, and an unfortunate jet bandeau which lay crooked on her brow.

"Respect has to be earned. What did the prig ever do to deserve it? I, for one, am glad I'll never have to listen to another one of his bloody lectures."

"At least he can't threaten to cut us out of the will anymore," an auburn-haired girl said with a sour smile. "Such an old bore. We got the last laugh, didn't we, Papa?" The poisoned apple did not fall far from the tree; this must be Alistair's delightful daughter, Gloria.

"Where in hell is William? I'm famished."

This was the welcome cue for the footman, who cleared his throat and stepped into the room with his laden tray. He set it on a hammered brass table, where it was pounced upon by Alistair and a pretty young woman who looked to be about eighteen. This must be Penny's daughter, Carola. She had her mother's coloring, but her skin tone was warmer and her eyes bluer, reflecting her father's Austro-Hungarian heritage. Her twin brother, Johannes—John to the family—didn't move, and was studying his watch as though he could speed up time and make a quick escape.

Their father, the graf, was not present. Rupert wondered how Edmund's death would affect Penny's reconciliation with her husband. The duke had never approved of her marriage, and Franz's previous entreaties to reunite his family had fallen on deaf ears for years.

He was in London now. Had Franz von Mayr pulled the trigger? It would be a neat solution to blame the murder on a foreigner—an enemy combatant, at that. Franz had distinguished himself on the Italian front fighting with the Central Powers despite having an English wife. As soon as the armistice was declared, Penny had taken the children and fled back to her father's house for a long-overdue visit.

For all the years of her marriage, poor Penny had never learned a word of German and was fed up with feeling like a stranger in her own home. Being swept off her feet at sixteen had not resulted in the same fervent feelings at thirty-six, for here she still was, six years on in Britain, her handsome husband billeted at the Savoy.

Like young John, the rest of the family avoided the hors d'oeuvres, but they were equipped with amber-filled glasses. Stephen, Lord Vere now, looked neither old enough to drink or shave, a mangy copper mustache on his pale face. His sister Gloria, a less-endowed—or perhaps more bound—version of her mother, was seated next to a striking young man Rupert had never seen before in his travels through society. A beau, probably— Gloria had grown up from the last time Rupert had clapped eyes on her. The baby of the family, Grace, was probably up in the schoolroom, champing at the bit to get to come downstairs and drink alcohol in a year or two.

Alistair's children were slightly older than Penny's. Judging from their unsuitably bright clothing and the girls' lavish makeup, all of them aspired to be Bright Young People, mourning be damned. Rupert had quite enough of their sort two cases ago, but suspected he'd be dragged into some foul nightclub to spy soon.

There was, apparently, no rest for the wicked.

Chapter Five

Mount Street

It was late, but not too late, Dev hoped. He was gratified to see lights on behind the drawn shades in the front room of Lady Adelaide's Mount Street digs. There was still a clot of reporters on the sidewalk, a few of whom he recognized, so they would probably recognize him, too. Dev pulled down his hat and edged down the alley to the mansion flat's service entrance.

He rang the bell, and after what seemed like forever, he heard a creative curse and the slide of a bolt.

The porter opened the door, looking pugnacious. "Oi, you've got yer nerve, bothering decent people. Go away or I'll call the rozzers."

Dev was prepared with his warrant card. "I am the rozzers. Lady Adelaide Compton is expecting me."

The man squinted at the card. "How do I know this is real? I wouldn't put anything past you lot. Got yer own printing presses, don't you? You could pass me a bloody maharaja's calling card, and how would I know different, eh?"

"I've seen you before in the building, so surely you've seen me. I've visited Lady Adelaide on several occasions," Dev said patiently. On the whole, he approved of this fellow's protective nature. A woman living alone might attract all sorts of male attention, and any discerning maharaja would be smitten.

"Maybe I have. Why are you here? Going to arrest her, too?"

"Not this evening." Dev debated whether he should admit that the Dowager Marchioness of Broughton asked him to prove her innocence, but decided against it. The man might trot right across the street to inform the press despite his apparent belligerence towards them. "Would you please call her on the house phone and announce my presence?"

The porter looked again at his name on the card. "Detective Inspector Hunter," Dev said, in case the man was illiterate.

"Hunter? Huh. That don't sound foreign."

Dev was used to such comments and held his tongue. He followed the man through a darkish hallway to a very tidy office, its glass door looking out into the marble lobby. Dev had interrupted dinner; a cup of tea, the steam still rising, and a half-eaten sandwich lay on a corner of the desk. Fish paste, by the smell of it. Dev suppressed a shudder. He ate most anything, but there he drew the line.

A switchboard sat against a dull green wall. "Sit, if you like, while I ring up my lady."

That was as much of a concession as Dev was about to get. He remained standing, however, while the porter adjusted the speaking tube, pulled out a cord, and inserted it into the proper hole.

"Uh, good evening, Lady Adelaide. This is Daniel, the night porter." He paused. "Very well, thank you, my lady. And yourself?... Terrible business about your poor ma. Don't you worry. I'll see to it that no one bothers you. And speaking of which, there's a strange man here who says he's from Scotland Yard. It never pays to be too careful, so I stopped him right quick before he could go up."

An utter lie. Old Daniel was making himself a hero at Dev's expense, but once again, his tongue remained in place. "Hunter, he says." Daniel glanced over at Dev. "That's right. Tall and dark. Don't know about handsome... All right, I'll send him by your private staircase... Aye, I'll tell him. Good evening to you, my lady. Tomorrow is another day."

With these philosophical words, Daniel pulled the plug. "She says she'll meet you at the kitchen door. When you get ready to leave, come find me. You can go out the same way you came in, and I'll lock the door behind you. Hush-hush, what? Wouldn't want the snoops to get wind of your visit."

Too right. "Thank you, Daniel. I shouldn't be long."

Unfortunately. There would be nothing Dev would like better than to spend what was left of the evening in Lady Adelaide's company.

He knew better, but it was difficult to convince his heart he should maintain his distance. He came pretty close yesterday to saying goodbye for good, though. He'd been stoic, marching off without a backwards glance until her sister burst out of the French doors onto the terrace.

One shouldn't wish for dead bodies to keep piling up so Dev could continue his acquaintance with Lady Adelaide—he wasn't a monster. But damned if he could see a way to carry out a friendship with a marquess's daughter without them.

Hell. Friends. He wasn't fooling himself for a minute. Dev shook his head at his stupidity and followed the porter through a labyrinthian hall to a set of stairs. To his right was an iron-grilled door that presumably led to Lady Adelaide's tiny brick-walled garden.

"Up you go, then."

"Thank you." Dev hoped he could find his way back to the porter's office. Encountering a weathered stick on the steps which had probably been dragged indoors by her terrier Fitz, he picked it up in order to prevent a mishap—he didn't need to break a leg, too.

The dog was in the country, where Dev would like to be. For a city boy, he was unexpectedly attracted to the Cotswolds. But perhaps that was because of a certain blond resident.

Dev tapped softly on the frosted glass door, and Lady Adelaide opened it at once. She wore a pretty dark-pink shift that suited her, and Dev was reminded of when he first met her. She was newly widowed then, pale, and swathed in black.

She looked much nicer in this shade.

"What on earth is that? Have you come to beat me?"

"I imagine it's your dog's, and I would never beat you, Lady Adelaide, or any woman, not even one of the Forty Dollies," he said, naming the notorious girl gang that was the scourge of London. Dev passed her the stick, and she tossed it in the trash.

"That's good to know. What news?"

"Not much, I'm afraid. I'm sorry I didn't come sooner—I had to write up the Fernald business. But I was able to secure some leave." He wiggled his arm, causing a stabbing pain to course through him. Biting his tongue for real, he needed to remember not to do *that* again.

"Oh! You poor thing! Is your arm broken? Oh, why are we standing here? Do come through and you can tell me all about it. Does it hurt very much? Can I fix you something to eat? Do you want a drink? Some tea or coffee or something stronger? Beckett is at the cinema, but I'm sure I could cobble something together."

From her rapid-fire sentences, he guessed she was as nervous in his presence as he was in hers, which was somehow gratifying.

Dev wasn't going to admit the truth that aspirin wasn't doing the trick. Breathing deeply was unpleasant as well. "I've a separated shoulder and a broken rib or two. Nothing that won't heal. I've been given two weeks off."

"Two weeks! Do you think you can solve Mama's case in so short a time?"

Dev smiled down at her, hoping to convey a confidence he didn't feel. "We've been successful before in less time, haven't we? And a coffee would be lovely." He was hungry, too, but then he always was.

He sat in a chair, resting his arm on the enamel table. Lady Adelaide whirled about the kitchen, putting Scottish shortbread and Garibaldis on a plate while the coffee brewed. It was just past nine, and all across London, the rich were sitting down in their paneled dining rooms to a multicourse dinner. Dev preferred Lady Adelaide's cozy kitchen and biscuits.

"Where is your sister?"

"I made her go to the pictures with Beckett. Cee thought it was a lark, borrowing one of her uniforms so they could sneak by the press. She'd make a terrible maid, though. She can't even brush her own hair." She poured cream into a glass pitcher and set it next to the sugar bowl. "Mr. Stockwell and Lord Barry were not at all encouraging this afternoon. I'm so worried." The coffeepot burbled, and she put it on the table on a trivet.

Dev fixed himself a cup. With some reluctance, he gave her the details of what he'd read in her mother's file, and Barnes's official interpretation of the events. Lady Adelaide's hazel eyes blinked behind her spectacles, and Dev was afraid she was going to burst into tears. From the shadows under her eyes, he doubted she got much sleep last night—Lord knows, he hadn't, either.

"This truly is awful, then," she said when he finished.

"I'm not going to put pearls on the pig. Your mother's chances might be better were she *not* a marchioness. Lovers quarrel all the time, and if the man can be proved to be a vicious brute—well, that's sometimes a mitigating circumstance. The duke's reputation is spotless, however."

"So is my mother's! Mama did not shoot the Duke of Rufford!" she said, slamming a dainty fist on the kitchen table, causing the coffeepot to wobble.

"I know, I know," Dev said hastily. He poured another cup and returned the pot to the stove where it was safer. "Because of her position in society, the police cannot be seen to show any signs of favoritism. Everything must be done by the book." There was enough civil unrest since the war; the poor already felt aggrieved and disproportionately punished. Allowing Lady Broughton to walk free would enrage them further.

Encouraging class warfare was not in the Yard's mandate.

"I'm not asking for special consideration. Is bail completely out of the question? She's led a blameless life. It's not as if she'll take potshots in the House of Lords from the Visitors' Gallery. The rest of the peerage is safe."

"It seems harsh, but you both must be patient. I know the avenue the police are taking, and we simply have to redraw the map."

Lady Adelaide removed her glasses and rubbed the bridge of her nose. There were a few faint freckles beneath the powder, and her rouge stood out against the natural pallor of her skin. Despite being exhausted, she was still too lovely for her own good. Dev concentrated on the plate of biscuits in front of him.

"What can we do? What can *I* do?"

"Would you consider speaking to the family?"

Lady Adelaide nodded. "I already planned to. If they'll see me."

"They may have newsmen camped out at their house, too. A neutral venue would be preferable."

"I can't very well invite them to the Ritz for tea."

Even with everything going on, she hadn't lost her wry sense of humor.

"What about your cousin?"

"Ian? What about him?"

"Does he have a house in Town?"

Lady Adelaide nodded. "Broughton Place. He never uses it, though. He prefers to stay at his club when he's here. Says the place is too big for a bachelor. Which it is."

"Do you think he could be prevailed upon to open it and arrange a meeting to help clear the family name? All this can't be a picnic for him, either."

"I don't know. I could call him." She wore the beginnings of a smile. "If he thinks it might help him in his suit with my sister, he just might."

"Is the wind blowing in that direction?"

"Not if Cee has anything to say about it. She's being very silly."

"Weren't we all at her age?"

She looked directly into his eyes. "I know I was—that's when I married Rupert."

Chapter Six

Tuesday

Addie awaited a call from Ian. Once she'd explained everything last night, he had agreed with alacrity to drive down first thing this morning and see what he could do to facilitate a meeting between her and the new Duke of Rufford.

He was as appalled as she was over the dowager marchioness's treatment. Ian was fond of Mama—she had eased his way into county society once he'd inherited the marquessate—and hoped she would become his mother-in-law before too long. The only fly in that organized ointment was Cee, but Addie expected she'd come around eventually. Ian had quite a lot to recommend him, and one day her sister would realize that. Like dukes, young marquesses didn't grow on trees.

It would be lovely if at least one of the younger Merrill women found happiness.

"Chin up, old girl."

Rupert. Addie contemplated throwing a scent bottle at him, but that would be a waste of a Lalique. She wasn't entirely dressed yet, and she did so hate having her mind read. However, she was anxious to discover how he'd got on in his invasion of Rufford House last evening.

"So, what happened?" she asked in an almost normal voice, adjusting her red Chinese silk robe over her slip. Rupert sometimes had an unwelcome—and far too belated—gleam in his eye when he caught her in dishabille. She ran a brush through her bob, hoping for the best. Beckett, who had a dab hand with hair, was out at the shops, and Cee had gone back to bed. The morning papers were still full of the murder and had given her another headache.

"It was…educational, to say the least. I stumbled into a nest of serpents."

"Really? So which snake killed Rufford?"

Rupert sank into a slipper chair. "The house is filled up to the rafters with possible suspects slithering about. The most obvious is Alistair. With his father dead, he's now the duke, with all the benefits that entails. No more paltry allowance for him and his grasping consort. Edmund was plump in the pocket, managing his holdings very well. No splashing money about, which is probably why you never heard of any of them. They were firmly under Edmund's fatherly thumb, which chafed Alistair in particular."

"Has he no income of his own?" Addie asked. There was often a bachelor great-uncle or godparent in these ancient families who came up to scratch in their wills. Rupert himself inherited Compton Chase from his grandmother, although there was no title to go along with it, or all that much money for its upkeep. It had been convenient that Addie's own godfather and great-aunt remembered her with considerable monetary affection so that Compton Chase's roof remained in good repair.

"If he ever did, he's gone through it. Elaine is an expensive woman, and their son and daughters have been indulged whenever possible. The old duke kept to the country most of the year in his draughty Norman keep and expected the family to do the same, close to his bosom, much to their disgruntlement. He lived quietly, only taking his seat in the Lords when matters piqued his particular interests. No headlines. Too bad for the poor bloke in death; he'd be horrified at the ballyhoo."

Addie paid very little attention to politics as a precaution to conserving her mental health. "I wonder how Mama met him."

"I happen to know. The family, I'm afraid, is not in her corner, as you might expect. She's viewed as a veritable femme fatale."

"Mama?" Addie asked, incredulous. There was no one on earth less *fatale* than her mother.

Oops. She had forgotten the duke was actually dead.

"They gossiped with considerable glee last night, much to my benefit. And it's a rather charming story, if you like that sort of thing."

Romance. Bah. In Addie's experience, there was usually a lie buried somewhere just waiting to bubble up.

"They met in New York," Rupert continued, oblivious to her mood.

"New York! I was with her in New York!" Addie cried. "And I thought you said he never went anywhere."

"Well, he made an exception last November. Took himself across the pond on a White Star liner, and once he got his land legs, went to the opening night of *Lady be Good!* on December 1. Quite out of character for such a dull dog. And that's when your mama decided to be bad."

"But we were there, Cee and I!" The musical was great fun—the Astaires were perfectly cast as a down-on-their-luck brother-and-sister dance team. Despite all the hijinks, mix-ups, and lies, everyone was happily paired off at the end. "I don't remember meeting him at all."

To be fair, Addie met a number of strange people on that trip, not to mention almost being caught in a speakeasy raid. As daughters of a marquess, she and Cee made a formidable social splash with the Americans, and they had not been short of male company. But surely she would recall a duke from her own country.

"You didn't. Your mother bumped into him during intermission, and by bumped, I mean she spilled her orange squash on the poor man's trousers. Handkerchiefs were produced. There was, uh, some rubbing involved."

Mama? Rubbing a gentleman's trousers? In public? Addie could not envision such a thing and said so.

"Doubt me not. At least that's what Rufford confessed to his family, the randy old devil. He intended to make your mother a duchess."

Oh! Now her mother's predicament was even worse, although Addie would have missed her if she had been sequestered way up in the back of beyond with a new husband.

Addie would miss her if she hanged, too.

"Do you think that's why he was killed? To prevent him from marrying again?"

Rupert shrugged. "It's as good a motive as any, although it's not as though she'd produce an heir at her age. Although women and their biological mechanics remain a mystery to me."

"Not for lack of effort," Addie said tartly. "Tell me more about your haunting."

"Alistair and his son, Stephen, are at odds. The boy has formed an attachment to a young Negro chanteuse. Needless to say, that's not the done thing in their circles."

Addie knew all too well. It was what stopped her from flinging herself into Devenand Hunter's arms—not for her sake, but his. The detective's life was complicated enough without incurring the wrath of a society that judged one on the color of one's skin and kept one confined to the appropriate box at all costs. It was ridiculous—odious, too—but then so many things were. Mr. Hunter was an ambitious man, brave, almost too diligent, and she didn't want to spoil his success.

It was time she put her infatuation behind her.

"Good luck with that," Rupert mumbled. He raised his hands in supplication. "I know, I know. I can't help it—you are clear as a bell on occasion. I shall endeavor to ignore your frequency and stick to the subject at hand."

Addie raised a frosty eyebrow. "Indeed."

"Anyhow, I can't see Stephen pulling the trigger on anything. He's rather wet. But I suppose if provoked, we're all capable of murder. If his grandfather got really shirty about his newfound love and threatened to cut him off financially, he might have found his gumption. His sister Gloria is a textbook redheaded firecracker, and far more apt to shoot someone. The old duke didn't approve of *her* boyfriend, either. Irish fellow, and not the northern kind. Rufford argued against Home Rule all his life."

This was precisely why politics made Addie queasy. "Was she about to lose her allowance?"

"Who knows? As far as I know, the young Irishman's not a bomb-thrower. And he is handsome enough so that her mother is not opposed to the match. Elaine is an inveterate flirt. Gloria had best watch her back."

Addie was shocked. "You don't mean—how could she—her own daughter!"

"Believe me, I wouldn't put anything past Elaine. She'd sleep with the devil himself."

"And you, too, I suppose."

Rupert examined his fingernails. "We're not here to discuss my regrettable past. Water under the bridge."

A deluge, more like. Honestly. Was there anyone in the United

Kingdom that Rupert had not conquered? Addie's hand would get tired making a list. She might run out of ink, too.

"How did Elaine get on with her father-in-law?"

"She knew which side her bread was buttered on. But she is a crack shot. As is Penny. No bird or stag is safe in Northumberland. I presume the Austrian grandchildren can hit a target as well as they tramp around yodeling in the Alps, and there seems to be no love lost there. They blamed their grandfather for their parents' estrangement, though Carola had a soft spot for the old man."

"And you said Penny's husband is in Town?"

"He is. At the Savoy. Not all that far from the Ritz. So that accounts for most of the family, except for the youngest, who's only thirteen. I suppose children can be bloodthirsty, too, but it's a stretch to accuse the duke's youngest grandchild of murder. She's still in pigtails. I saw a photograph on the piano."

"What about the servants?" Addie asked. The butler was always conveniently guilty in the mysteries she read.

"I'd say not. The staff is loyal, and most of them traveled down to London from the family seat—Rufford was too tight-fisted to keep two places fully staffed. They could have killed him up there with far less fanfare. Granted, the French chef is temperamental, but then, he *is* French."

"It could be a business associate, too. Or someone from Sinn Féin who objected to the duke's votes."

"The Irish question is settled in their favor—what would be the point? And as far as the duke's finances, he was not one to rashly speculate. But perhaps a visit to his man of business is warranted. I'll see what I can do."

Which meant that Rupert would once again trespass. It might not be cricket, but murder called for extreme—and sometimes ghostly—measures.

Chapter Seven

Tuesday evening

Addie could not decide what to wear, putting Beckett through her paces. It would be hypocritical to wear black; after all, she didn't know the duke, had only seen his picture in the newspapers.

She could understand his appeal for her mother. He had been an attractive man, if a trifle severe, with unusual light eyes. He didn't smile for the camera, coming from an age when that would be considered frivolous. As dark as her father was fair, Rufford had very little gray to show for his age, and could have been mistaken for a man a decade younger. The duke looked absolutely nothing like Addie's father, Herbert, an avid huntsman who spent most of his days chuckling with good humor and chasing game of one sort or another all over Gloucestershire.

As Addie came from Compton Chase at such short notice, she barely packed a bag. So she was left with her old city standbys in her closet, and most of them were meant for a pleasant afternoon of shopping, or an evening of dining and dancing in a fashionable boîte. Bugle beads were definitely dispensable to meet Alistair, Duke of Rufford.

But they *were* to dine. Ian had flown into action once he arrived in Town, pulling off Holland covers himself and inviting the new duke to a quiet private dinner at Broughton Place "to discuss family matters." The man just didn't know Addie would be there, too.

"I don't see why you're doing this." Cee lay on Addie's tufted white velvet chaise, holding an ice bag to her forehead. "And not that one. It's too green."

How could a dress be too green? It was one of Addie's favorites, and brought out the emerald chips in her hazel eyes. Addie rolled those hazel eyes in Beckett's direction, and her maid hung it back in the wardrobe.

What did one wear when one was trying to convince a son that her mother didn't kill his father? Addie needed to appear sympathetic yet confident of her mother's innocence. Perhaps Alistair was in possession of information that would help solve the case, even if he didn't know it.

It would be too much to hope that he'd confess.

She had memorized Mr. Hunter's suggested questions. The police detective had gone to Berwick-upon-Tweed by train this morning in hopes of ferreting out something useful about the family's background. There, he hoped to find a way to Rufford Castle and make discreet inquiries without attracting the Yard's attention. As far as Mr. Hunter knew, Phil Barnes had no plans to waste time and venture north. He was certain he had his villainess.

"What about this blue gown, Lady A?" Beckett held up a sleeveless navy chiffon dress trimmed with fluffy dyed feathers at the hem.

It did not sparkle. But the last time Addie wore it, she had sneezed her head off. Sneezing had got her into quite a lot of trouble lately. "No. As a matter of fact, I think you should have it, Cee."

Her sister frowned. "It's too long. You know I'm shorter than you are." And not as modest. Addie imagined Cee wouldn't be happy in it unless there was a foot less fabric.

"I bet Beckett could take it up for you."

Beckett sighed dramatically, putting the offending garment back. Really, she should be on the stage instead of in service.

"It will have to be the dove-gray crepe, I think." It was a left-over from the end of Addie's mourning period, very simple but embroidered in black chain-stitching around the neckline and elbow-length sleeves to give it some interest. "With the double strand of black pearls."

"Very good choice. Dull as ditchwater," Cee said.

"Just what I'm aiming for. I'm not planning to seduce the Duke of Rufford. Or Ian, for that matter."

Cee sat up straighter, forgetting her ice bag as it tumbled into her lap. "Ian! I should think not. He's not your type at all."

"And what is my type?" Addie asked, muffled as Beckett dropped the dress over her.

"You know. Tall and dark. Like Rupert. Like Insp—"

"That's enough, Cecilia," Addie said, emerging like Athena from Zeus's head. She examined herself in the mirror, wondering if gray ever suited any woman. Her poor mother was wearing a prison-issued gray dress right this very minute, so Addie's lack of enthusiasm for the dress was selfish. "I don't have time for men, tall or not. Beckett, I'll need all your prowess with the powder puff. But not too much makeup—I don't wish to look like a Bright Young Person."

It was time for Cee to roll *her* eyes. "As if you could. You're too old."

"That's enough again. Honestly, when I was your age—"

Cee raised a hand. "Spare me. There was a war on. You were rolling bandages and knitting lumpy jumpers and baking tarts for the wounded, which I'm sure were inedible. The tarts, not the poor boys. I'm so sorry I cannot follow in your illustrious foot-steps. Perhaps that dreadful Hitler in Germany can start another war now that he's out of jail so I can be brought up to scratch."

"Cee!" Addie said, shocked. "Don't even joke about such a thing!" Sometimes her sister was so provoking, Addie was at a complete loss as to what to do with her. But at least Cee had been reading something other than gossip in the papers. The world was a terribly dangerous place. They hadn't even gotten over the Great War yet, and already there were martial rumblings on the Continent.

"Now, now, miladies," Beckett interjected, unlocking Addie's jewel case and drawing out the pearls. "Don't borrow trouble, as my mam used to say."

Addie thought trouble was bound to come anyhow, borrowed or bought. Cee pouted in the mirror behind her as Beckett fastened the necklace and worked her hair and maquillage magic with efficiency. Much improved, Addie buttoned her short white gloves and rose.

"Wish me luck. Ian's driver is due any minute. Shall I give him a message from you, Cee?"

"A message! What do I have to say to him? How are the crops he's always going on about? As if I care about yields and drainage."

"Papa did. You might convey your thanks for trying to help Mama."

"Pooh. He's only holding this summit so the Broughton name won't be besmirched. For the future marquesses on to infinity."

"He'll have to marry first. I wonder which of our acquaintances would make him a suitable bride. Those Jordan twins at Hugh's were very taken with him, you know."

Cee shot her a malevolent look, so Addie knew her dig had succeeded. Really, she was being difficult, but at this point Addie expected nothing less.

Deciding to wait in the building's elegant lobby, she found a filmy wrap from the hall closet and took the flight of marble stairs to the ground floor. Daniel was on duty, and he informed her that he'd chased off the last of the newspapermen not a quarter of an hour ago.

"Bound for the pub, I expect," the porter said with satisfaction. "Vultures. As if anyone here would ever speak to them."

Addie certainly hoped not. She opened her black satin evening bag and pressed a fiver in Daniel's hand. "Thank you for all your help. My sister and I appreciate it."

"You're much too generous, my lady."

Yes, she was. Five pounds was a lot of money. Addie tipped all the mansion flat's staff with regularity, not waiting for Boxing Day. It was remarkable what dosh could do to smooth the way.

But she couldn't bribe her mother's way out of gaol.

Ian's chauffeur drew up, and Daniel, after checking the street, escorted her to the car. Addie sat back against the buttery leather and rode the Mayfair miles in silence to Broughton Place. She had not been inside the house since well before her father died, and once again felt the tug of grief for times past. She'd been presented to the king and queen from this address, remembering her debut season as a swirl of pearls and white dresses. The idyllic spring of 1911 stretched on endlessly in a cloud of blossoming trees and lime-green city parks, and then the return to the Cotswolds meant even more parties.

Life was so much simpler then—before war and marriage and misery and widowhood.

Ian greeted her in the double drawing room that hadn't changed at all since her parents were in residence. Her cousin was happier in the country and put forth all his modernization efforts into Broughton Park. Addie knew she was remiss at not visiting him there, but even after five years, her father's death was still painful. She hadn't brought herself to step over the threshold in all that time.

She was silly but couldn't seem to help herself.

"I didn't expect to see you quite so soon," Ian said, giving her cheek a kiss. Only three days ago, he'd come to give her a most unexpected confession.

"I admit, the circumstances are not ideal, although it's always lovely to see you." Ian was a few months younger than she was, with the Merrill fair curls and an open, honest countenance. Misleading, as she now knew he had the ability to keep significant secrets of his own. Had she been born a boy, he would be a poorish distant relation and she'd be the current marquess. She didn't hold a grudge, but it was annoying, nonetheless.

"How is Cecilia?"

"To be frank, she's being rather a pain. She's at awfully loose ends, and was, even before Mama's predicament."

"You know I'd like to change that," Ian said quietly, fixing her a glass of soda water and a slice of lemon. He knew her general aversion to alcohol.

"And you have my blessing, for what it's worth. But we need to get this murder business sorted. You're sure the duke is coming?"

He poured himself several fingers of whisky. "It took some convincing, but yes. I've only met him once, but he did remember, or said he did."

"What's he like?"

"You know I'm not much for the social conventions. It was just a fleeting encounter at Cheltenham right before I shipped out. I was with your father." The race course had been turned into a Voluntary Aid Detachment hospital in the fall of 1914. For a while, the races continued, much to the convalescents' delight, until the need for horses at the front soon stopped the sport throughout the kingdom.

Addie knew how agitated her father was when Ian went off to war, worrying that the lad he was truly fond of and grooming to take over the title might meet an untimely death. Addie had remembered Ian in her prayers every night, even if she resented his male birth.

The doorbell pealed, and she set down her glass. *Once more, unto the breach, dear friends, once more.*

Chapter Eight

En route to Northumberland

Dev enjoyed long train travel as much as the next bloke—which was to say, hardly at all. All day his lungs were irritated from the belching coal smoke and his arse was stiff from the hard Second Class seat. He supposed he might have bought a First Class ticket and listed it on his expense reckoning, but he was frugal by nature. The lawyers had given him far too much money on behalf of Lady Broughton, so he was as flush as he'd never been before.

But it was other people's money. Dev couldn't dream of earning so much as a policeman in a year, whereas Lady Adelaide could probably dip into a tea caddy in the kitchen and pull out a fortune.

Leaving from King's Cross Station this morning around six, he made the three-hundred-forty-plus-mile journey, changing trains only once. The stop gave him a chance to stretch his battered body and wire ahead to secure a room for the night. He tried not to inhale too deeply on the station platform, for the combination of summer heat and fumes was seriously unpleasant.

Dev couldn't say the jolting locomotive was much fun, either, particularly on his shoulder. He did garner some sympathetic looks with his sling, but more often he was made to feel as if his very presence was suspicious. The farther north he went, the more he felt out of place.

The sun was too bright when he stepped off at Berwick-upon-Tweed, although the air temperature was cooler. Starving after an unsatisfactory train sandwich and sinfully weak tea, he warred with himself but didn't stop at the station café. The sooner he could get settled, the happier he'd be.

On the ride up, Dev learned from his guidebook there were more castles in Northumberland than any other county, due to the constant Border wars, but exploration would have to wait for a later date. The Debatable Lands were once the bloodiest and most lawless region in the country, and had caused governmental headaches for decades. Rufford Castle was listed as a place of historic interest, changing hands several times over the centuries between the English and the Scots. He was to stay at the recommended—and only—pub near the castle's gates, and less than two miles from Scotland.

The faint scent of the sea over the fug of the train was welcome. Holy Island was not very far away, and tempting for a man of his spiritual bent. However, time and tide waited for no man, and twice daily the causeway flooded. Dev was not about to get stuck so far from home when he was supposed to be working.

He didn't expect to find a motorized taxi, and was not wrong. Climbing onto a wooden cart, he informed the driver of his destination, agreed to the exorbitant fare—and had to pay in advance—and inured himself to the bumps in the winding dirt road outside of the town. There were glimpses of sparkling water between the hills and farmhouses, and eventually a grim crenellated tower rose above the trees in the distance.

"There it is, guv. Rufford Castle. Not far from the Rose and

Thistle, if you don't mind the climb. You a newspaperman?" the driver asked over the rumble of the wagon.

News traveled quickly; Dev had seen the broadsheets at the stand in the station. Posing as a reporter struck Dev as a rather genius idea—he was sorry not to think of it himself first. Since he hadn't quite worked out how to approach the Berwickers, it seemed as good a way as any.

"Something like that."

"Come up all this way from London for the story on the dook?"

Dev nodded. That much was true.

"Shame about old Edmund. Who'd think he'd be catting around at his age? Bully for him, though it didn't work out so well, did it?"

"Women! Guess you can't trust a pretty face," Dev said, hoping for dirt.

"Oh, I'd not say that, or my Mary'd hear of it and give me what for. She worked for the second duchess, God rest her soul, and a nicer and prettier woman you couldn't find. Too bad about her daughter, Penny. Can't hold a candle to her ma, looks-wise, but she's nice enough, I guess. Married a bloody Hun, though. Her pa was fit to be tied, and so he should have been. Proper family feeling Edmund had. Kept his relations close. You won't hear a bad word about him from me."

Dev pulled out his policeman's notebook as though he was doing an interview. "Popular roundabouts, was he?"

"Will I get my name in the papers?"

"Not if you don't want to. I can always say 'a local source.'"

"I'm as local as they come. Bill Neal. That's N-E-A-L, not N-E-I-L-L. Lived here all my life."

"So you're the expert about everything and everybody."

Neal shrugged. "I wouldn't go so far as to say that. But if you've come to nose around up at the castle, you've wasted your time.

The old man took the servants to his house in Town with him. Careful with his coins, he was. No point to keeping two places running. You're just asking for abuse and waste. You know what they say—when the cat's away the mice will play."

Damn. "Is there no one left behind?"

"Oh, a maid or two, I suppose. The bootboy. Nobody of consequence who'd know anything worthwhile."

Not like Bill Neal. "Where would you suggest I nose around?" Dev asked with a grin.

"Why, you're going there. The Rose and Thistle. It's not much, but it's all there is away from Berwick proper to the border. Edmund himself used to come down every few weeks for a pint or two. Now, mind you, he was never one to chew the fat with us lot, but he'd give a friendly nod and stand us all a drink."

"Were any of his family ever with him?"

"Sometimes. He was right fond of his granddaughter. The German one. Even if she *was* German."

Austrian, actually, but who was keeping track, as the map of Europe lay in tatters? "What about his son and heir?"

"Alistair? Too busy chasing the ladies to hang out with his old pa. Didn't even sit in the family pew once a week—probably thought he'd be hit by lightning. There are more than a few village girls who know to steer clear of him now. The man was and still is nothing but trouble."

Dev wondered if Alistair had children in the area that he never acknowledged. Had they approached their "grandfather" for a share of the family fortune and been turned away? Money coupled with revenge were classic motivations to murder. But why should Edmund pay for his son's sins?

In Dev's opinion, a man who was unfaithful to his wife lacked character and was probably capable of breaking other vows. His own parents had set an excellent example of mutual marital devotion, and if Dev was ever lucky enough to find the right person...

At the rate he was going, he'd never wed. With a most recent exception, encountering decent people in his line of work was nigh onto impossible. And despite his mother's efforts within the Anglo-Indian community, he'd failed to form an attachment to any of the young women she introduced him to. Dev consoled himself with the fact that it took his father forty years on earth to meet and marry his mother. He still had five years to go before things became desperate.

"Almost there, guv." By Dev's reckoning, they'd traveled a few miles from the station so far, passing a modest cluster of cottages and a few shops hugging the road. The aforementioned church was set back behind a stone wall, its ancient gravestones tilting between tassels of overgrown grass. The resident vicar, if there was one for such an unpopulated place, needed to get the push mower out. The rest of the village was neat enough, but a bit forlorn. Dev noted black bunting on a few doors.

What would it be like to live here year-round? Stupendously boring, he reckoned.

"Will the duke be buried here, do you think?" Dev asked. The body had not been released yet, as far as he knew.

"We hear the funeral's to be in London so the muckety-mucks can attend. But Moretons—that's the family name, ye ken—always come home. We've got a graveyard full of 'em. Here we are."

The Rose and Thistle was the very last whitewashed building before the road narrowed and rose between elaborate stone pillars, the gate tantalizingly open. "That's the way to the castle. I can drive you up later if you like."

Dev climbed down from the worn padded bench, grabbing his small travel case. "I think I'd like to stretch my legs after the day I've had. But you've been a big help, Bill. Do you live here in the village?"

"Aye, just down the road. My Mary runs the notions shop, and we live above it. She's a wiz with a needle, used to sew all the second duchess's clothes." He sniffed. "The first one went to Paris for hers, very snooty, she was. Nothing was good enough for her up here. No one shed too many tears when she passed on, not even Edmund, I'd wager. Poor fellow. Two dead wives and now this. Didn't have much luck in love, did he?"

Dev didn't think love had much to do with the duke's death. Reaching into his pocket, he gave Bill a tip despite the ridiculous rate he'd been charged to bring the driver practically to his own front door. He expected Bill would pop in for a pint and pave Dev the "reporter's" way into local society. People might be more inclined to confide in the press than the police, or so he hoped.

The landlord led him to a remarkably spacious room on the first floor. He told Dev the inn was empty of guests at the moment, but was hopeful more newshounds might follow in Dev's footsteps. Noncommittal, Dev shrugged, wondering how he'd manage to remain incognito amidst a pack of savvy London reporters. His recent murder investigations had garnered him some unwanted attention—he didn't like being singled out, although his mother saved all the clippings. With any luck he'd be at the train station tomorrow on his way back home.

As he'd suspected, Bill was holding court when he went downstairs. The locals were prepared, and didn't startle at Dev's brown face.

"Here he is! What paper did you say you worked for?"

"I didn't. We're not one of the major ones, I'm afraid. You've never heard of us. My bosses would like to change that, though. That's why they sent me all the way up here, sparing no expense, so I might get an exclusive. May I buy you all a drink?" Dev waved the landlord over. "What's your pleasure, gentlemen?"

The four men didn't ask for anything fancy. He ordered a half-pint of Double Maxim, first brewed to celebrate the homecoming of the Northumberland Hussars from the Second Boer War. Nursing it while his new friends were somewhat less circumspect on his tab, he sat back as they related the Moretons' history in colorful detail, and promised to spell everyone's name correctly when he filed his imaginary article.

After a decent meat pie and an apple tart drenched in double cream, he went upstairs to splash some water on his face and read over his copious notes. The trip had been worth it, thus far. But he would walk up to the castle anyway while the light still held.

Dev wondered how Lady Adelaide was faring this evening. Had she met with the new duke? He couldn't wait to tell her what he'd found out.

Chapter Nine

Awkward. Awkward. Awkward. Addie's mother raised her to master most any situation, but this evening was proving to be a challenge.

She gave the new Duke of Rufford credit. When introduced, he could have headed right back out the door, possibly tossing a scathing remark over his well-tailored shoulder. Instead, he blinked his ice-gray eyes just once, then offered a hand to shake, as though Addie was just any woman he might meet in any drawing room in any civilized house. And to *his* credit, Ian was unembarrassed at the surprise he engineered, as if it was the most natural thing in the world that he broker such a meeting. Usually quite shy, he seemed at ease in what was the most bizarre situation she'd ever found herself in, and that was saying a lot of late.

Including discovering Rupert was still lurking about after she'd buried him with all the pomp and ceremony he didn't deserve. Addie took a quick peek around the room, praying he was not hiding behind her mother's old drapes. She was nervous enough without worrying about her dead husband's unsettling presence.

The room could use a refresh. Lady Broughton's taste was exquisite, but it had been a decade and a half since the house had been redecorated for Addie's come-out. She supposed if Ian married, his wife would have a free hand, erasing a link to the past.

The present loomed, however, as did the duke, who was rather tall. She took a sip of her soda water to relieve the sudden dryness in her throat.

"May I get you a sherry? Gin and tonic? Or a whisky and soda?" Ian asked, standing at the gilded eighteenth-century sideboard that served as a bar.

"Whisky. Neat, I think. Broughton, you didn't mention Lady Adelaide would be here."

"Would you have come?" Ian asked, handing the man his drink.

"I'm not sure." Rufford drained the glass in one long swallow and placed it on a table.

"Thank you for accepting my cousin's invitation, Your Grace. And please accept my condolences on the loss of your father," Addie said, without stuttering too badly.

"Loss? He's not a misplaced parcel in a freight office. He's dead, and from what I understand, your dear mama shot him." His pale eyes were so piercing that Addie shivered.

"She didn't! You must believe her, and me. This is all a dreadful misunderstanding." Addie's words sounded weak even to her. What must Rufford think?

"Let's not get off on the wrong foot." Ian poured the duke another drink. "I've arranged to have a quiet dinner *à la française* in the study, where we may help ourselves and not be disturbed. We are all interested in the truth, are we not?"

Addie's stomach was in revolt, no matter what was served or how. But she was sure she wouldn't get another chance to speak to the duke again and needed to make the most of her time with him. No hiding in the cloakroom and begging for bicarbonate of soda, no matter how wretched she felt.

It was clear he detested her, but he looked to be the sort of man who detested most people. Rupert didn't like him, and he'd been a fair judge of character in his day. Addie needed to tread carefully with her questions and not put the duke's back up. Her best bet was to appear confused and a bit naïve, which was not all that far from fact.

Ian offered his arm, and they traversed the hall to the back of the house, where Addie's father's study lay. Despite the windows thrown open to the garden, the smell of leather, old books, and tobacco nearly brought her to tears. She'd spent a great deal of time in here—not doing much serious reading, if she was honest. Her mother discouraged intellectual tendencies in both her daughters, though Cee had rebelled of late. But Addie often kept her father company as he tended to his accounts in Town, curled up in a window seat flicking through her mother's copies of *The Lady* while the marquess grumbled good-naturedly about the outlandish bills his wife and girls toted up.

It was here in this oak-paneled room that Major Rupert Charles Cressleigh Compton asked the Marquess of Broughton for his eldest daughter's hand in marriage. Addie had waited in the drawing room with her mother with rising anxiety, as the men were sequestered for over an hour. But when they both finally emerged, full of brandy and goodwill, Rupert presented her with the sapphire-and-diamond ring she still wore.

She was grateful her father had not lived to see their unfolding unhappiness.

A small round table stood in front of the open windows, and a slight evening breeze brought in the scent of the shrub roses that lined the garden walls. She was glad the outdoor space was still well-tended. Her mother had been as proud of her pocket city patch as she was of the vast Cotswold country estate. Even if Ian rarely spent time here, he was a good steward.

He pulled out a chair for her, and Addie sat. Wine had already been poured into crystal goblets at each place setting, and she stopped herself from guzzling it—nothing good would come of *that*, no matter how upset she was. The broad desk was cleared, covered with a white cloth, and held shiny silver chafing dishes.

"May I serve you, Addie?"

She nodded, as she thought she might drop her plate. He seemed to understand the state of her stomach, as he gave her the merest taste of each dish. Then he and the duke helped themselves to much more generous portions.

"I hope you find the food to your satisfaction, even if you object to the company," Ian said with a wink in her direction.

"One must eat, I suppose. Plead your case, Lady Adelaide. I have another social engagement tonight and won't be able to tarry long." Attacking his food with gusto, the Duke of Rufford's hunger was on full display—unlike Addie, death had not diminished his appetite at all.

Apparently, he was not one to observe the niceties of mourning. In some respects, she understood that, resenting her blacks for the year honoring her unfaithful husband, eschewing all sorts of amusing opportunities. And when she finally tried to emerge from Rupert's shadow, a dead body in her barn had quite killed the evening.

"My mother has sworn to me she did not harm your father. She was, uh, quite fond of him."

Rufford picked up a spear of asparagus and waved it at her before ripping off the tip with his teeth. "Well, she would say that, wouldn't she? Why should *I* believe her? My father was losing his marbles, you know. Getting on in years. Any scheming woman could have taken advantage of him with ease. The last thing the old duffer needed was a third wife." He cut into his lamb with vengeance and shoveled it and a cube of perfectly roasted potato into his mouth.

Addie bristled, but kept her tone conciliatory. "My mother is not a scheming woman, Your Grace. She is a dowager marchioness with more than adequate income and property of her own. She was faithful to my father's memory for over five years, and has the most sterling reputation."

"Had, I'm afraid. It's too bad for you and your sister—and Broughton here—but murder cannot be batted away like an inconvenient moth in the blanket chest. The police are satisfied she did it, and who am I to argue?"

"Can't you think of anyone else who might have disliked your father?"

"Enough to shoot him? Sorry. The old fool was annoying but did not incite homicidal maniacs until he took up with your mother. And before you can accuse me of the dastardly deed, it's true we weren't the closest father and son. But I didn't sneak into the Ritz Sunday morning—I was otherwise occupied with a lady friend who will vouch for me if necessary. Obviously, I do hope it won't come to that—my wife might object."

Addie resolved to somehow find out who this mistress was. "He was on good terms with the rest of his relatives?"

"Of course. He had this absurd notion we were one big, happy family, and insisted we all share the same roof when we could. It broke his heart when my sister flounced off to the Tyrol after her misguided marriage, and of course I was in Town during the war."

"You didn't serve?"

It was Rufford's turn to bristle. "Not that it's any of your business, but I was an aide to Asquith."

Asquith had resigned as prime minister towards the end of 1916. Plenty of war left, but with those connections, no wonder Rufford didn't have to fight in France.

"Did your father have any misadventures in business or finance?"

"What, you think he owed money to his bookie and got 'rubbed out,' as the Yanks say? You are reaching, Lady Adelaide. I understand your sympathy for your mother, but it's misplaced. The woman did it, and that's that. Hard to accept, I'm sure. We always idolize our parents until reality sets in, as it inevitably does. My father was no hero. Your mother's not a heroine." He tossed his napkin over the plate. "Don't think you or your cousin can approach my family—I'll warn them off. You've got gumption, I'll grant you, but it won't get you anywhere."

He rose, and Ian scrambled up. "You won't mind if I don't stay for port and cigars, Broughton. My compliments to your cook. I can see my way out." Rufford strode to the door and slammed it behind him.

Ian sat back down. "Well. I'm sorry. That was a cock-up."

Addie reached for his hand. "It's not your fault. You were never able to get a word in edgewise. Thank you for trying. For opening the house for me."

"What a total prick."

Addie had rarely seen Ian angry and was remorseful for causing all this trouble. "I hope for my mother's sake his father was nicer."

"Aunt Constance wouldn't be taken in by such a viper. She's got too much good sense. Do you think the old duke meant to marry her?"

Addie couldn't attribute confirmation to Rupert, so she shrugged. "His family seems to think so. I don't think he was gaga, either. Mama said he read the whole of *The Times* every day first thing and was a shrewd investor."

"No," Ian said. "I wouldn't believe anything Rufford said. We'll get to the bottom of this, I promise. Is it awful if I still want to eat the pudding? It's raspberry fool, my favorite."

Chapter Ten

Wednesday

Addie was not inclined to take no for an answer, particularly when it meant her mother's life or death. Sitting on her garden bench to get some much-needed fresh air, she tossed one of Fitz's mangy tennis balls into the sky, pondering how she could infiltrate the duke's family to finish asking her questions. Detective Inspector Hunter was not due back until this evening (she had received a terse telegram), so she couldn't consult with him on strategy.

It wasn't as if she could don one of Beckett's uniforms and storm the Maddox Street kitchen. The newshounds remained on her front doorstep, although there were fewer of them, thank goodness. Beckett managed to mingle briefly on the pavement this morning, stepping on as many toes as possible as she tried to pass with faux clumsiness. She reported they were bored, which was a very good sign.

Addie disliked the new Duke of Rufford intensely, and would be very satisfied to pin the murder on him. Patricide was common enough in literature—why not in real life? He was despicable, and a womanizer to boot. Men like him—

Rupert caught the ball one-handed and threw it up again. "Hush, now. Don't tar us all with the same brush. Alistair doesn't even *like* women."

Addie hardly flinched at Rupert's reappearance. "You mean he's a homosexual?" A concept she had not entirely understood until recently, sheltered idiot that she was. The ball landed in her lap, then rolled away towards the ivied brick wall.

"Nothing like that. I have—had—an acute appreciation for those of the fairer sex. Alistair simply wants to dominate, and is disinterested in his partners'—or should I call them victims'?—needs. Pleasure, if you will. I can say with some modesty one could never attribute the same sort of callous behavior to me. Even you must agree."

Addie was not about to discuss Rupert's vaunted skillfulness in the bedchamber at this stage of the game. "He says he has an alibi for the time of the murder. Some woman."

"Do you want me to find out who? You know I'm eager to help."

"And get closer to those apricot custard clouds. Yes, see what you can do. Maybe he has an assignation book or something."

Rupert rubbed his hands together with glee. "In code, like what's-his-name, the banker from our first case together! I do love to solve a puzzle. If I hadn't been in the Air Corps, I'd have been right at home in the War Office unscrambling the Kaiser's cables *auf Englisch*. I'll pop round there this afternoon. Perhaps I'll hear something fruitful quite by accident." He blew her a kiss and vanished.

Rupert did have his good points, especially now that he was dead. But his presence in her life couldn't go on forever, could it? The whole "till death do us part" was a complete lie otherwise. What if a widow took multiple husbands—after proper periods of mourning, of course—and they each met an unfortunate end? If they all haunted her at the same time, it would be very uncomfortable.

That was an ecclesiastical problem for another day. With Rupert heading for Maddox Street again, Addie decided to go to the Savoy. Not for tea and scones, but to speak with Graf Franz von Mayr, if he could be located. The last time she'd been to the hotel, her sister had been poisoned, but surely such bad luck could not strike twice.

She went back inside to change into something suitable for the visit and the warm June day. The back stairway from the garden door to her flat was dimmer than usual—a bulb had burned out in the sconce. She must remember to tell one of the porters to replace it, not that she frequented these stairs often unless she was going out with her dog. He preferred a brisk walk and all the delicious street smells, but if she was feeling lazy—or Beckett was—they frequented the private yard. Fitz liked to romp around, and was likely doing just that in the country. It had been an age since she'd entertained in the little London garden, and at present the future did not look promising for cocktails and conversation.

Addie swore to herself she'd avoid all social events if, in fact, she was ever invited anywhere again. The house party she'd attended just last week had resulted in death and drama, not to mention Mr. Hunter's injuries, and now she was embroiled in yet another scandal. It was...exhausting. Perhaps she might be better off taking vows as an Anglican nun and hiding away in some cloister, though her knowledge of the Bible was not all it could be.

But first, she had to save her mother from the hangman's noose.

Addie had locked the kitchen door behind her when she went out, as Beckett and Cee went in their maids' uniforms to a double-feature matinee to try to cheer themselves up. She reached into her pocket for the keys but came up empty. Bother. She'd left them in the downstairs door so she'd remember to secure it; it was usually left open so Fitz could shoot straight outside in case of a doggy emergency. So much for *that* plan.

She turned to go back down, then heard a shuffling noise below. This stairwell was for her exclusive use to enter the garden—the service stairs for deliveries were across the hall. Addie wouldn't be one bit surprised if some ambitious (and athletic) journalist jumped over the wall in an attempt to access the building and get up to her flat.

"Who's there?" she called.

The other light in the sconce went out.

That tore it. She wasn't some stupid gothic novel heroine going into the cellar with a candle that was destined to blow out *no matter what.* Wishing she still had Fitz's stick to throw down the steps, she hurried to the main staircase and ran down to the lobby. There had been talk amongst the residents of installing a lift, but Addie was glad she was not trapped in a moving box right now.

Mike, the day porter, was on duty and gave her a beaming smile, no doubt hoping for even more gratuities to come. "Good afternoon, my lady. May I hail you a taxi?"

It was clear he was not familiar with women's fashion if he thought she was going out in public like *this.*

"No, thank you, Mike. I think someone's lurking on the stairway to my garden. The lights are out down there, too, so you must take a torch with you."

He looked alarmed. "You want me to investigate?"

Addie nodded. "Unless you prefer to call the police and wait. Though by the time they come, the person might be long gone. And the other residents will be upset at the fuss." They must already be beside themselves—members of the press were still outside, and Addie knew she was persona non grata amongst her tony neighbors. Even Angela next door had failed to call her, and gossip was usually her bread and butter. "Think of the bad publicity for the building. I'll go with you."

"Indeed you will not, Lady Adelaide! I know my duty."

"Pooh. There's no reason for me to stay up here like a wilted daisy. It might only be a stray cat that slipped into the open door, and we'll have a good laugh about it." A cat which was especially dexterous at shutting off lights.

Perhaps she was being overly suspicious. The bulbs may simply have burned out. The noise might have been a leaf skittering in a draft in the stairwell. She hadn't seen anyone outside—the space was much too small to hide behind a shrub without being noticed.

Mike picked up a torch from his office, and Addie followed him down through the twists of the back corridors, passing the boiler room and storage spaces for the tenants. He had to unlock the door to her little staircase, so that blew her theory that a deliveryman got turned around looking for the exit and wound up at her back door.

He shone the light ahead. The garden door stood open, and there were no keys dangling from the lock.

Chapter Eleven

Mike gave Addie a spare set of keys so she could get into her flat. She called several locksmiths, none of whom could come until tomorrow morning. She would have Beckett and Cee help her push furniture in front of all the doors tonight in case the key thief decided to make a visit. In the meantime, she had plans.

Dressing quickly in a sunny-yellow linen dress that matched the brightness of the afternoon, she scribbled a note to her sister. Mike got her the taxi he was ready to hail earlier, and after getting stuck in hot, heavy traffic, she arrived at the Savoy more in time for a sidecar than a cup of tea.

She doubted von Mayr would be alert to her existence. From what Rupert said, Alistair, much like his father, was not close to Penny's husband. He might be able to threaten the rest of his family, but the graf was probably immune to intimidation. The man had a fortune and a castle of his own. Addie was curious about the person who had such nerve and charm he eloped with a duke's daughter when she was barely out of the schoolroom.

Though perhaps his charm had waned, as his wife had been in England since the war ended. Familiarity did breed contempt.

Addie had reason to know that, after the first blush of attraction, real life tended to penetrate the rosy haze.

She arrived at the Savoy somewhat wrinkled but determined. Greeted by name by the concierge, she knew she attracted the attention of a few people in the plant-filled lobby. Addie had experience with uncomfortable social scrutiny—Rupert's infidelity had been the worst-kept secret in the kingdom. Raising her chin, she sailed into the maître d'hôtel's outer office and spoke to his secretary. Mr. Reeves-Smith had been attentive after Cee's accidental poisoning, sending flowers and treats from the famous kitchen to Broughton Park's dower house during her recovery. The hotel was in no way responsible for the incident, but went above and beyond to assure the Merrill family's goodwill.

Mr. Reeves-Smith welcomed her into his organized office, greeting her with a warm smile. "Lady Adelaide! What a very pleasant surprise. What may I do for you?" His tone was sympathetic, as he undoubtedly knew the current state of affairs. He was also no doubt grateful that her mother chose to have her rendezvous at the Ritz instead of his establishment.

"I hope I'm not intruding."

"Not at all. I was about to ring for tea. Would you care to join me?"

As tempting as that would be, Addie declined. "I have a favor to ask of you. I'd very much like to be introduced to one of your guests, the Graf von Mayr, and speak with him privately."

Mr. Reeves-Smith's smile faded. "Are you sure that's wise, Lady Adelaide?"

"Wise or not, it's something I must do to try to help my mother. It's insupportable that anyone can think she's guilty of murder."

"Of course not!" he said hastily. "It's just that such a meeting is bound to be discomfiting."

"It's more discomfiting imagining my mother being convicted

of a crime she did not commit. How long has the graf been staying with you?"

Reeves-Smith looked discomfited himself. "You know our guests' privacy is paramount to us."

Addie wondered whether batting her lashes would be worth it. The hotel manager was a consummate professional, probably impervious even to bribery. She did so hate to attempt to use her atrophied feminine wiles—the result was often humiliating. "I know I'm placing you in a difficult position, and I appreciate your discretion. The Savoy is lucky to have you."

Not meeting her eyes, he looked to the pebbled glass door separating him from rescue by his secretary.

"*Please*," Addie continued. "It's just an introduction. And perhaps a quiet room in which to speak to the man. I promise you I won't cause a scene."

"It's very irregular, Lady Adelaide."

She was always reluctant to play the daughter-of-a-marquess card, but needs must. "Everything about this is irregular, don't you think? You've known my parents—my mother—for years. Papa loved to dine here when he was in Town, and one can't count up the number of charity events Mama chaired at the Savoy."

He pointed to a filing cabinet. "One can, actually. We keep meticulous records. The hotel appreciates your family's business over my tenure here, but I do not wish to find it—or myself—in the midst of a scandal. The Dukes of Rufford are valued clients, as well. I do not wish to be accused of favoritism."

Addie deflated. "Naturally not. I suppose I can go to the front desk and have Graf von Mayr paged."

"That might be best. Thank you for understanding, Lady Adelaide. You know I wish you nothing but the best. And your mother, too, of course."

Damn damn damn. Addie hoped for help, but it seemed she

had to do this on her own. Leaving Mr. Reeves-Smith to enjoy his tea, biscuits, and integrity, she stood in line before the registration desk in the crowded lobby like any ordinary person. A young man beckoned her forward, and she approached.

Addie smiled brightly, crossing her fingers behind her back. "Good afternoon. Is Graf von Mayr in? We had, um, an appointment, but I'm afraid I mixed up the time."

The desk clerk picked up the house phone. "Allow me to check for you, madam. Who may I say is calling?"

"Uh, Miss Beckett. Maeve Rose Beckett." Cee was not the only sister who could pose as a maid. She would tell von Mayr who she really was at once if he came down to meet her. She stopped herself from tapping her gloved fingers on the veined marble counter as the clerk turned away from her.

His conversation was remarkably brief. "You're to go straight up, Miss Beckett."

"I beg your pardon?"

"Graf von Mayr is expecting you."

"He is?"

The clerk nodded. "As per usual. Do you remember the room number?"

"I'm afraid it's slipped m-my m-mind," Addie stuttered.

"Room 348. The lifts are that way."

"Thank you." Obviously there was some mistake, but Addie was not going to argue. She dodged a bellhop with a pyramid of luggage, entered the lift, and told the operator the floor number.

The doors opened. "Three four eight. Three four eight," she muttered to herself, noting she had a fair walk on the floral carpet ahead of her. With each step, the butterflies fluttered in her stomach. She slowed her pace a bit, mustering calm. She wasn't here to accuse von Mayr of killing his father-in-law, just to gather information. She hoped Mr. Hunter would come to Mount Street tonight and they could compare notes.

If she survived the next fifteen minutes.

She arrived at the correct door and raised a fist to knock. Before she could, it was opened by a tall, extremely handsome blond gentleman with a dashing dueling scar slashed across his right check. He was wearing…absolutely nothing. Addie took a step backward and closed her eyes.

The desire to scream—or flee—was powerful.

That simply wouldn't do.

He was still naked when she looked at him again, and frowning. "*Du bist nicht, Rosie.*" He pronounced the name with a soft *c* sound as opposed to a *z*.

Addie noted that this Rosie was a "du" and not a "Sie" to him, familiar or beneath him in social standing. She struggled to keep her eyes on the scar, shining silver on his tanned cheek. "I believe there's been a misunderstanding," she croaked. All her mother's deportment lessons had not prepared her for nude men in hotels. In fact, Lady Broughton would probably not approve of Addie going to a strange man's room under any circumstances, even if it might exonerate her.

"*Ach,* well." He looked her up and down, and Addie felt as if she was the naked one. "Come through." *Come true.* "You will do."

She certainly would *not*. But the graf pulled her in by an elbow and shut the door. "Is Rosie unwell?"

His English was excellent except for his difficulty with "th," so Addie presumed he would understand that whatever arrangement he had with Rosie, it definitely did not apply to her.

She clutched her bag tightly to her bosom. "Forgive me. I'm afraid I've gained entry under false pretenses. If you'll permit me to explain—"

He moved to a fully stocked drinks table, and Addie noted that his bottom was as firm as the rest of him. It came as somewhat of a belated shock to her that she'd only ever seen one man completely undressed. There had been museum trips, of course, but that was not quite the same thing. No artwork hanging on a wall or standing on a plinth conveyed such smoothness of skin, the musculature beneath, the patches of golden fur. And none Addie ever encountered were blessed with von Mayr's considerable male protuberance, which in her opinion would require two or more large fig leaves for a semblance of decency. Goodness, this detecting business certainly was expanding her horizons at a rapid clip.

He poured himself a whisky and added a splash of soda. "Your colleague and I have agreed to terms. Do not think because I am a foreigner that you can take advantage. Shake me down, as it were. I went to Eton College."

Bully for him. "I am not what—um, who—you think I am." Should Addie be offended to be taken for a woman of easy virtue? A—a—courtesan? Her charming Reboux hat cost the earth, and the Lord knew the buttercup-yellow dress was not cheap. But perhaps real money could be made in the oldest profession if one had the appropriate clientele.

The drink stopped midway to his lips. "*Gott in Himmel!* You are not one of those bloody reporters, are you?" He put the glass down, snatched a decorative jacquard pillow from the sofa, and held it strategically in front of the von Mayr family jewels.

Addie felt a brief stab of disappointment that her education was being curtailed. "Oh, no! Nothing like that. I had hoped Mr. Reeves-Smith—the Savoy's manager, you know—might introduce us, but I was unsuccessful in persuading him. I'm so sorry I gave a false name to the clerk, but I thought if you knew who I really was, you might not agree to see me."

"Who the devil are you, woman?" His face paled. "Wait! Did my wife send you?"

She saw a narrow avenue open. What had Mr. Hunter said? They had to redraw the map. She'd acted in a handful of school plays at Cheltenham Ladies' College. Perhaps it was better not to tell him who she was. She was a terrible liar, but if she was playing a part…

Addie tutted and shook her head sadly. "Poor dear Penny. I don't know what I shall tell her about all this."

If possible, he grew paler. "Wait right there. Do not move," the graf ordered. He nearly ran to the door that closed off the bedroom from the drawing room, slamming it behind him.

He couldn't mean that she should actually stand in place while he slipped into something less comfortable, and in truth, her knees were knocking a little at her brazen scheme. Addie dropped into a wing chair in front of a fireplace that was filled with fragrant flowers. The room was beautifully appointed; she'd expect nothing less at the Savoy. The soft furnishings were a soothing combination of cream, ecru, and ivory, which must be a challenge for the housekeeping staff to maintain. She certainly had regrets regarding the décor at Mount Street, which was altogether too fashionably white and caused Beckett to complain endlessly.

Clad in a striped silk robe, the Austrian emerged from the bedchamber sooner than Addie expected. She had hoped he would come out in a suit, for it would be easier to be businesslike. The man was still barefoot, for heaven's sake.

He picked up his abandoned drink and swallowed it in one go. "Explain yourself."

"It's you who needs to explain. I thought you were trying to reunite with Penny," Addie said, conjuring up her old governess and giving him a stern look.

"Are you from an inquiry agency? How much is she paying you?"

"Certainly not! Please sit down, Graf von Mayr. Perhaps we can come to an arrangement."

He continued to loom over her. "Blackmail so you won't tattle on me? What kind of friend are you? I have nothing to hide. Nothing. Rosie is my, uh, masseuse. Our afternoon appointments are all perfectly innocent. My war wound is a constant bother." He rubbed a silk-covered shoulder for emphasis, but Addie wasn't fooled. Rosie was no doubt skilled at rubbing everything.

"Penny doesn't trust you, and I see she is justified."

"I told you there is nothing going on! I love my wife! The children visit me here in the hotel since I arrived, but it's not like us all being together at the *schloss*. You must persuade Penelope to forgive me." He paused, looking down at his feet. "I suppose she has told you what her father did, may he rot in hell. Almost six years he has kept my family from me, the miserable bugger."

Now they were getting somewhere. "So you're glad he's dead."

The graf snorted. "I would have shot him myself if I'd thought of it first."

"But you didn't?"

"Of course I didn't! That woman did. What is her name? Brighton? Brougham? You read the papers."

"One cannot always believe the gutter press. Where were you when the duke was killed?"

"Right here! And before you ask it, alone. No Rosie. No anybody. Please tell me Penelope does not think I murdered her father! I did not like the man, but Penelope is—was—very fond of him. I would do nothing to hurt her."

Addie raised an eyebrow. "Nothing?"

He raked his hands through his fair hair, inexplicably appearing even more handsome when he was finished. "Liesl and Murli were mistakes. They meant nothing to me, and Penelope knows it. I was so lonely, you understand. And to find out the duke set me up and sent his spies to take those photographs! The man deserves to be shot all over again for what he did to my family. Tell her I will do anything to get her back. Anything."

Had he resorted to murder to save his marriage? Addie wouldn't rule it out just yet.

Chapter Twelve

"You enjoyed yourself far too much, old girl." Rupert pushed past her and clambered into the taxi before she could slam the door in his face. Addie slid in after him and took out her compact. She looked just the same—no Pinocchio nose for her. No rosy flush of guilt, either. Keeping the mirror over her mouth so the driver would not think she was insane, she whispered, "You were there?" He might have warned her about the graf's dishabille.

"Not until the end. I just popped in in case you needed moral support. There was no need for me to step in. You did very well prevaricating. I'm proud of you."

Rupert *would* reward her with praise for the same devious skill he possessed. She had tricked von Mayr into thinking she was a friend of his wife's and hadn't even been required to give her real name. Addie snapped the compact shut and, despite her dead husband's prodding and provoking, refused to speak to him until they got out at Mount Street.

She opened her bag and fished out the borrowed keys which were tied together with a rather dirty string. "Did you take my keys?"

"What keys?"

"My house keys! I left them in the garden door and now they're missing."

"Of course not. I don't need keys to gain entry."

This was true. Rupert appeared at will when he was least wanted. Did he walk through walls or just materialize? This ghosting was complex, and even Rupert appeared uncertain at times.

"What's for supper?" he asked, as they climbed the stairs to her first-floor flat.

"Whatever Beckett has thrown together. You're not invited." Her maid's head was often in the clouds after sitting in a dark movie theater all afternoon, so dinner was apt to be an afterthought.

Addie would be satisfied with a toasted cheese dining in a nightgown anyway. She corrected her mental sentence. *She* would be wearing the nightgown, not the cheese. What was that? A misplaced modifier? Rupert's presence always mixed her up. But, with any luck, Inspector Hunter would pay her a visit this evening, so the nightgown would have to wait.

"I'll just pop into my club then," Rupert said.

"Your club? You mean 'the Senior?'" The United Service Club had been formed in 1815 for senior officers, and once Rupert became a major, he'd been nominated and accepted for membership.

"No. Not that one. They're nothing but a bunch of bores resting their stringy bottoms on their laurels. All they do is drink to excess and drone on about whichever war they served in, one-upping each other for guts and glory. This new club is more of an informal post-life group. We meet at Highgate Cemetery when we're not out fulfilling our respective missions and compare notes."

Addie wished she was no longer part of Rupert's "mission," but it was intriguing to think of other dissatisfied ghosts wandering around London in Limbo along with her late husband. At least he had company. "Have fun."

Rupert gave her a wave and disappeared before she could put the key in the door.

She realized he'd neglected to tell her if he learned anything new at Maddox Street.

"There you are!" Cee cried, rushing into the hall. "We thought you might have been kidnapped."

Addie stood before the mirror and removed her hat. Her sister did tend to be dramatic. "Kidnapped? Why would you think such a thing?" She fluffed her bob with her fingers, trying to recover her curls. Not that she cared what Inspector Hunter thought of her looks whatsoever.

He might not even come tonight.

"Well, your note said your keys were gone. We've been on tenterhooks since we came back from the picture show thinking some brute might have broken in and was marauding through Mayfair with you. We very nearly called the police!"

That was all they needed. "I told you I went to the Savoy. Nobody's invaded—the keys have only been misplaced. They might have fallen out of the lock and some squirrel made off with them."

"A magpie, more like," Beckett said from the dining room, where she was laying the table with Addie's best china. "Your Mr. Hunter just called from the train station. It was hard to hear him over the crowd noise, but I invited him to dinner. I hope he heard *me*."

He was not hers. Why, just a few days ago he was saying good-bye forever.

"We'll make ourselves scarce. Beckett is taking me to a Lyon's, and then we're going to see that new movie, *The Lost World*. It's based on Arthur Conan Doyle's book, you know. Dinosaurs!

Ape-men! It all sounds too thrilling. Imagine, three movies in one day. After that, we might look in at a nightclub that maids and butlers visit on their evenings off. Beckett's a very bad influence on me." Cee grinned, looking perfectly happy to be corrupted. Addie knew her sister was every bit as worried as she about her mother, but was glad she found sufficient distraction. It was an improvement over the headaches and listlessness.

"Dinner! How have you had time to cook anything?" Addie asked, her heart skittering. Did she have time to change? Her dress was dreadfully crushed.

"Oh, I ordered from the Connaught and put it on your account." Beckett said, folding a napkin into a fanciful rose. Lady Broughton would not approve such a departure from tradition. Plain was always best. "Crab cocktail, cold peach soup, Dover sole, rice timbales, lamb cutlets, potatoes au gratin, asparagus, minted peas, a cheese board, and strawberry-rhubarb pie. They'll deliver it in the next half hour, and you'll just need to keep the hot food hot and the cold food cold. The wine is decanting, and the coffee's ready to perk. I think that should be enough, though who can tell? Mr. Hunter has a healthy appetite."

Addie felt stuffed just listening, and even he could not do justice to such a feast.

"You should change into the beaded teal chiffon," Cee said helpfully.

"You're sure it's not too teal?"

Cee stuck her tongue out, and she and Beckett left Addie to her own devices.

The teal chiffon was far too fancy for a quiet dinner with a policeman, no matter how elaborate the meal was. Or how attractive the man. Addie changed into a plain coral georgette sheath with a handkerchief hem, wishing she hadn't given her coral jewelry away.

Impulsively, she removed her engagement and wedding rings. It was time, wasn't it? Her hands looked strange without them. She wasn't especially vain—how could one be when one had to wear tortoiseshell spectacles to find one's way out of bed? But she did love jewelry. She locked the rings away and tried to make some headway with her flattened hair.

When the porter rang to announce the waiter from the Connaught, she swiped on some lip rouge and went to the kitchen door. The poor fellow was bogged down with boxes right up to his nose, and Addie unburdened him by taking a few of the top layers away.

Once the man's mouth was exposed, he asked, "Do you want me to stay and serve, my lady? I'm sure they wouldn't mind."

Addie considered the offer briefly, but rejected it. She and Mr. Hunter required privacy. It was up to her to control her silly *tendre* without a chaperone, and stick to the investigation.

Left with containers on nearly every surface, she tucked covered dishes into the warming oven and icebox. Now all she had to do was wait.

She sat in the drawing room flipping through one of Beckett's magazines. None of the upcoming features appealed to her much; she preferred live theater to films. She hadn't been to a play in a long while, and really couldn't go in good conscience until her mother's situation was settled.

Addie was glad Cee was able to find some amusement, and hoped Ian would be able to take advantage to strengthen his suit. It was also time that Addie stopped feeling so responsible for her sibling—Cee was twenty-five, more than old enough to take care of herself.

And a family. Addie was quite looking forward to becoming an aunt. Children growing up again at Broughton Park would be delightful.

The flat phone rang again with Daniel informing her of the imminent arrival of Detective Inspector Hunter. She no sooner hung up when the doorbell sounded.

Mr. Hunter appeared tired, still carrying a travel case with his good arm. Really, he should be resting rather than going all over creation to help her mother. But he smiled, and Addie smiled back.

He set the case down and removed his hat. "Excuse my dirt. I came straight from the station."

"You look fine." He looked more than fine, even if his tweed jacket was rumpled.

"Something smells delicious. I hope you're not annoyed with Beckett for inviting me."

"Not at all! But neither she nor I can claim credit for the meal— it's the Connaught to the rescue again. If you'd like to sit down in the dining room, I'll bring everything out to the sideboard."

"Let me wash up first. I'm hungry enough to eat the sideboard."

Addie directed him to the powder room off the hall, and went into the kitchen. Donning oven mitts, she trekked back and forth until all the food was on display in the chafing dishes.

Mr. Hunter entered, his thick dark hair combed and his tie properly knotted. "This looks fantastic. Thank you, Lady Adelaide."

"Thank Beckett. She did the ordering—I think this meal could feed half the tenants in the building. May I serve you? I'm sure it might be easier."

"You may. I haven't mastered cutting up my food with only one hand available, either. This sling is a nuisance."

"But necessary. How is your shoulder?"

"I'm all right."

He probably wasn't telling the truth; men were meant to be stoic, weren't they? To never complain. To be strong and silent, to stifle their feelings. It was ridiculous, really. Addie mounded the crabmeat on a lettuce leaf and spooned the Marie Rose sauce on the side.

"Was it worth the trip?" she asked, setting the dish in front of him. She poured a splash of wine in both their glasses and served herself.

"I believe so. I have a great deal to tell you but don't wish to speak with my mouth full. I haven't eaten since breakfast, so—" He gave her a boyish grin.

"By all means, tuck in." The crab was chilled to perfection and disappeared from both their plates in a short amount of time.

By the time he'd eaten half his soup, the edge of his hunger was dulled, and he was ready to talk.

"A local man drove me to the settlement outside Rufford Castle. It's not that far from Berwick, but they're in their own world up there. Most depend on the duchy for employment, and everyone knows everyone else's business."

"Like Compton-under-Wood," Addie said. She loved her adopted village, but maintaining one's privacy was difficult, if not impossible.

"Like most any country place in the kingdom," Dev agreed. "Gossip comes in handy for police work. Anyway, the fellow introduced me to some men in the pub where I stayed, and it didn't take much to get them to air the duke's dirty linen."

"Which one?"

"Both. Edmund was pretty well thought of, though. Very strict, set in his ways, but mostly fair. Old-fashioned noblesse oblige and all that. His son, on the other hand, is not at all popular. In fact, it's the general opinion that Alistair killed the old man to get free of him."

Addie shook her head. "Not according to him. He was in the arms of his lover when the deed was done."

"Do you have proof?"

"Only his word, and I don't trust him an inch. He's a very unpleasant man. Ian went out of his way to be helpful and organized a dinner for us as you suggested, but I'm afraid I did nothing more than put the duke's back up."

"Well, you can't expect him to thank you for ambushing him. I wondered how the evening would go."

"Not very well. Why do people believe he murdered his own father?"

Mr. Hunter helped himself to the fish course. "Edmund regularly clipped Alistair's wings, and not only financially. He interfered with the raising of his grandchildren and generally thought he knew what was best for the family. I imagine that gets tedious over time."

"I know Graf von Mayr thinks so."

Mr. Hunter raised an eyebrow. "You *have* been busy in my absence, I see. How did you manage to meet him?"

"I went to the Savoy." Addie felt her cheeks go warm. "There was a mix-up, and he thought I was someone else and let me come up."

"What kind of mix-up?"

"Um." How much to explain? It was rather embarrassing. "He is visited regularly by a...a masseuse. Or so he says. For his war wound, but to be frank I didn't see any blemishes. And I had ample time to look as he greeted me at the door without a stitch of clothing on. I think he was waiting for another sort of female."

Mr. Hunter broke out into laughter. "Good lord. He thought *you* were a pros—um, lady of the night?"

"It was teatime. More like lady of the afternoon, and only at first. Then he thought I was a detective come to gather dirt about him, but I pretended to be his wife's friend instead. He told me the duke—Edmund—had kept them apart unfairly, and he would have liked to shoot him. But he assured me he did not."

"Do you believe him?"

"I don't know. He had ample reason to be angry at his father-in-law. He claims to love Penelope, though I gather he's been unfaithful, too. He blames Edmund for tricking him into affairs. Apparently, there is photographic evidence. But honestly, if you weren't already inclined to break your marriage vows, how is it possible to be tricked?" At least Rupert didn't blame anyone else but himself for his wayward ways.

"You are full of surprises. You got more accomplished than I, and probably had more fun doing it."

"I wouldn't say that," Addie replied with modesty, though the afternoon had been somewhat stimulating.

"I would. You interviewed two principal suspects, and I trust your instincts. I only got second- and thirdhand information."

Addie sliced a lamb cutlet and passed it to him. "What else did the locals have to say?"

After he cleared his plate, Mr. Hunter sat back in his chair. For a one-handed man, he was pretty efficient in putting the food away. "You're right about Alistair being unpleasant. He's debauched more than his fair share of young women over the years. It's fair to say he was a disappointment to his father, who was a stickler for the proprieties."

Like Mama, Addie thought.

"His sister—your pretend friend Penelope—is far more well-regarded, even if she was married to, and I quote, 'a bloody Hun.' She takes an interest in charity, particularly the education of girls, and sponsors some sort of reading group at the castle. Making up for her brother, I'd say. Her children are better liked than Alistair's, even if—and I quote again—'they talk funny.' The old duke preferred them, too. And he didn't much like his daughter-in-law, and let everyone know Alistair was a fool for marrying her. Alley cats have better morals than the new duchess, according to my driver, Bill Neal. That's N-E-A-L, by the way."

Elaine. But Addie couldn't explain how she knew anything about the woman without revealing Rupert's spying.

"So what you're saying is the old duke didn't really like any of them except for Penelope and her children. But the Austrian contingent might not have been sanguine about Edmund's interference, no matter how much he favored them." Addie set the cheeseboard between them.

"Correct. We really have not eliminated anybody. It's curious why he was so set in being surrounded by his family when their behavior was so unsatisfactory to him."

Addie spread soft cheese on a wafer. "Control. Or maybe he tried to keep them out of trouble."

"Well, he failed there. I have it on good authority—Bill Neal again—that Alistair's son, Stephen, married an American Negro singer. Hopped over the border to Gretna Green a few weeks ago. Needless to say, his grandfather was not pleased. According to Bill, he came down to London to seek legal advice. The boy isn't twenty-one yet, but Scotland does not require parental permission."

Honestly, at this point Addie was so annoyed with Edmund she was almost glad he was dead. What had her mother seen in him? He sounded like a rigid, manipulating, arseh—

"Is there custard for the pie?" Mr. Hunter asked hopefully.

Chapter Thirteen

Dev contemplated going back into the powder room to release his top trouser button. He'd been an absolute glutton. If the unlikely occasion ever arose, he'd recommend the Connaught's kitchen to anyone.

They sat now in Lady Adelaide's very modern white drawing room. There were touches of color—reds and pinks—and she matched, looking like a flower in the snow.

He was too tired and full to think straight, and his ribs and shoulder were throbbing. Best to excuse himself and go home.

"More coffee?"

He should say no. But he held out his cup. "Yes, please." Despite his weariness, he always enjoyed Lady Adelaide's company. Too much. For months, he'd been unable to forget that kiss, one she'd initiated, when he visited her in April.

That was a problem.

Amongst many. They were no closer to gathering evidence to exonerate Lady Broughton. If anything, the cast of potential killers had expanded.

"Have you been to the new private club called the Southern Belle?" If Neal was correct, that was the new Lady Vere's current place of employment. He'd been shown a crumpled poster touting the "Jazzy Jones Sisters" that had somehow made its way up to Berwick-upon-Tweed.

Lady Adelaide frowned. "I have not. The Thieves' Den was enough for me. But Cee has. She says it's all the rage now, and joined last month. There are magnolias on the tables, and waitresses in hoop skirts, which must make navigating the dance floor with a tray of mint juleps next to impossible. Why?"

"Stephen's wife is performing there. Unlike the Thieves' Den, I've never visited the establishment in an official capacity, so I'm not known there. I wondered..." Was he being too brazen? But it wasn't a date, not really. And there would be no kissing involved. "...if we might go together and meet the young woman. Perhaps run into Stephen as well. From what I understand, they are not yet living together as man and wife in the family home. Edmund wanted the marriage annulled, and I have no reason to think Alistair is any different."

"Racial prejudice," Lady Adelaide murmured.

"Yes. Not uncommon," Dev said, knowing full well its effects. "We could ask your sister to join us."

Lady Adelaide smiled. "*She* act as chaperone to *us*? That would make for a pleasant change."

"Lady Cecilia is well?" Lady Adelaide's sister was a bit madcap, and a menace on the road. Unlike her sister, she refused to wear spectacles.

"Yes, more or less. She and Beckett have been keeping each other company, but I'm sure she'd like to feel useful. She's taken Mama's arrest hard, and with Cee, that means she's even flightier than usual. She needs to grow up."

All over Britain, young people Lady Cecilia's age needed to grow up. There was a wildness, an idleness, that didn't sit well with Dev's generation, men and women who were rushed into maturity by a devastating war. Their sacrifices had been rewarded with a complete lack of seriousness and rather desperate silliness from their juniors. Dev had little patience for them.

"Perhaps tomorrow night then. I plan on visiting your mother as well to let her know of our progress, or lack thereof."

"I'll go with you, if they'll let me visit."

Dev set his cup down. "If you don't mind, I'd like to speak to her alone. She might be…reluctant to be totally frank in front of you."

"You're right, of course. I still can't get my head around the fact that she was having an affair. I'm no prude, but it's just that she is—was—so very proper. And from what I'm learning about the late Duke of Rufford, he didn't deserve her regard. My father was his exact opposite—not so stiff-necked or straitlaced. He was *fun*."

"Spoken as a devoted daughter. It's hard to see our parents as real people sometimes with their own needs and desires. I look at my mother and marvel that she left everyone and everything she knew behind when she married my father. Moved halfway across the world for love. I'm fond of the man myself, but he's hardly Rudolph Valentino. It hasn't been easy for her, but she never complains. She's done her best to raise me as an English gentleman."

"And a good job she's done, too." Lady Adelaide rose with a smile. "If you'll excuse me a moment, I'm going to powder my nose."

Dev was left with his empty coffee cup. Well, he could make himself useful, too. He went into the dining room and gathered up the serving dishes and plates. A field mouse would be hard-pressed to make a meal out of the scrapings. He carried everything to the sink, filled the dishpan with washing powder and water, removed his jacket and tie, and rolled up his shirtsleeves. The service door opened before he had a chance to get his hands wet.

"Inspector Hunter! What on earth are you doing?"

Caught in the act! "Good evening, Lady Cecilia, Miss Beckett. How was the picture?"

"Get away from there. Sir," Beckett added to soften the order. She practically shoved him across the kitchen into a chair. "It was all right. Lots of dinosaur-fighting and not enough romance for my money."

"The little monkey was darling," Cee said. "Of course, the whole film was ridiculously inauthentic, though I suppose they did try. Then we went dancing for a bit, but I twisted my ankle. Did you fix the locks?"

"I beg your pardon?"

"Didn't Addie tell you? Someone stole her house keys—probably a reporter climbing over the garden wall. Let's hope that's who it was and not a crazed killer—they want our story, and it would be silly to murder us in our beds. Although," she considered to Dev's dawning horror, "that would be quite an exposé—*Murdering Marchioness's Daughters Discovered Dead.*" She stuck a finger into the custard bowl and licked it.

"Lady C!" Beckett tossed a dish towel in her direction.

"Oh, don't worry, Beckett. We'll barricade ourselves in for the night once Mr. Hunter leaves."

"I'm not leaving," Dev said with resolve.

The kitchen door swung open. "What's this all about?" His hostess had reapplied her lip rouge, and now licked her coral lips nervously.

Dev tried to rein in his temper. "Lady Adelaide, why didn't you tell me about your keys going missing?"

She didn't meet his eyes. "Please don't make a fuss. I probably dropped them in the grass."

"It's not safe for you three to stay here if you cannot lock your doors. What were you thinking?"

"I was thinking there is a night porter."

"Not if someone has access to your private staircase! Whatshisname will never know if someone sneaks in." The porter was a good fellow in his way, but hardly up to Dev's standards as a guard dog.

"Really, you're making too much of my carelessness. I doubt even the most dedicated journalist would scale the garden wall at midnight and try to gain entry and catch me in my pajamas. If the keys have been stolen—and I say *if*—someone might use them when we weren't home to snoop around. But there's nothing here."

"Nothing but silver and jewels and furs," Beckett muttered, bending over the sink.

"It could be a common thief, or one of those Forty Dollies," Lady Cecilia piped in. "Maybe Inspector Hunter is right. We could go to a hotel. Room service is always delectable. Eggs Benedict. Croissants. Those cute little pots of jam."

"I'm not packing a bag at this hour. We'll be fine," Lady Adelaide said, looking especially stubborn.

Dev stopped himself from poking a finger in her face. He knew from experience women didn't like that much. "Yes, you will. I'll spend the night."

One could have heard a pin drop in the tiled white kitchen. After at least thirty seconds, Lady Adelaide got over the shock and said, "What? You can't do that!"

"It's no inconvenience. I have my suitcase with me, and I won't be a bit of trouble. It's warm enough for me to sleep on the sofa even if you don't have a spare blanket."

"Of course I have a spare blanket!" Lady Adelaide cried. She glanced over to Beckett, who was trying hard not to grin. "We do, don't we?"

"Oodles. Blankets enough for a blizzard. And pillows, too. It'll be nice to have a big, strong man around the house. We want him to be as comfortable as he can be, don't we, Lady A?" She returned to the dishpan and scrubbed something with vigor, her shoulders shaking.

"I can give up my room and sleep with Addie if that helps, so that Inspector Hunter can get his beauty sleep," Cee said, not trying to smother *her* smile.

Dev couldn't be annoyed that they—except for Lady Adelaide—found the situation amusing. But he did not take any comfort that they seemed to encourage what was clearly inappropriate.

Impossible.

"The couch will be adequate," he said firmly. It was closer to the front and kitchen doors than the bedrooms were, and if there was an incursion, he'd hear it.

He didn't plan to sleep anyway. There were books in his case that he'd been neglecting, and it was time he focused. His self-improvement project was lagging of late. For some reason, ancient philosophers did not have the advice he currently needed.

Chapter Fourteen

"Isn't this a fine kettle of fish? So near, yet so far. Ah, the course of true love never did run smooth."

"Shut up." Addie didn't even bother to punctuate the utterance with an exclamation point. Rupert wouldn't pay attention anyway. He lived—so to speak—for teasing her about Mr. Hunter. And Cee was nearby; the last thing she needed was to explain to her sister that she frequently talked to her dead husband in the middle of the night.

Addie had been unable to fall asleep despite a cup of cocoa, and never would now, as Rupert lazed upon her chaise, his suit sharply pressed, cuff links gleaming in the bedside lamplight. Thank heavens Cee was in her own room, although perhaps if she had been sharing Addie's bed, Rupert might have thought twice about barging in.

No, Addie acknowledged, he was a barger now, appearing when one least wanted or expected him. He'd only find it amusing to see her spit and sputter trying to get rid of him without Cee getting wise to Addie's perpetual Rupertilian predicament.

She'd left Beckett with an armful of fresh linens to make up the sofa while she pin-curled her own hair. The thought of Inspector

Hunter just across the hall separating the bedrooms would have undone her.

She was undone no matter where the man was sleeping.

Mr. Hunter was practically undressed already, having lost his suit coat and tie when he tried to wash the dishes. Beckett had been suitably horrified, but was it really such a bad thing that a man showed his domestic side? After all, he lived alone. Unlike Rupert, he was probably used to taking care of himself. Addie wondered if he liked to cook—he certainly liked to eat.

"I'll have you know I managed quite well during the war. There were no maids and valets and gourmet meals in the officers' quarters, you know. You would have shuddered at the fodder they served us on occasion. Turnip this and turnip that. Tinned muck that deserved to be lobbed over the barbed wire to bean some Jerry in the brainbox. Might have killed him even quicker if he ate it. You may think I was spoiled and demanding during our marriage, but I was making up for lost time."

Rupert *had* been particular at table. Addie sighed. "I do wish you'd stop listening in."

"And I wish you'd give me some credit! I did have my good points."

"I don't want to argue. What have you unearthed in your travels?"

Rupert shot his cuffs. "I had no luck at Maddox House earlier—they were all out."

"*All* of them?"

"Well, except for little Grace. She was upstairs conjugating French verbs with her governess, and none too happy about it, I can tell you."

There was Rupert and his infernal mind reading. But it did come in handy on occasion. "You spied on a child and invaded her thoughts?"

He shrugged. "She's thirteen. Neither fish nor fowl. If we were in the Middle Ages, she'd be married and a mother, running a peel tower on the Borders while her husband was off on crusade. Mostly, I just encountered badly accented, fractured French and deep resentment, but I did manage to spirit away her diary." To Addie's horror, he tossed it on her bed.

"You stole her diary? That's low, even for you." She had kept a diary herself at that age, and as she recalled, it was full of her longing for her handsome neighbor Lucas Waring.

"You never know what Grace has observed. She's very bright, despite her difficulty with languages. You may thank me yet. But burn it or return it if you like, I don't care. Anyway, I paid a visit to Rufford's private banker's office before my little graveside meeting. There were no financial irregularities to be found in all the boring files—going back to the first Boer War when Edmund came into the title. The fellow was as sound as a bell when it came to his investments. Conservative, yet canny. Parsimonious when it came to disbursements, as you are already aware, although about a month ago he withdrew a substantial amount of money from one of his accounts. Perhaps he planned on buying your mother an engagement ring. A big one. Alistair must be dancing upon his father's grave with glee to get at his father's dosh. Metaphorically, of course—the police have not yet released the body. I believe the funeral is scheduled for Friday at St. George's, and will be private, by invitation only. Family and close friends, so don't expect to crash it."

"As if I'd try to crash a funeral!" Addie had some standards left, although the list was diminishing lately.

"Well, you know what your precious inspector says— oftentimes the murderer can never resist his—or her—victim's funeral. But I don't see how either of you can go—you can't very well disguise yourselves as gravediggers. Infiltration might be a job best left for someone of my special talents."

"Suit yourself. But the more we sleuth, the more suspects we uncover. Did you know Alistair's son has married his singer?" Addie was gratified to see the stupefaction on Rupert's face.

"Good lord! Does the family know? They didn't say as much when I popped in the other night. There was just a great deal of bluster and hand-wringing."

"They knew. Or at least his grandfather did. It was one of the reasons Edmund came to Town. He was to consult with his lawyers about dissolving the union somehow. Mr. Hunter found out it was a Scottish marriage on his reconnaissance trip north. One of the locals drove the couple over the border, and he was quite proud of his part in aiding young love."

"Over the anvil," Rupert murmured. "The boy's not of age, but it doesn't matter. Interesting. The various Dukes of Rufford have long believed themselves to be above everyone but the king, and I wouldn't be surprised if they found *him* wanting. Such an unequal pairing must have driven poor old Edmund around the bend."

"Why? Because the girl is American, an entertainer, or Black?"

"All of the above, I'd imagine. If he was set on annulling the marriage, he'd somehow find a way to do so. More often than not, dukes get their way. A misplaced marriage certificate would be child's play. Money exchanged, and a page torn from the records. Poor Stephen. His independence was about to be squelched."

"Do you think he could have killed Edmund?" Addie asked.

"I shouldn't have thought so, but then love has the power to turn the most mild-mannered man into a dragon-slayer. And Edmund was a bit of a dragon, to be honest. I'm surprised your mother fell for him."

"I am, too. Mama is many things, but she's never been small-minded. I mean, she's a woman of her times—not a radical by any means, obviously—but still has a generous heart. Edmund doesn't sound as if he had a heart at all."

"He was a duke," Rupert said. "A species of its own. And perhaps he was good in bed."

"Rupert! Ugh." One did not want to think of one's parent in the throes of ecstasy. In fact, sometimes Addie wondered how she and Cee had come into the world at all. She had received a mystifyingly oblique marital duty chat from her mother the morning of her marriage, so it was a good thing Addie learned something in her Cheltenham Ladies' College dormitory to help her maneuver her wedding night.

Of course, Rupert had enough skill for the both of them.

Gosh, Addie hoped he didn't hear her compliment. His self-regard was more than sufficient.

"So, I think we can rule out Edmund's running afoul of his banker. The prime motives for murder are usually love, money, or revenge, you know. So far, I can't think of anyone in the duke's social circle who had reason to feel betrayed enough to shoot the man—he was well-respected by those he cared to associate with. It does look like someone in his family pulled the trigger, but who?"

"Inspector Hunter and I are going to see Miss Jones sing tomorrow night." Addie squinted at her bedside clock. "Tonight. I really need to go to sleep."

"Shall I take the hint and shove off?"

"Please." Not that Addie was tired enough to let go and relax, despite the trying day she'd had.

"Very well. But I'd like it known I was prepared to sleep across the door like a guard dog to prevent the good inspector from taking liberties."

As if that would ever happen, Addie thought glumly. They merely had another professional relationship, insofar that she was helping him with an investigation. Fingers crossed it would lead to the release of her mother.

And then they'd never meet again.

She placed Grace's diary in a drawer, promising herself she'd try to send it back somehow. Addie would be absolutely mortified if someone read her diary from her youth, especially Lucas, who would tease her to death. She picked up her new book and found the place where she'd left off. Mrs. Woolf was an evocative writer, but Addie found *Mrs. Dalloway* to be both depressing and confusing. The bouncing back and forth between the years required more of Addie's concentration than she was able to spare at the moment, so she slipped her stamped leather bookmark back in amongst the pages. Another time, perhaps, when her mind was less scattered.

She switched off the light. The bedroom windows were cracked open, but the air was still and much too warm for this time of night. A fan was stored in her closet, though Addie was too lazy to get up and plug it in. She threw off the blanket and wriggled around for a bit trying to get comfortable. If she and the inspector were going to the Southern Belle tonight, she'd need some rest, hard as it was to come by.

She was reviewing in her head exactly which of her beaded evening dresses to wear when she heard a crash and cursing. Leaping from her bed, she wished she had her revolver. Though the last time it was in her handbag, she remembered ruefully, it had been no use to her whatsoever and had nearly got Mr. Hunter killed.

Leaving her robe behind but putting on her specs, she rushed down the hall to the drawing room. It was too dark to see, even if an electric torch had rolled under the coffee table and was beaming up at the recently vacated sofa. A fracas seemed to be occurring on the floor. She turned on the light just in time to watch Mr. Hunter punch the waiter from the Connaught in the face.

"What on earth?"

"We've found your thief, Lady Adelaide," the detective said

somewhat breathlessly. His dark hair was disordered in a rather delightful manner, although his face was thunderous. Hauling the man up to a sitting position, he nearly choked him by his tie. Not far away, her keys gleamed on the carpet on their sterling silver ring.

"There's b-been a misunderstanding," the waiter stuttered.

"Surely the hotel didn't send you to collect the dishes at this time of night," Addie said, perplexed. And that still didn't explain the sudden appearance of the keys. She scooped them up and put them in her pajama pocket.

"The hotel?" Mr. Hunter looked as confused as she felt.

"This is the waiter that brought our dinner."

The man flushed. "About that. I'm not really a waiter. I paid the fellow a fiver to let me bring up the food. He was happy he didn't have to climb up the service stairs with it all. Said his knee was bothering him. Shrapnel."

"I don't understand." For several reasons. The Connaught staff knew there was a dumbwaiter in the building to facilitate deliveries, so a waiter person wouldn't have to tote everything up on foot, just fetch it in the hallway.

He still would have to climb up the stairs, though, injured knee and all.

Should she call the hotel and report their employee was susceptible to a bribe? The man would get fired, and in these times, it was difficult to find employment. The real waiter probably had no idea the malevolent lengths this intruder would go to.

"If this brute lets me go, I'll explain everything."

"This brute declines," Mr. Hunter growled. "Who are you?"

"Joe Lombard. *The Daily Star,* London bureau. Society beat. You may have read my byline a time or two when you were in New York last winter, Lady Adelaide. I even wrote about you and your ma and sis cutting a swath through what passes for the elite in the Big Apple. See, I've done my homework."

He was American! And pretty good with a lower-class British accent earlier as the earnest waiter who wanted to stay and serve. "You're a reporter? Since when is it allowed to break into people's homes? That can't be allowed even in the States," Addie said. She'd read enough about the Wild West, and the Wild East for that matter.

"I didn't break in, did I? Used the keys. Would have returned them, too. Ow!"

Mr. Hunter had given Lombard a violent shake, which mottled his relatively handsome face. "Hold on, hold on. I'm not dangerous, I swear. I can barely breathe. You're killing me!"

"Good."

"I didn't mean any harm! Figured you might be having a night on the town to dance off your dinner and I'd just pop in for a few minutes sub rosa. All I saw before was the kitchen, and not a lot was going on in there. I wanted to get some background material for my big story on the marchioness. Humanize her, so to speak, with the odd titbit. Describe the posh digs where she lay her head. The golden knickknacks and whatnot she might have handled. Americans lap that royalty stuff up. I heard she usually stays here when she's in Town, and I wondered if she might have left something personal behind that would be of interest to the readers."

A hat? A garter? Or something even more unmentionable? Addie was appalled.

"A fellow's got to take a chance to get ahead in this business— your tabloids are even more competitive than ours. Dog eat dog, don't you know. I came into a bit of luck when I climbed into the garden and found the keys still in the door. It was almost like an Act of God."

Mr. Hunter snorted. "I don't know where you worship, but I'm calling the police."

Lombard's expression turned sly. "I wouldn't do that. You *are*

the police, aren't you? I recognize you from that nightclub murder case a couple of months ago. And won't it be another society
scandal to learn that Lady Broughton's daughter is slumming and
shacking up with an ordinary copper? Nice pajamas, by the way."

Lombard didn't have much time to gloat before Mr. Hunter
punched the man in the face again.

Chapter Fifteen

To add to the current absurdity, Beckett entered the drawing room in her pink chenille wrapper and pincurl bonnet, wielding a rattan rug beater in her small fist. "What's all this then? Who's that blighter asleep on the floor?"

"Never mind, Beckett. Mr. Hunter has it all under control."

Did he? Not very likely, Addie admitted to herself. The blighter would wake up and ruin all their lives unless she could think of a way to prevent him.

Killing Lombard was out of the question, wasn't it? Mr. Hunter might object. It rather went against whatever oath he'd taken at the start of his career, even if the man was American.

"So I should just go to my room?" Beckett sniffed. "I don't think I can unless somebody tells me what's going on. I could be murdered in my bed yet. The night is young."

"We have the keys. You don't have to worry about this bloke or anyone else disturbing you," Mr. Hunter said. "He and I will come to terms once he is himself again. In the meantime, you might fix us a pot of coffee if it's not too much trouble." He sat back down on the sofa, massaging his shoulder.

Had Mr. Hunter hurt himself in the scuffle? With his injuries, this was not an ideal time for him to be engaged in fisticuffs.

"I'll do it," Addie said quickly. The sooner Beckett went back to bed, the better. Fingers crossed Cee was still dreaming. Her sister had the capacity to sleep through almost anything, even the bomb-dropping zeppelins during the war. It was amusing when they were younger—Cee had been the perfect canvas for painted beards, mustaches, and third eyes. Once upon a time, Addie had been rather naughty, but adulthood had tempered her sense of adventure.

Mr. Hunter had awakened it. However, at the moment all she could see was a grim future for them all.

Addie shooed a grumbling Beckett away with a promise to explain everything in the morning. She prepared a coffee tray and carried it carefully into the drawing room. Lombard now sat up on the carpet, his wrists and ankles tied up with what appeared to be Addie's silver-braided curtain cords. A handkerchief had been shoved into his mouth, and he looked very cross indeed.

Mr. Hunter's suitcase lay open, his pajamas neatly folded on top. A very quick-change artist, he was now dressed in his suit, although he had not knotted his tie, and his feet were bare. Addie saw the significant scarring and discoloration of his war wound, and marveled how he could walk with only the slightest of limps.

"Do you want to press charges?" he asked. He shoved his feet into his argyle socks, never looking away from his captive.

"I don't think that would help Mama," Addie said, handing him a cup of coffee, after adding sugar as he liked it. She turned to newsman. "*You're* the reason Detective Inspector Hunter is here, Mr. Lombard. He was concerned about our safety after the keys went missing. After you *stole* the keys," she amended. "I was unable to arrange for a locksmith to come until tomorrow, well, today, I guess. So he volunteered to stay and protect us. He was sleeping on the couch. Furthermore, though you missed her, I am fully chaperoned by my martial maid, who would beat you like a rag rug if sufficiently provoked—she has a fearsome Irish temper. And my sister is also in residence." Who could sleep through incendiary bombs, but Lombard did not need to know that.

The man mumbled into the handkerchief.

"Perhaps you should let him speak," Addie suggested.

Mr. Hunter ripped the handkerchief out of Lombard's mouth none too gently.

"You know how he takes his coffee."

"I beg your pardon?"

"You didn't ask. One and a half sugars. No cream. I'll take some of that java, too, if you're pouring. Black is fine. You'll have to get rid of the ropes, though."

He was observant, she'd grant him that. Addie supposed it was a good skill to have if one was a reporter.

"Unbeknownst to the public, Lady Adelaide has assisted me in several cases," Mr. Hunter said stiffly. "There is absolutely nothing untoward in our relationship. Unsavory. Unsuitable. It would be ridiculous. Absurd. Laughable. As you said, I'm just an ordinary copper. Lady Adelaide is a marchioness's daughter and the widow of a famous Great War hero, far above my common touch or most men's, for that matter. If she does in fact know my coffee preferences, it is only because she was raised to be an exceptional hostess and has an excellent memory."

Rubbish. Mr. Hunter was seriously underselling himself. Addie was about to say so, but was prevented by Lombard. Considering he was still tied up, he looked quite smug.

"So you say, buddy, but I've seen the way you two look at each other. There's something going on here, I know it—I didn't get this far by being a dumb cluck. Star-crossed lovers. You're from the other side of the railroad tracks, as we say in my country, but don't let that stop you. Go full steam ahead. We're all equal in God's eyes, or should be. Say, did you read the Horatio Alger books when you were a kid? They should be right up your alley."

Addie felt her cheeks catch fire, while Mr. Hunter's dark face took on a grayish cast. Could it be this dreadful Yank had the right of it, and Mr. Hunter held her in as much esteem as she held him?

But then why hadn't he kissed her again?

It was too late in all respects for this kind of conversation. Addie summoned the spirit of her pre-incarcerated mother. Raising her slightly freckled nose and righting her shoulders, she stared down at the fellow with contempt.

"You mistake yourself, sir. Inspector Hunter has been hired privately by my mother the Dowager Marchioness of Broughton to discover the true perpetrator of the heinous crime of which she is accused. Of course we are in concordance—we have a mutual goal. I respect the detective's experience and acumen, and if I have been any minor assistance to him in the past, it has been entirely through lucky happenstance."

And Rupert.

"I know what I know," Lombard said, stubborn. "What's it worth to you to keep me quiet?"

"Are you threatening *blackmail* to an officer of the law?" Mr. Hunter asked, incredulous.

Lombard chuckled. "That's a harsh word, don't you think? I was thinking more along the line of an information exchange. Quid pro quo, as they say in ancient Rome and modern-day Washington. You rub my back, I rub yours."

"No one is rubbing anyone's anything. With Lady Adelaide's connections, I imagine she can have you deported before tomorrow's evening addition. Who is your godfather, Lady Adelaide?"

"The Chancellor of the Exchequer," Addie said promptly, hoping Lombard would not ask his name. She was almost positive it was Winston Churchill, though she didn't follow politics much. He would have been a little young to be a god-father when she was born, but Addie hoped Lombard was too ignorant—or American—to know it. In truth, her father's oldest school friend Rollo Lavenham had served in that role, and he was as dead as dear departed Papa. A charming Old Etonian, he might have been able to send a strongly worded letter on steel-engraved Smythson stationery to the United States, but not send back a man.

"So? I can pull strings, too. Look, I admit I made a mistake reconnoitering here. As you Brits say, it wasn't cricket. But I guar-antee all the other newshounds would do the same thing if they got the chance. Strike while the iron is hot—you're not gonna catch any worms of you sleep till noon, eh? What do you say we let bygones be bygones? There's no need to drag the authorities into this. I'll keep mum about the hanky-panky for the time being. And if you hear anything interesting in your investigation, give me a call. My direct line is on my business card, which I'd be happy to hand over if you untie me."

"There is no hanky-panky!" Addie exclaimed. Not for her lack of trying.

"I will not allow you to besmirch Lady Adelaide's reputation. You are aware of this country's libel laws, are you not? If you write one false word, I'll have you in the dock." Mr. Hunter clenched his fists. "I should arrest you anyway. It's people like you who give the press a bad name."

Lombard smirked. "But you won't. I might even be able to help you out right now."

"What do you mean?"

"Maybe your mother didn't do it. Rufford's family aren't a bunch of angels. Full of Huns and wastrels. The new duke is as mean as a snake, too."

"Everyone knows that," Addie snapped. "But he has an alibi. Or says he does."

"I wouldn't be too sure. His lady friend is in the south of France with her husband."

"Mr. Lombard, I hate to burst your bubble, but it's highly possible the man has more than one lady friend. I've just come back from the ducal seat in the North. The locals didn't mince words about his numerous affairs," Mr. Hunter said. "But more power to you if you can find out who he claims to have been with last Sunday morning. The police are not pursuing that information, taking the duke at his word."

"All right. I accept the challenge. But you'll have to let me go. Deal?" He held out his wrists in supplication.

Mr. Hunter sighed, and pulled out his well-worn army knife. "This goes against my better judgment. If you disparage Lady Adelaide in either speech or print, I'll be more than happy to give you another set of black eyes." He sliced through the curtain cords, and Addie made a mental note to ring her decorator for more.

Chapter Sixteen

Thursday night

Mama had spent four nights in gaol now, and tonight was the fifth. Considering everything, she was holding up remarkably well, impressing Addie and Cee during their brief visit this afternoon. Every hair was in place, and her rough cotton dress was pressed. Addie had the feeling her mother could subdue any pesky wrinkles by sheer determination, probably facial ones, too.

Mr. Hunter had been in to see her mother earlier to explain their findings, such as they were, so the Merrill women were able to chat about more pleasant things besides murder. All that was missing was a pot of tea and a plate of biscuits, although Addie left a generously stuffed hamper for the prison guard's perusal. Hopefully her mother would get some of the treats once all possibilities of poisons and pistols were eliminated.

Last night, Mr. Hunter escorted Joe Lombard to his lodgings, whereupon he spent a further hour threatening the man into discretion. He had omitted that news from his report to her mother, not wanting her to worry about her daughter as well as her own neck, so Addie had to watch her words. It was hard not to praise Mr. Hunter for his right hook, but she could be discreet, too.

Feeling somewhat buoyed by her mother's indomitable attitude, Addie dressed for her evening. She and Mr. Hunter were to be accompanied to the Southern Belle by Cee and Beckett in the hope that four heads were better than two. Addie wasn't sure how to approach the new Marchioness of Vere, who was still performing nightly to great acclaim, so they would all go as regular patrons of the establishment.

Cee, of course, had a membership, as the club had eclipsed the Thieves' Den as *the* place to be. Addie had never been, and was curious to see how barmaids in hoop skirts could traverse the dance floor without mishap. As a child, she had played in her grandmama's cage crinolines and could barely drag herself from one corner of the attic to the other.

The whole premise was a trifle silly to her, as the Old South had much to answer for. It had not been and was still not very gay for a large portion of its residents of color. But Bright Young People were hell-bent on ignoring unpleasant realities like slavery, lynching, and poverty, and were swilling mint juleps at an astounding rate.

Addie had settled on a midnight blue shimmery dress and did not put on all the sapphires she could have, not wanting to overwhelm Mr. Hunter. The detective was bound to feel out of place. Beckett, on the other hand, loved to go undercover with the Merrill sisters, and was borrowing one of the dresses Cee left in the spare bedroom closet for "emergencies." She and Cee were doing each other's bobs and makeup, so Addie was left on her own, which suited her. Beckett always wanted her to make more of a splash than Addie was comfortable with. The maid said it reflected poorly on her if Addie went out looking matronly, but Addie was not in the mood to be bullied tonight.

Their arrival, no matter how subtle Addie's costume, was bound to cause a stir. Everyone knew who they were and would wonder why they were out and about while their mother languished in gaol. But no one knew—yet—that one of the singing Jones sisters was married to the grandson of the man Mama was accused of murdering. Surely the four of them would figure out a way to approach her.

They'd get the lay of the land first. Have a drink, just one, at least for Addie. Perhaps even dance. Addie would like a chance to dance with Mr. Hunter, although she expected to be in competition for his attentions from Beckett and Cee.

Months ago, on their very first case together, he had acquitted himself very creditably foxtrotting with her childhood friend Barbara, then with her minder, Miss Schober. Babs and her nurse were in a fancy Swiss clinic at the moment while Babs tried to break some bad habits. Addie received a breezy postcard from her every couple of months. She hoped the new health regime was working, and wondered who Babs might fall in love with next. Her past romantic history was complicated, to say the least.

One might say the same for Addie. She was haunted by her unsatisfactory and insufficiently dead husband, and had no realistic prospects for a live one, not that she was at all anxious to marry again. And if she couldn't prove her mother's innocence, she and Cee would be social pariahs.

They might even be already. She'd received some sympathetic notes from friends since she arrived in Mount Street, but people were not knocking down her door in droves to provide support. No doubt they didn't know quite what to say; etiquette books did not provide instructions for this kind of occasion.

She heard the doorbell and Beckett's yelp of dismay across the hall.

Addie stuck her head in. The room looked as if a tornado had recently blown through. Several dresses lay on the twin beds, and both girls were still in slips. "I'll get it. You two will be ready at some point this evening, won't you?"

Cee made a rude gesture Mama wouldn't like, and Addie left them to it.

The real action in any of the current crop of popular private clubs occurred closer to midnight. Addie sincerely hoped their business would be concluded by then. After last night's excitement, she had difficulty sleeping and wished she were in bed right this minute.

The smile on her face froze once she opened the front door. Holding a top hat in his hands, Mr. Hunter wore well-tailored black evening clothes, exceeding all her expectations, or anyone's. His collar was high, white, and starched, his silk bow tie perfect, his waistcoat embroidered in silver thread. A black paisley scarf served as a sling. Of all things, he wore a large carved jade pin of an elephant with a tiny diamond eye in his lapel, giving him a most insouciant air. She tried to imagine Rupert or Lucas wearing such an adornment and failed.

"Oh!" she breathed.

He grinned, breaking the spell a bit. "Oh, good, or oh, bad?"

"Oh, definitely good. Definitely. Wherever did you get the suit?"

"This old thing? Believe it or not, it belongs to my father. He hasn't had much opportunity to wear it since his retirement dinner. Thirty years at the Yard counts for something—it was quite the grand occasion. Fortunately, we're roughly the same height. My mother had to take the trousers in, but she was happy to do it for the cause. She said it's her fault to begin with the waist was so large. She is a very accomplished cook, and my father is a very accomplished eater."

Addie smiled. Like father, like son. Mr. Hunter always spoke of his parents with affection, and she knew his family was important to him. It was something they had in common. Cee might drive her mad with her fads and impossible crushes, but Addie would do absolutely anything for her. And she owed everything she was to Mama. Her mother might be strict, but had given Addie her strength and standards.

She needed to focus on the mission, and with Mr. Hunter by her side in his considerable finery, she allowed hope to enter her heart.

"Do come through. I'm afraid Beckett and Cee are not ready. Would you care for a cocktail? Sherry?"

Mr. Hunter shook his head. "I'll wait. There will be temptations enough at the Southern Belle. We'll have to blend in, though I expect you'd rather order a pot of tea."

"I would. But I promise not to be a total killjoy, even if we're engaged in a serious investigation. A glass of champagne never hurt me." Never really helped, either. Addie took comfort that she'd never be so impaired she'd ever drive into a stone wall like some people she knew.

Oops. Mustn't think of Rupert now. Perhaps she'd inadvertently conjure him up and the evening would be far more complicated than it was already.

"Is your shoulder still troubling you?" Addie asked, sitting on the edge of the sofa.

Mr. Hunter glanced at his arm and shrugged. "A bit. My ribs are still sore, too. I don't think I did myself any favors dealing with Lombard. You didn't see or hear anything from him today, did you?"

Addie shook her head. She'd swiveled it around like a spinning top when she was out with Cee, expecting to cross paths with him. "I didn't, and I made sure to look behind me everywhere I went. In front, too."

"Somehow I don't think he's the type to take no for an answer. I may have frightened him out of his wits last night, but in the light of day I'll bet anything he hasn't given up. Are you sure you still want to go out with me? It will cause talk."

It certainly would. All of society was bound to wonder who her dashing escort was.

Chapter Seventeen

Dev had nothing against liquor. Nothing against dancing. But somehow the combination produced a frenzy that set his policeman's instincts on edge. He waited for a wobbly spin or spilled drink to set these young idiots at each other's throats.

The gaiety seemed forced to him, a veneer so thin one could nearly see through it. In his time, young men had purpose. The country had been at war, and duty—and often death—called. Most of his generation was lost on blood-soaked fields, and the living were changed forever, some by invisible injuries that were just as pernicious as the loss of a limb or an eye.

How did one turn off the endless reel of horror in one's head? Dev knew many who could not. Drugs and drink blurred the misery, but nothing could cure it. Even the children here tonight—for Dev could not think of them in any other way—had suffered, and sought some respite from Britain's postwar bleakness in pranks and private clubs.

To give the Southern Belle credit, it was certainly outfitted to a higher standard than the Thieves' Den, another venue he'd come to know too well in the course of an investigation. Centered on the lace-covered tables, lavish silk magnolias with glossy cellophane leaves lay amongst crystal votives. Against the walls, papier-mâché columns sported artificial wisteria and ivy. Spanish moss—or something like it—trailed from a giant carved tree in the middle of the dance floor, a bench around its circumference in case one became too exhausted to dance an additional step. Iridescent stars twinkled above on a dusky violet ceiling. Dev felt as if he'd wandered into a production of *A Midsummer Night's Dream*, only instead of fairies, waitresses dressed in picture hats and hoop-skirted ensembles gingerly maneuvered around gyrating couples.

The band was loud and lively, though the Jones Sisters had yet to appear. Beckett and Lady Cecilia were somewhere on the dance floor. Lady Adelaide had nursed a glass of champagne so long it had gone flat. Dev was on his second bourbon and branch water (whatever *that* was). A specialty of the house, it was alleviating some of the discomfort of last weekend's wounds.

It was hard to believe that last Thursday he was presenting evidence at an inquest; the events at Fernald Hall felt like a life-time ago. He wondered what Sir Hugh Fernald had made of his letter, and how his young son was coping with the loss of his mother. The case had tried every ounce of Dev's resolve, and he was almost grateful for the respite of this "working vacation." Though if he didn't make some progress soon, Lady Broughton would regret asking for his help.

Lady Adelaide polished her eyeglasses with a handkerchief, then returned them to perch on her nose. "I don't see anyone I know, which I must say is a relief." She was seated so close to him there was no need to shout over the music.

"This doesn't appear to be your sort of crowd," Dev said. Or his. The reveling girls reminded him of the glittering Jordan twins, overly made-up and wearing precious little material on their lithe frames. The young men looked as if they only shaved every other day. By God, he was ancient by comparison.

"I wonder if I even *have* a crowd. My friendships have turned very strange lately."

"Humans are not very dependable, are they? I suppose that's why people have dogs."

"Fitz isn't dependable, either." She squinted through her lenses. "That boy over there sitting alone by the pillar—do you know him? He's staring at you."

Dev turned. An auburn-haired youth with a joke of a mustache quickly averted his eyes and picked up a pink drink.

"I've never arrested him." Much to his chagrin, Dev's photograph had appeared in the newspapers in the past. It was possible despite his natty costume than he'd been sussed out as a copper. "Perhaps he was staring at *you*." Lady Adelaide was extremely stare-worthy this evening, in a dark blue gown and what he was pretty sure were not paste sapphires.

"I think he might be Stephen Moreton. There's a resemblance to his dreadful father. Not the coloring, but the chin and nose. And those icy-gray eyes."

The band ended in a shrieking flourish, and the club's manageress took the microphone. "Good evenin', ladies and gents! I'm your hostess Miz Dorothée Baptiste, from way over yonder in N'awlins. Y'all will want to sit a spell and catch your breath," she said in an awful faux drawl—Dev thought the woman was a Cockney from briefly speaking to her earlier as she led them to their table. She waited a minute or two for the dancers to disperse, toying with a long strand of fake pearls. The waitresses, resembling schooners buffeted by the wind, moved en masse to the tables to take orders from the perspiring guests.

"Y'all are about to be blessed. Blessed, I say. What we have here tonight are two of the most sublime singers y'all ever did hear, all the way from Georgia, in the good ole U. S. of A. Sent to us by the angels since they couldn't stand the competition, I reckon.

These gals are sweet as peaches. Smooth as molasses. Hot as a sultry southern summer night. Let's give them a warm welcome. Put your paws together for the Jones Sisters! The beauties Bettie and Bobbie!"

The spotlight moved to a flower-decked archway to the rear of the raised band platform, and two very young women appeared from behind beaded curtains, holding hands and smiling. They looked no older than schoolgirls, save for the flashy dresses and elaborate stage makeup. Hoots and prodigious foot-stomping followed—they were known to the audience and evidently very popular. Some of the young men stood up and whistled, including the red-haired fellow that Lady Adelaide had pointed out. One of the girls noticed him, and gave a modest wave.

The new Marquess of Vere? Was Lady Adelaide right? Which meant that one of the singers was his marchioness. Bill Neal had not known the given name of Stephen Moreton's wife, if wife she could be called. Dev wasn't certain about the legality of the marriage which had brought his grandfather the duke to Town. But the boy's presence tonight could not help ease any contact he might make with Miss Jones. No doubt he'd object if he thought Dev was moving in on his territory. Lady Adelaide was perhaps better suited to make an approach.

Bettie and Bobbie were not twins, but the family resemblance was clear. Both were of medium height and very slender, with marcelled hair capped close. Not a strand was out of place, almost as if it was shellacked on. Dev was reminded of Josephine Baker, whose style the sisters were emulating. And when they opened their mulberry-red lips and began to sing in the too-bright spotlight, the hairs on the back of his neck rose.

They began with what was sometimes played as an up-tempo foxtrot, Irving Berlin's "What'll I Do?" but slowed it down. The harmony that only comes from related vocal cords hushed the room. The sisters truly did have angelic voices, and they eased into another Berlin ballad, "All Alone."

One of the girls stepped forward on the second verse, her hands folded together as if in prayer.

> *Just for a moment you were mine, and then*
> *You seemed to vanish like a dream.*
> *I long to hold you in my arms again.*
> *My life is very lonely*
> *For I want you only.*

Her sister joined her on the refrain, the blended notes exquisitely sad. The raucous crowd was totally silent and in thrall to the music. It was as if these callow Bright Young People in the audience knew true heartbreak, which Dev rather doubted.

He shot a glance at Lady Adelaide. A single tear slipped down her cheek, and Dev longed to wipe it away. She must miss her husband, even if he'd broken his vows. The man hadn't deserved her, war hero or not.

And then the mood broke, as the Jones Sisters segued into a lively version of "I'll See You in My Dreams." Even though the lyrics were similarly downbeat, the girls turned the song into a joyous celebration, shimmying along with the band. The spotlight bounced around the ballroom, and couples sprang up to dance their sorrows away, Beckett and Lady Cecilia included.

Dev untied his sling with fumbling fingers. "Want to give it a go?"

Lady Adelaide's blond eyebrow raised. "Are you sure? You won't jolt anything?"

If he did, it wouldn't matter; in his old age—probably in his cups—he could say he danced with the divine Lady Adelaide Compton.

"Be gentle with me." He winked.

They took to the dance floor, staying near the edge for safety's sake. As much as Dev would have liked to take her in his arms, he enjoyed watching her kick and wave her arms about, a smile blossoming on her face. He sensed she wasn't entirely comfortable with the gay abandon demonstrated by their compatriots, though, but she was a good sport. He knew she was game for a great deal more than most women of her class. He'd seen her bravery and grit, and respected her insight.

He really, really liked her, which was a damned nuisance.

The sisters sang another exuberant number, but Dev and Lady Adelaide gave up after the first few bars and settled back into the velvet-cushioned gilt chairs. They were immediately approached by a tray-bearing Southern Belle—who was probably raised in Hackney—as Lady Adelaide refastened his sling, having some difficulty with the knot in the flickering candlelight.

Dev didn't want any more to drink, but he did want information. Upon learning that the Jones Sisters' set was almost at an end, he turned to his companion.

"You'll cause much less fuss if you visit their dressing room. Are you willing to speak to Miss Jones in a few minutes?"

"Of course. Or try to. See which way the wind is blowing."

"I'll see if I can occupy her swain if he looks like he's going after her."

"Her swain?"

"That fellow you noticed earlier. They've exchanged a few discreet glances, and I'm betting you're right and he's Stephen Moreton. No, don't turn and look—it's too dark anyway to see much." Putting a lie to his words, the spotlight swept over their table and lingered too long.

Would they be recognized? Why, damn it, yes they would. That blighter Joe Lombard was making his way through the dance floor towards them right this very minute.

Chapter Eighteen

"Go! Now! Don't ask questions." Inspector Hunter gave her knee a rough squeeze.

Addie was stunned by this unexpected behavior, but she didn't hesitate. The detective must have his reasons, and heaven knows, she was not going to argue when his face was so stormy. She grabbed her evening bag, since she had the forethought to stuff it with several ten- and twenty-pound notes as well as her Helena Rubinstein's Cupid's Bow lipstick. She'd had fair success in the past with bribery, and there was no reason to think it wouldn't work again. Money was a universal language, and pounds and dollars were not so far apart.

Addie had done a little reconnaissance earlier after she visited the ladies' loo. The performers' dressing rooms were down a half-flight of stairs. There had been a rather large man with a crooked nose stationed in a folding chair at the top, but that's what one of the tens was for. Judging from the exceptionally enthusiastic reception the Jones sisters had received, he was probably there to repel stage door johnnies. Well, Addie was a female, and posed no threat to their virtue. While the band was made up of handsome fellows, she had no designs upon them, either.

What she wanted was information. Now, if only she knew what questions to ask.

She was in luck. There was no sign of the bouncer, just his chair, and she slipped into the shadowed stairwell. She could still hear the music, so she needed to find which dressing room the girls used. The first door she opened was a closet filled with boxes of linens and glassware. The second was a largish room, with instrument cases strewn about, the scent of hair oil and aftershave quite pungent. Third time was the charm.

The sisters shared a small space, but it was pin-neat, a profusion of flowers taking up much of the flat surfaces. Several matching glittery dresses hung on a movable rack, with coordinated shoes lined up below. The dressing table contained a basket of jumbled makeup, the brands of which were mostly French.

Perhaps the girls had appeared in Paris first. The French were having a love affair with American Negroes. There was even a word for it—*négrophilie.* Entertainers and artists achieved far more accolades abroad than they did in their own country. Addie had read that many black ex-soldiers from the States decided to stay abroad where there was a degree of freedom—at least inside the Parisian jazz clubs—that was not to be found at home. Previously playing at the iniquitous Thieves' Den, Ollie Johnson and the members of his All American Band were there now. Addie wondered how he and his new wife were doing; perhaps the Jones sisters could tell her. Likely it was a small world amongst expatriate American entertainers.

There were only two bentwood chairs before the mirror. Addie didn't want to presume, so she waited, leaning into a corner to prop herself up. The truth was, she was very nervous and her knees were being uncooperative.

It was only five minutes or so before she heard the thud of footsteps and good-natured laughter as the band sought their well-deserved break. The paneling was thin and uneven between the two rooms, so the thumping and scraping of chairs was audible, as was muted conversation. Soon a harsh, unfamiliar odor drifted through the cracks, and Addie wrinkled her nose. French tobacco? Burning rubbish? Whatever it was, it was vile and made her a little dizzy just breathing.

She'd never taken up smoking, although there was a certain glamor involved with long ivory holders and gold lighters, attentive gentlemen at the ready. The act gave one something to do with one's hands, and filled awkward conversational gaps as well. But one didn't want to smell like an ashtray all day. Addie was far too fastidious and preferred a fragrant cloud of Chanel No 5.

Where were the singers? They seemed very young to be on their own an ocean away from Georgia. She didn't know the legal age to marry in the States, but neither one of them appeared to be over twenty-one. If that red-haired boy in the club was Stephen Moreton, he lacked the gloss and vivacity of his wife, and Addie was hard-pressed to see his attraction aside from his title. Did the girl care—or even know—about a marquessate? Addie presumed Stephen's income was still controlled by his father, which would definitely dull the romance.

She checked her sapphire-and-diamond-studded watch. How long did the band have to refresh themselves? Perhaps the sisters were taking their break with the musicians, which wouldn't suit Addie at all. She didn't quite dare to go next door. It was one thing to attempt a visit with two young women, altogether something else confronting a roomful of strange men and the fug of smoke.

Really, though, she had faced much worse over the past year, from Rupert's unexpected death to being held at gunpoint. Just a few days ago, dead bodies were turning up with dismaying frequency. Surely she could tap on the door, hold her breath, and ascertain the whereabouts of the Jones Sisters.

Happily, it turned out she didn't need to. The dressing room door creaked open, and one of the girls entered. Addie tried to smile.

Huge brown eyes fringed with false lashes widened. "May I help you?" Her speaking voice was as mellifluous as her singing.

"I do hope so." Addie stepped forward and held out a hand. "Forgive me for trespassing, but I'm so anxious to speak to you. Or your sister."

The young woman did not take her hand. "Why? Who are you?"

"Lady Adelaide Compton. You've never heard of me, I expect. Are you Bettie or Bobbie?"

"Roberta, actually. And Bettie is Elizabeth. Named after our folks, but that doesn't sound as cute on the marquee. What do you want?"

"May we sit down?"

"I haven't much time." Roberta made no effort to move to a chair. She did, however, examine her reflection in the freckled wall-length mirror, patting down a rebellious spitcurl. "What's this about?"

"Perhaps we can meet after the show, Roberta. My treat. I can take you and your sister out to dinner, or wherever you'd like to go."

"I have plans, Lady."

Gracious, did the girl think her first name was Lady? The encounter was proving to be more awkward than Addie had dreamed. She patted her handbag, feeling all too obvious. "I can make it worth your while."

"Can't. We're going to nibble one with a big-time British news-hawk after we're done. Won't hurt the Southern Belle none to get a little positive press. Good for business, and good for us. What's your beef?"

"It's important. Do you know the Duke of Rufford?"

Roberta's lips twitched. "The dead one or the new one?"

"The future one, really."

"That'd be me." She slid a hand under her bodice and drew out a ring dangling from a chain. She held the plain gold band up under the light. "His family send you to scare me away? Too bad. You're wasting your time. Stevie knows I've never skated around. I'm no chippie. His daddy can call in a hundred lawyers but they'll all tell him the same thing. We're married all right. All square. And I *was* a virgin."

How blunt the girl was! "I'm not here to question your marriage," Addie said with earnestness. "Someone shot your husband's grandfather, and I want to find out who."

"The fuzz caught the broad red-handed, and she's in the jug now. Gonna dance soon at the end of a rope. Why are you so interested?"

It would not help Addie any to smack this slang-spouting girl, but it was tempting. "She did not do it."

Roberta shrugged. "That's what they all say, isn't it?"

"In this case, I'd stake my life on her innocence."

"Then it's your funeral. Stevie says it's an open-and-shut case."

"Maybe he says that because *he* did it," Addie blurted most undiplomatically.

Instead of getting angry, Roberta erupted in a gale of laughter. "My Stevie? First of all, he wouldn't harm a fly, even a grumpy one like his grandpa. The man was a snob, and a cheapskate, too, but Stevie loved him anyhow. And besides, we were together that morning. Honeymoonin', y'know."

An alibi Addie simply couldn't quite trust. "Has he said anything about his grandfather's murder to you? Perhaps he knows something that might be helpful to the police. Something he's not even aware of. I would really like to talk to him."

Roberta shook her head scornfully. "Look, Lady, I don't know who you are or why you care so much that one old man is dead. We've all gotta go sometime. You're not roping me and Stevie into any of this. You got some nerve sneaking in here."

Addie extended a hand again and Roberta darted away. "Perhaps I didn't explain myself properly. The woman in gaol, the Marchioness of Broughton, is my mother. I'm sure you would do anything you could for your mother if she was accused of a crime she didn't commit. I *know* she's not guilty."

"No flies on my momma. If you'd ever met her, you'd know she'd be smart enough not to get caught. Tough luck for yours, but I can't help you. Truly. We don't have any more details than what the news rags say. Stevie didn't even have a clue where his grandpa was staying—he made the whole family come down to London on the train and then took off. Bonus for me, since I get to see my man again without having to traipse back up to the middle of nowhere. That castle is creepy as hell."

Another reason to be grateful that Addie's mother wouldn't become its chatelaine.

"You didn't like the duke?"

"Never met the man. Didn't stop him from not liking *me*. I'm sullying the bloodline, don't you know. Stevie says he came to see the show last week and was not impressed. I never noticed him in the crowd."

Addie was sure the Southern Belle was not his usual haunt. "Do you know if my mother was with him?"

"Sorry. Ask her."

"I will." Although Addie felt her mother might have mentioned it if she'd accompanied the duke on a secret mission to observe his grandson's bride. Mama had said he was concerned about a grandson but not that he'd married. Perhaps Edmund never told her.

There was a knock on the door, and one of the band members stuck his head in. "Time to sing for your supper, Bobbie."

"On my way." Roberta turned to Addie. "We're done here, right?"

Unfortunately, it seemed they were, and Addie was no wiser.

Chapter Nineteen

It had taken all of Addie's powers of persuasion to extract Beckett and Cee from the Southern Belle. Of course, listening to the Jones Sisters for their second set was no hardship; their voices really were extraordinary, and the band was quite good, too. Mr. Hunter was persuaded without too much effort to dance again with all three of them. It was only when she shamed Cee for enjoying herself too much while their mother was still rotting behind bars that her sister saw the feeblest of lights.

Rotting was perhaps an exaggeration, but the word had been reasonably effective. Cee now sulked in her room, and Beckett, still in her borrowed dress, was grudgingly making up a tea tray before she headed off to bed herself.

After the very briefest reports in the taxi, Addie waited until she and Mr. Hunter were alone to compare notes. "So how did you get rid of him?" she asked. That horrible reporter was at the nightclub, too, and had approached him with unsurprising brazenness.

"I didn't, actually," the inspector replied. "He got rid of *me*. He ditched me and buttonholed the Jones Sisters the second they left the stage. They looked very deep in conversation off in a corner. Very chummy. Either Lombard is a big fan or he's met them before."

"Do you think he knows about their relationship to the Rufford family?"

"Impossible to tell. He said nothing of it to me. Just threatened to 'expose' us again if we made a fuss about him to his superiors."

Us? There was no us. And if there was, would it be so horrible? Inspector Hunter was an intelligent, attractive man. He might not be titled, but he had dignity and an honorable career. A woman could do far worse.

She could marry Major Rupert Charles Cressleigh Compton, for example.

Addie frowned. "Roberta—that's Bobbie—mentioned meeting a reporter, but it was supposed to be after the show for drinks. My hunch is it wasn't Lombard. She said he was an Englishman."

"One of them didn't stay in the huddle too long. Roberta, I presume."

"Yes. I surprised her in her dressing room. It is she who's married Stephen. But I'm afraid I got nowhere with her. Apparently, the duke went to the Southern Belle to see her perform last week. She says she didn't know it and never met him then or any other time. She still had nothing much good to say about him, even if Stephen held him in some affection. She claims they don't know any more about Edmund's death than what they read in the papers. Her husband is convinced Mama is guilty and has not considered anything or anybody else. As for Sunday morning, the newlyweds were together and serve as each other's alibis."

"Do you think she was telling the truth?"

"She's very composed—it's unnerving, really—for one so young and in a foreign country. I wonder how she met Stephen. I didn't have a chance to ask. They seem a most unlikely couple."

"Because of the race difference?"

"Oh, no! Not that at all. She strikes me as an old soul. Independent and no-nonsense. Stephen has been ruled by his overbearing family his whole life."

Mr. Hunter smiled. "And now he'll be under his wife's rule."

Beckett shouldered her way through the door from the kitchen, and he leaped up to take the tray from her.

"It's very good of you to do this, Miss Beckett. I'm sure you've had a long day."

"Not as long as I'd like, but under the circumstances, I suppose the party had to end sometime. How do you want me to keep your sister out of trouble tomorrow, Lady A? We've seen all the new pictures."

"Maybe you both should go back to Broughton Park and wait."

"She won't like being left out."

And neither would Beckett. Addie could hear their objections now. They were both even more stubborn than she herself was.

"We'll visit Mama tomorrow. Perhaps she can encourage Cee to go home. It can't help my sister's reputation any to be seen out and about. If she's amusing herself, she'll be called callous. Or clueless. And attract unwanted notoriety. Have any of her friends called?"

Beckett shook her head. "Rats deserting a sinking ship, I'd say. Lady Cecilia hasn't said anything, but I know she's hurt."

"All the better to get her back to the country. You won't mind going with her?"

"Not at all. But maybe we should lay low at Compton Chase. There's less of a chance for the papers to camp out on the doorstep." And her beau Jack Robertson was there.

"I'm sure Ian can handle them at Broughton Park." Her cousin was proving to be an unexpected comfort. He had telephoned every day since their blighted dinner party to check on her. "But either place is preferable to being in Town. It's so hot."

Beckett rolled her eyes. "Don't bore the poor inspector talking about the weather. I'm going to bed."

Addie poured them both a cup of tea as Beckett went to her quarters. "Can you think of a way to occupy Cee here?"

"I confess, I can't think of a way to occupy *myself*. I was sure after going north we had a decent motive. Stephen Moreton's marriage might not have pleased his grandfather, but can you see the boy shooting him dead?"

"From what I've heard about him—" from Roberta and Rupert—"it would be out of character. Of course, we've seen stranger things happen."

"We have indeed, and quite recently, too." He returned his cup to the tray and absently kneaded his shoulder. "I'm letting your mother down. She's counting on me to solve the crime, and I'm no closer than I was from the beginning."

"It's only been a few days."

"The most important few days. I'll go to the Ritz tomorrow and see if I can jog anyone's memory about Sunday morning. Their security is good, but according to Phil Barnes's notes, no one noticed anyone suspicious entering the hotel at that early hour. They do remember a very jolly—Phil wrote 'rowdy'—group coming in from some all-night party, but with a little polite prodding from the management, they went straight upstairs to sleep it off. Apparently, drunk Americans escaping Prohibition are unwelcome to lounge about the lobby and let loose."

"Maybe the murderer *wasn't* suspicious," Addie said, suddenly struck. "He, or she, might have dressed as a maid like Cee's been doing these past few days. No one notices maids."

Mr. Hunter's eyebrow lifted. "You think a woman could be the killer?"

"Maybe. But who's to say a man couldn't dress up as a woman?"

"Now that's a film plot if I ever heard one. It reminds me of the one we talked about last week, only in reverse. And a rather ingenious idea. Lady Adelaide, you never cease to amaze me."

Addie's cheeks warmed. "I imagine the Ritz is awash with maids and housekeepers, even on a Sunday. One more wouldn't stand out. They must have their own entry in the rear of the building."

"I suppose we can eliminate any bearded gentlemen—even Stephen Moreton's sad mustache disqualifies him. How would someone get a hotel uniform?"

"Oh, that's easy. They're not all that different from the run-of-the-mill maid's outfit. And as I said, lots of people don't really see servants or pay much attention to them. What's an extra ruffle or button? You expect that person dressing as a maid *is* a maid. Cee walked by a whole host of reporters. Not one of them recognized her, and she's had her photograph in the papers a time or two, much to Mama's dismay."

"Bred, wed, dead," Mr. Hunter offered.

"Exactly. Those are the only announcements permitted in Mama's world. I hope she doesn't have access to the current crop of papers. She'd find them unbearable." Every day, the headlines grew more lurid.

"You've given me a good place to start. Barnes's investigation included the fact that no visitor had inquired about seeing the duke at the front desk that morning—as if the murderer would reveal himself, or herself, in such a way. He never considered hotel staff, or anyone posing as staff." He paused, looking troubled. "But really, someone staying at the Ritz might have had access to Rufford's room, too. It would be an impossible task to interview every guest even if I could convince the management to supply me with names. Which most assuredly they would not. My feeling, though, is that the duke's death can be blamed on someone closer to home."

Addie skimmed the edge of her saucer with a fingernail. "Could we find out where his family members were Saturday night?"

"I'm not sure how. You've been barred from coming near any of them, and I doubt I'd be successful getting through the front door. Or the kitchen door, for that matter."

Infiltrating the household again might be a task for Rupert. "The servants always know everything, and no one's even spoken to them. I do wish the police had been more thorough."

"Phil Barnes doesn't have much imagination. He saw what he expected to see, just as you said. Why explore further when all the evidence points in a certain direction?"

"I know what it looked like—it's just so frustrating."

"I concur. I'd like to report something positive when I see your mother tomorrow."

"Well, we are eliminating suspects."

"Are we?"

Addie nodded. "I believe Stephen and Roberta are probably innocent. Probably Franz von Mayr, too."

"That's two probablys, which means two possiblys."

He was right, and she knew it. "The new duke claims he was with his mistress. Maybe you can find out who she is and confirm that."

"I didn't have the chance to tell you. I spent some of the day at his club trying to track down Alistair's various mistresses. Naturally I couldn't get near the members, but the manager was helpful after suitable remuneration. Lombard is right—one of them has been in France the past month and sending him love letters in care of the club. I saw the postmarks." Inspector Hunter rose. "Well, we both have our work cut out for tomorrow. I confess I'm ready for bed myself."

And it was a pity he would be in it alone.

Chapter Twenty

Addie walked him to the door. It *was* late, and she was tired, too, and couldn't wait to remove her spangled shoes. The days since Sunday had been one long, blurry nightmare, but sleep—when it came—was still unhelpful.

They were in the midst of saying goodnight in the hallway when the doorbell rang, causing her to jump a foot. "Who on earth...?"

Mr. Hunter stayed her hand, and she ignored the pleasant tingling sensation. "Let me open the door. It could be Lombard, or some other miscreant."

Addie didn't argue. It was rather nice to be able to stand behind a tall, strong man. Why hadn't the night porter Daniel rung?

"You should have a peephole on the door, you know," Mr. Hunter said. Until this business with Mama, Addie had never given her safety and privacy much of a thought. Beckett was perfectly capable of getting rid of any unwanted guest that might have slipped past the porters. But now?

The detective eased the door open a crack, then swung it wide. Standing in the hall were the current Marquess and Marchioness of Vere, clutching hands and looking like a pair of guilty children skipping school. Stephen was still in evening clothes, but Roberta had removed her lashes and glittery costume. She now wore a smart houndstooth check suit, a jaunty beret, and sensible lace-up Oxfords. She could have been coming home from an office job instead of the most glamorous private venue in London after the Embassy Club.

"Oh!" Addie said, which was most inadequate.

"May we come in, Lady Adelaide?" Stephen Moreton asked, his voice rather reedy.

"Of course, please do." She led the way to the drawing room, Mr. Hunter taking up the rear. "Make yourselves comfortable. May I get you anything? It will be no trouble at all to brew a fresh pot of tea and fix some sandwiches." A few biscuits Mr. Hunter had somehow overlooked remained on an Imari plate, and she was prepared to rummage for more.

"I'll take a whiskey if you have it," Stephen said, adding another layer to the surprise.

The mirrored drinks cart in the corner was well-stocked as usual, even if Addie rarely partook. "Inspector, will you do the honors?"

Roberta stiffened on the sofa. "Inspector? Are you the police?"

"I am, Lady Vere." Addie noted he called her by her title, which was the respectful thing to do. "I'm Devenand Hunter from Scotland Yard. As you know, Lady Adelaide and I were at the Southern Belle tonight for your show. The mistress of ceremonies was not wrong—you and your sister sing like the angels." More respect, if not downright flattery. He poured several fingers of whiskey in a cut-glass tumbler and delivered it to the marquess.

"Cheers," the young man said, and drank it in one go. Both his wife and Addie shuddered.

"Roberta, would you like a drink?" Addie asked softly.

She shook her head, "Nothing for me. Stevie seems to be

drinking for both of us." She glanced at her husband, then took in the modern glamor of Addie's flat. "Nice place."

"Thank you. I confess, I'm surprised to see you."

"I told Stevie about your visit after we were done. I was the one who was surprised when he said he'd talk to you."

"I'm very grateful, Lord Vere," Addie said, meaning it.

"It will cost you, what I know," the boy blurted. "I can't even pay my tab at the Southern Belle. My father's cut me off. Haven't got a farthing, and nobody except for my Aunt Penny seems to care. A romantic, she is, but she's got no more influence with him than I do."

"I'm sure something can be arranged," Mr. Hunter said smoothly. "The Dowager Marchioness of Broughton has engaged my services to investigate what really happened to your grandfather. Any insight you might have will be invaluable."

Vere frowned. "What are we talking about for money?"

"It rather depends on the quality of your information. Do you really know something useful, or are you just trying to extort Lady Adelaide? She is, as you might expect, desperate to help her mother. Vulnerable. You are a gentleman, my lord. I'm sure you don't want to take advantage, and must be as interested in the truth as she is."

Ouch. More flattery, if in a backhanded way. Vere had the grace to blush. "It's not so much what I know, although I have an idea or two. But I bet I can find out. Keep my ear to the ground. My family—well, I wouldn't wish them on anyone. Any of them could have done the deed—except for my little sister Grace, I guess—if your mother really didn't do it, Lady Adelaide."

"She really didn't do it, Lord Vere." Addie had completely forgotten about Grace's diary. Perhaps she should hand it off, but how could she explain where it came from?

"Call me Stephen. Lord Vere is still my bloody father to me."

Addie had to be honest. "I had dinner with your father the other night. He forbade me to talk to you or any of your relatives and threatened legal action."

Roberta snorted. "Typical. That man thinks he's God ordering people around."

"More like Satan," Stephen mumbled. "I'm not afraid of him." He didn't sound convinced of his own words.

"We can get by on what I earn, Stevie, 'specially if we go back to Paris. You don't have to grovel and go to the man hat in hand."

"I won't be kept by my wife!" Stephen said with more spirit than he'd previously shown. "It's I who should be taking care of you. You're being exploited, and it's criminal."

Roberta sighed, as if she'd had this discussion before. She squeezed Stephen's shoulder, and he captured her hand in his. "Nobody's exploiting us. I could be home helping my daddy sharecrop his field and singing to pass the time from row to row. Isn't it better that Elizabeth and I are getting paid good money to do what we did every Sunday morning and Wednesday night in church for nothing? And in much nicer clothes than feed-sack dresses."

"You deserve more," he said stubbornly.

Addie felt some sympathy for both of them. As unusual as their pairing was, it was impossible to miss the connection between them. Mr. Hunter might be right that Roberta was in charge, but she did appear to care deeply for the young man sitting next to her on the divan.

Still, they were both terribly young. What would happen a few years down the road?

Ah, Addie thought to herself, what a silly question. No one could predict the future, and there were no guarantees in life. One would just have to try to make the best of the present.

"We all deserve more," Roberta said.

Addie agreed, although she knew she was already extremely lucky. But if she could get her mother out of this dreadful situation, she'd never ask for another thing.

"Stephen, your father told me he was, uh, with someone Sunday morning. Would you happen to know who that might be? The police have no interest in corroborating alibis, but I do."

"It wouldn't be my mother," Stephen replied with bitterness. "He's stepped out on her the whole length of their marriage. Of course, she's done the same to him. They haven't set a good example. I mean to be different."

"You were not home yourself, I understand," Mr. Hunter interjected.

"He was with me," Roberta said. "I already told Lady, that is Lady Adelaide. We have a room at the Albert. Lots of musicians and actors stay there. The management is not so picky if there's a little noise, and it's not too far from the club."

"I know of it," Addie said. That's where Ollie and Trix Johnson stayed while they worked at the Thieves' Den.

Ever the detective, Mr. Hunter asked "Can anyone confirm that?"

"All of us walked back after we closed. My sister, a bunch of the fellas. If you're asking if anybody was in the room with us, no, of course not. My sister bunked in with another girl to give us some privacy. But folks saw us come down to breakfast."

"What time?"

Stephen's face darkened. "When we woke up! I didn't shoot my grandfather, Inspector Hunter. What was the point? My father likes my marriage even less than he did. Grandpapa only threatened to cancel my allowance. My father's actually gone and done it, and he's still meeting with the family's solicitors to try to break us up."

"It won't work. We have the papers from Scotland," Roberta said.

And how easily they could go up in smoke.

Mr. Hunter was thinking along the same lines. "I hope they're in a safe place. Scottish marriage laws are honored in Great Britain, but I understand your family has influence in high places, Stephen. Do be careful."

"We will. They'll just have to learn to love me." Roberta gave a confident smile.

Chapter Twenty-One

Friday morning

Dev left the gaol feeling inadequate. Lady Broughton had been all that was kind—remarkable under the circumstances—but he still felt he was failing her. The cooperation from the Veres was at least something positive to report, but not enough. He hoped he'd have better luck when he visited the Ritz later.

She signed off on the monetary "reward" that Stephen insisted on, saying that Edmund had been fond of the boy, even if he didn't approve of his love life. The duke hadn't told her of the marriage. If he'd voiced his objection, Lady Broughton said, she would have tried to persuade him to accept it. In her experience, young people could rarely be swayed from their passions, no matter how much one nagged and needed to learn from their own mistakes. Whether Stephen had made one, she was not prepared to say.

Disheartened, his head was down and he didn't see the man until the collision on the pavement. He saved his hat from flying off, and bit his tongue at the jolting pain that swept through his shoulder.

"You!"

"We meet once again, Inspector." Joe Lombard smiled smugly. He wore a camera on a leather strap around his neck, and Dev was tempted to grab it and strangle him with it.

"Are you following me?"

"Naw. Just got lucky today. And last night, too. I hope you had a good time. You cut a pretty good rug."

"I beg your pardon?"

"Dance, man, dance. You're not half bad. What happened to your arm?"

Dev adjusted his sling. He'd taken several aspirin this morning to not much avail. "I fell off a horse."

Lombard whistled. "You are a man of many parts. I wouldn't think a copper had time to ride around the park."

He was not going to explain what happened last weekend. "Why are you here?"

"Oh, just wondering who might visit her ladyship in the pokey today. Thought maybe I could get a snap and quote from one of her pretty daughters, but you're almost as good."

"If you know what's good for you, you'll leave Lady Adelaide and Lady Cecilia alone." The reporter had a very punchable face, and it was all Dev could do to calm his good fist.

"That sounds like a threat, Inspector, and we wouldn't like that immortalized in my next dispatch now, would we? Your bosses won't like knowing you're off the clock and mucking about their investigation."

No, they certainly wouldn't. Damn.

"What do you want, Lombard?" Dev asked, beyond irritated.

"Information, of course, like we agreed. And I might have something for *you*. Let's get a cup of coffee and compare notes."

"I never agreed to anything." As far as Dev was concerned, the man belonged in gaol himself for breaking into Lady Adelaide's flat. But they were in fact across the street from a dismal-looking café.

He'd had another late night. A cup of coffee might wake him up and sharpen his edges so he wouldn't stumble into any more reporters.

Lombard shrugged. "Well, you should. If we put our heads together, maybe we'll solve this thing and get Connie out of the clink."

Constance, Lady Broughton, would not care for this appellation. "All right."

He followed Lombard as he darted through the heavy morning traffic. Unfortunately, the man was not hit by a passing taxi or omnibus. Once they were settled inside at a sticky table, a dispirited waitress took their order. Dev took out his handkerchief to brush off the crumbs on his side. Lombard could take care of his own.

"Persnickety, are you?"

Dev supposed he was. Keeping company with Lady Adelaide was bound to rub off. There was something to be said for a clean, well-run home. He'd grown up in one. But due to his schedule, his bachelor flat was not as pristine as it could be. Dev refused to allow his mother to come in and tidy up as she frequently offered to do.

"Let's get down to business. Do you really know anything to Lady Broughton's advantage?"

Lombard pulled out a notebook very similar to Dev's own. "Maybe. But my readers prefer that she's guilty as sin. They don't like high society dames much, and for good reason. They're coated in diamonds with their noses in the air, walking all over the riffraff, *expecting*. Expecting to be obeyed, expecting to get away with sh—stuff, expecting to be at the top of the heap without doing a lick of work like the rest of us. A lady like Connie Broughton— why, they think she needs her comeuppance. From riches to rags, so to speak. Very satisfying to the poor saps just making ends meet. The Germans even have a word for it. *Schadenfreude*."

"I assure you, Lady Broughton has done nothing in her whole life to warrant her current predicament." One shouldn't be sent to gaol just because one was so very proper. The woman had been involved in charitable endeavors forever to help the very people who apparently hated her.

"So you say. But even if she's pure as the driven snow, you have to admit it's an irresistible storyline to the unwashed masses. A dead duke shot by his marchioness mistress. Blood everywhere in a ritzy hotel. Ritzy, get it? You must see the appeal. Why, it's practically Shakespearean. Your colleagues like it well enough to lock her up and throw away the key before the trial. No bail, no special privileges."

Dev couldn't argue. The coffee came, and it was as vile as he expected. He tried to overcome its defects with too much sugar and milk, and was amazed to see Lombard down the brown scum straight.

"How about a sandwich or eggs or something? I'm starving. Gotta get to the funeral later and I'll miss my lunch."

Dev had observed the other customers' plates and declined on principle. He had toyed with the idea of attending the funeral himself. Not in the church, as it was private, but outside, just to observe. Maybe he should buddy up with Lombard, if he could stand it.

The reporter waved the waitress back. After a lengthy discussion over a stained menu, the reporter settled on a cheese omelet, sausages, and whole wheat toast.

"So, what were you doing at the Southern Belle last night?"

"Just escorting the Merrill sisters," Dev answered. "They needed a respite."

"Must be tough on their previously perfect lives."

Dev stared the man down. "You have no idea what you're talking about. Lady Adelaide lost her husband."

"Oh, I know all about that," Lombard said, grinning. "Her old man crashed his fancy car, a French tootsie at his side. No love lost there by the widow, I'll wager. Even if the man was in the Royal Flying Corps and not the Navy, he had a girl in every port during and after the war. The man was a stallion. Legendary. His death should have been more of a splash, but it was all hushed up. Friends in high places. Can't tarnish the name of a famous hero, eh?"

He was glad Lady Adelaide wasn't here to hear her personal tragedy so easily mocked. "Why were *you* there?"

"A little birdie told me the Rufford family is going to be rocked by an even bigger scandal than the duke getting bopped."

Dev kept his tone neutral. "Oh?" Could the Jones Sisters have spilled the beans last night?

"Yep. I don't see how it impacts the duke's murder, but it might." Lombard grinned as the waitress delivered a greasy plate with an omelet the size of an elephant's ear, revolting gray sausages, and a rack of burnt toast. "You sure you don't want some? I don't mind sharing."

Dev generally had a healthy appetite, but not this morning, and not in this place. The newsman had no such qualms, and attacked his breakfast with relish. Dev sat back and pulled out his own notebook, which was painfully blank.

After a few minutes, Lombard pushed his plate aside. "You haven't asked me a thing."

"I expect you'll tell me when you're ready." He was not in the mood to play cat-and-mouse games.

"Can I trust you to do the same?"

"Nothing I've uncovered merits the interest of a journalist," Dev lied. The Veres' marriage would be front-page news, for sure. It was true that several peers had married actresses and singers over the years, but never had a beautiful American Negro joined their ranks.

"But you *have* uncovered something."

"Nothing that is for public consumption. Yet. The story is not mine to tell."

"Huh. Well, you're making me regret inviting you to breakfast," Lombard said, frowning.

"I can pay for my own coffee if you like."

"Oh, don't go all stiff upper lip on me. You Brits are so damned touchy."

He didn't know the half of it. "Let's not waste any more time. If you do in fact have information that might help me help Lady Broughton, I'm more than ready to hear it."

"She paying you well?"

Dev rose, and tossed some coins on the table. "Good day to you, Lombard."

"Oh, for chrissakes, sit down. I won't snitch on you to Scotland Yard for double-dipping. A fella's got to look out for himself; I respect that."

Dev had already decided he would return to Lady Broughton whatever money was left over from the expenses he'd accrued. He was a friend of the family, wasn't he? Doing them a service, using his so-called expertise, only from a different perspective than usual. It did not seem honorable to accept payment.

Especially if he proved to be unsuccessful.

"I am on medical leave."

"Sure, sure. Stop looking at me as if I'm some kind of worm. Mrs. Lombard loves me."

"Your wife?"

The man laughed. "Naw, my mum, as you would say. I don't have time for any shebas at the moment."

Neither did Dev. He sat back down in the hard booth and glanced at his watch. He was to stop at the marchioness's solicitor's office in an hour to discuss strategy and get a check for

Stephen. And then—the funeral? He was afraid he'd stand out in the crowd. "I'm listening."

"You know the dead duke's granddaughter?"

This was not what Dev was expecting. "Which one? He has three."

"Gloria. Her pa's the new duke."

"What about her?"

"She's light-fingered. Her grandfather bribed the woman she stole from to drop the charges against her and gave a substantial sum to your lot to keep quiet."

"My lot?"

"The coppers. You know half of them are as bad as the crooks they arrest."

Dev didn't argue. Couldn't. Corruption within the department was widespread and well-known, despite the commissioner's crackdown, and he was as much out of step as a nun on a chorus line. Frequently teased for his honesty, Dev wondered if somehow Alistair had paid Phil Barnes to *not* investigate.

"What is it that Lady Gloria was accused of stealing?"

"She and her mick boyfriend were at some fancy house party in the country, and the hostess's jewel case went missing. There were tiaras inside. More than one, apparently, and who knows what else. Sapphires as big as robin's eggs, no doubt. Naturally the local police were called in. The box was found in Gloria's luggage. She was all packed and ready to go—claimed her mother was sick and she had to leave early."

"When was this?"

"A few weeks ago. Went back to the castle in disgrace. I'm surprised the old duke let her come down to Town with the rest of the family."

"Maybe he wanted to keep an eye on her," Dev suggested.

"How could he do that when he was at the Ritz with Connie?"

Dev gritted his teeth. He could no more imagine calling Lady Broughton Connie than addressing the king as Georgie.

"How did you learn about this?"

"Trade secret." Which probably meant he'd bribed a servant at Maddox Street.

What would make Lady Gloria—or her boyfriend—shoot Edmund? He'd gotten her out of a jam. Even if he'd lorded it over her—and after hearing about the duke's personality, Dev expected he might have—it didn't constitute a sufficient motive.

But one never knew all the particulars, did one?

Chapter Twenty-Two

Friday evening

"I despise funerals."

They had already established that Rupert had not been present at his own, but Addie understood. They'd both attended too many in the past ten years. In his ghostly capacity, he'd attended Edmund's service this afternoon, and was looking unusually downcast.

"Was St. George's full?" Sitting in her drawing room with a cup of lukewarm tea, Addie could ask in a normal voice without fear of discovery. Cee and Beckett had left for Gloucestershire on a late afternoon train. Her mother had been persuasive, even encouraging Addie to return to Compton Chase. In this instance, however, she refused to obey her mother.

"To the rafters. A profusion of politicians and peers. I'm surprised they didn't hold it in Westminster Abbey. That ghastly little worm Lombard lurked outside with his camera, and I believe I might have caught a brief glimpse of your inspector in the curious crowd before I shimmied in."

"Stephen was there?"

"Oh, yes. Minus the old ball and chain. The lad's terrified of

Alistair, and justifiably so. I wouldn't put it past him to rub out Miss Jones if he gets the chance."

"Rupert! Do you really think so?" Addie had developed a fondness for the young couple, and objected to her dead husband's slang. Was Alistair a cold-blooded killer as well as a cad?

"Anything is possible—you know that. Alistair's a rum cove. I can't see what the Prince of Wales sees in him. The fellow's got damned bad judgment, even if he'll wind up our king someday. Who knows who he'll befriend next? Al Capone? That little stinker Hitler? Mark my words, he's up to no good."

Addie was unsure whether Rupert was referring to Alistair, the Prince of Wales, the American mobster, or the German politician, but wanted to stick to the subject at hand. "Tell me what happened at the reception after."

"The food was pretty good."

"Rupert!"

"All right, all right, hold your hosses, as they say in Miss Jones's neck of the woods. A select few went to Maddox Street after for funeral meats. There was a lot of blather about the government, which nearly put me to sleep. Penny was so distraught she went upstairs to lie down all afternoon with an ice bag. But I took special note of her niece Lady Gloria, since your inspector claims she may be a person of interest."

Mr. Hunter telephoned her to discuss his impromptu meeting with Joe Lombard. Addie wondered how she might speak to the girl without running afoul of her father. "And?"

"I took the opportunity to listen in to her thoughts. Yes, I know you find that egregious, but needs must, eh? It was an uncomfortable period of time—I longed to wash my brain out with Vim Scouring Powder. The girl has a most unpleasant mind. Avaricious. Devious. Rapacious. Reminds me of her mother."

He would know. "Did she do it? Steal the jewels?"

"I don't know for sure. She wasn't thinking about the past, but shagging her handsome boyfriend in the present. That is, when she wasn't being unnecessarily vicious to her brother and cousins and tossing off cutting remarks to unnerve them in their hour of grief. I bet they'd all like to set her naked on an ice floe and watch her disappear over the horizon."

"Charming."

"She is the perfect amalgamation of both her parents. I don't know how Stephen escaped the family curse. She's quite pretty, though."

"Handsome is as handsome does. She sounds absolutely appalling. Can she be the murderess?"

Rupert shrugged. "She's as good a candidate as any, I suppose, as is her potential fiancé. To be honest, he was a bit of an enigma to me. As you know and dislike, I can usually detect someone's thoughts, but he was inscrutable. I will vouch for the von Mayr twins' innocence, however. They sincerely regret their grandfather's passing, although they did view him as the chief obstacle to overcome in getting their parents back together."

"What about your old flame?" Addie asked.

He stopped himself from asking which one—no doubt there were several present at the reception. "Elaine? I'm certain she could shoot someone between the eyes and then go off to get her nails done."

The more Addie learned about the Moretons, the more grateful she was that her mother would not be marrying into the family. It was a shame—Mama deserved happiness. When this was all settled, Addie was determined to find a suitable husband for her.

"But not for you?"

Mind-reading once again. "I see no advantage to acquiring another husband. You were more than enough, Rupert. I like to think I've learned my lesson."

"Not all men are such rogues, my dear. I was one of a kind, to my regret."

"Water under the bridge," she said, nearly honest. "How can I bump into Lady Gloria and discover for myself how horrible she is?"

"Despite his father's death, Alistair is due to attend the opening of Canada House next week. I expect Gloria will accompany him—she's not one to miss an important occasion. The king and queen will be there."

Next week. Could it wait that long? Addie wondered if they were running out of time. Mr. Hunter would return to Scotland Yard at the end of it. Maybe Stephen could fix something up sooner.

"In the meantime," Rupert continued, "I'll continue to cast my net. One never knows what one will catch. Slippery eels. Goblin sharks." He shuddered.

Addie knew nothing about disgusting aquatic creatures and meant to keep it that way. "Hurry up, Rupert. I'm feeling a bit desperate. Mama is being incredibly brave, but this must be torture for her."

"And for you, too, I'm guessing. I know how protective you are of your family."

A few sleepless nights were not going to kill her, but if something didn't turn up soon, her mother might actually lose her life. Addie felt sick to her stomach.

Rupert put a chilly hand on her cheek. "Now, now. It will turn out all right. I'm here, aren't I? The Fellow Upstairs is depending on me. And there's a great deal at stake for me as well—like escape from eternal damnation. I wouldn't want to blot my copybook at this late date."

Perhaps he was right. The Marchioness of Broughton did have unusual assistance not granted to most prisoners. A brilliant Scotland Yard detective *and* a nosy ghost were bound to unearth something in her favor.

"And don't discount your own instincts, Addie. Why, you might turn your hand to writing mystery novels when this is over," Rupert teased.

The thought had actually flitted across her mind. But she was no Mrs. Christie.

"You don't have to be," Rupert said, still eavesdropping. "Just be yourself."

"I can hardly be anyone else," she said tartly.

"By the way, I think your idea of the killer dressing up and sneaking into the hotel is genius. I confess I can't see Gloria getting rigged up in such an unflattering costume—she's quite the fashion plate. But I suppose she might have."

"She would have needed to get access to Mama's pistol," Addie said. "Maybe she visited the duke earlier in the week when my mother was getting her hair done."

"Someone did. Unless Edmund simply turned the weapon over to the person who shot him."

"I wonder if Mr. Hunter asked about the duke's visitors during the week when he went to the Ritz today." He'd been busy. Mr. Hunter had visited Mama, been accosted by Lombard, gone to her mother's barrister's office, stood on the street outside St. George's, and then the Ritz. He'd told her on the telephone his inquiries with the hotel staff had not been propitious. No one had noticed a strange maid or waiter in the early hours of Sunday morning.

That didn't mean there wasn't one, though.

"Ask him. Call him up right now and invite him over. Change into something slinky."

Addie lifted an eyebrow. "Are you playing Cupid, Rupert? It won't work. Mr. Hunter looks upon me as a semiprofessional colleague at most."

As usual, Rupert's cackle of laughter was very aggravating.

Chapter Twenty-Three

Addie did not change into something slinky. She was wearing perfectly good Japanese silk evening pajamas that were slinky enough, even though they buttoned right up to her chin. But she did call Mr. Hunter.

He said he'd already had dinner, as had she, but she assembled a tray of cheeses, crackers, nuts, and fruit just in case. Beckett had placed a grocery order before she left for the country, so Addie was well-stocked for the next few days and shouldn't have to bother going out to shop. Of course, if she entertained Mr. Hunter regularly, she might run out of food.

She felt they were at a standstill, just waiting for *someone* to do *something*. Something to happen that would make all the clues—precious few that they were—fall in place. For Stephen to introduce her to his sister and possibly his mother. For Mr. Hunter to receive more information from that dreadful reporter. For the killer to trip up or confess.

The last, she conceded, was too much to hope for.

Daniel rang up on the house phone to say Mr. Hunter was on his way up. The porter had also been apologetic about last night, allowing Stephen and Roberta to come up unannounced. Addie had put a stop to the groveling. Everyone made mistakes, and his was to be in the basement changing a fuse for another flat, which was certainly not a mistake at all. Who would expect guests so late? Addie's Town neighbors were a conservative lot, and right about now they probably wished she'd move.

After turning on the fan in the drawing room, Addie went into the hall, twisting her curls. It was a nervous habit; she missed her longer hair. Addie was not sure short hair was actually less fuss. There were some days when she awoke looking as if she'd been electrocuted overnight. Since Beckett left with Cee, she and her hairdo were on their own.

She threw open the door before he had a chance to knock. "Thank you for coming. I know you had a long day."

Mr. Hunter removed his hat and left it on the hall credenza. He followed her into the well-lit drawing room. "I don't mind catching up. But I think I told you all there was to tell on the phone." He glanced at the tray on the table, and helped himself to a handful of nuts.

"You didn't say much about the funeral."

"I didn't actually attend it, Lady Adelaide. I was outside watching the family and the other mourners enter, hoping no one would watch *me*. No one appeared obviously guilty, I'm sorry to say. I didn't tarry till the end, but went to the Ritz to test out your theory. And, as I said, nothing came of that."

"I've had another idea. Did you ask if any of the staff remembered if anyone visited the duke the week before his death?"

"Of course. I'm assuming that's how the murderer got hold of your mother's gun. I'm afraid I came up blank there, too. They recalled the duke left the property nearly every day for a few hours—alone, they thought. Presumably, he went to see his lawyers, and we know he went to the Southern Belle briefly one evening without your mother."

Addie's heart dropped. "Perhaps the visitor wasn't noticed. It is the Ritz, after all. Too many comings and goings to keep track of, no matter how vigilant they are. I wish Mama had paid more attention to the contents of her purse. Could one of the house-keeping staff have stolen the weapon?"

Mr. Hunter gave her a sympathetic look. "And then shot the duke for no reason? Your mother's belongings are in police cus-tody, Lady Adelaide. She had quite a bit of cash in her handbag, as well as a small pouch of jewels. Why would a maid take only the gun?"

"Because..." Really, no matter how demanding the duke might have been during his stay, the motive was extremely thin for a Ritz employee to kill him. Unless there was some bizarre history that might provide a reason. Maybe the maid was an illegitimate granddaughter, one of Alistair's abandoned by-blows, forced into service at a tender age, resentful and vengeful.

In which case, the girl should have shot Alistair instead.

Addie was grasping, and she knew it. "There is no *because*, is there? I do appreciate you coming. I should have known you'd ask the right questions."

Mr. Hunter slathered some soft cheese on a cracker. "I don't mind. Questions are really all I have at the moment. Stephen thinks any one of his immediate family could have committed the crime, but which one? His father allegedly has an alibi. We don't know where his mother or Lady Gloria were that morning. We can presume the younger sister didn't sneak out of the schoolroom, but really, why not? Children are such bloodthirsty creatures."

Which reminded Addie she was still in possession of the poor girl's diary. To her shame, she'd flipped through it very briefly but had learned nothing except Grace had a pash for a boy whose name began with a *V*. There had been many, many exclamation points and random capitalized words, which gave her a headache.

Grace also didn't appear to believe in dating her entries, but at some point Addie would read towards the end and see if there was anything useful.

She was about to join the inspector in a slice of cheese when the house phone shrilled.

"Are you expecting anyone else?" Mr. Hunter asked.

"No, I'm not. It's a little late for a surprise visit. I do hope it's not Mr. Lombard again."

"It had better not be."

Addie picked up the phone. Daniel was in something of a state, and it took her a little to understand what he was saying.

"Send them up. Of course it's all right. They're perfectly respectable. Yes, yes, I understand." Addie hung up, her heart speeding up.

"A problem?"

"I think so. Miss Jones and a friend of hers want to see me. I wonder why?"

"We'll find out soon enough."

He walked to the front hall, Addie right behind him. At the first tentative knock, he opened the door.

It was indeed Miss Jones, but not Roberta. Her sister was very similar in looks, but there was enough of a difference for Addie to recognize Elizabeth. Wearing one of the sequined dresses Addie had seen on the dressing room rack, she was accompanied by a heavyset Negro man. If Addie was not mistaken, he played the trombone in the Southern Belle's band, and very skillfully, too. They both looked upset, and Addie ushered them in instantly and bade them sit. They refused any offer of refreshment, ignoring the platter in front of them.

"What is it?"

"You're the policeman?" Elizabeth asked, turning to Mr. Hunter.

"I am."

"My sister is missing. I haven't seen her since rehearsal this afternoon. She had some shopping to do, but she didn't have that much money on her to spend—I keep our kitty. When she didn't get back at the usual time, I got ready, thinking she might have met up with Stevie. I waited and waited, and then the band just went on without us. It's not like her to miss a show. Miss Baptiste is fit to be tied."

"Have you spoken to Stephen?"

She nodded. "He came to the club tonight expecting to see her. She wasn't with him all day, and now he's wild—the poor fool's not thinking straight. He's gone to confront his father and he might do something stupid."

"Now, honey, don't go thinking the worst," the large musician said, patting her hand.

"I can't help it, Walt. I don't know what to do. Lady Adelaide, can you help us? My sister said you're all right. I don't know Stevie's people—they probably wouldn't let me in the front door."

"Could she have met with an accident?" Mr. Hunter asked.

"I called around to the hospitals before I came here. There were no Black girls brought in this afternoon. They would have noticed. It's not like we blend in."

"I know," Mr. Hunter said softly. "Where did she go shopping?"

"Oxford Street. She needed new gloves. Stevie kept one of her old ones in his pocket. He's an awful romantic." Elizabeth's voice shook.

Well, Addie wanted something to happen. But not this.

"She hasn't been missing long enough to file a police report," Mr. Hunter said. "Is it possible she ran away?"

"Why would she do that?" Walt asked.

"Please don't take this the wrong way, Miss Jones. Could she regret her marriage?"

"Why should she? Stevie worships the ground she walks on. It's almost sickening, if you want the truth. And she couldn't have afforded a ticket to anywhere. As I said, she didn't have much cash with her."

Addie had to know. "Does she love him?"

Elizabeth smiled for the first time. "Yeah, she does. He's not my cup of tea, but he's a good egg. He'll do right by her when he comes into his own."

Which could be decades from now. What if Roberta simply wasn't that patient? She'd been impetuous making a marriage in a strange country, perhaps not realizing the consequence of her husband's family.

Or if she'd been threatened, as Rupert suspected—

"Has anyone from Stephen's family contacted her?"

"I don't think so—she'd tell me. We tell each other most things. I do know Stevie's grandfather came to a show, but we never knew it. Nobody's sent her a wedding present, that's for sure."

"The marriage is still a secret?"

"They were hoping his family would come around and stop fighting it. If they met her, they'd like her."

Addie saw Walt roll his eyes, not equally optimistic. "He has a year to go before he comes into a little legacy from his grandmother," Elizabeth continued. "Enough to set up a household, if they're careful. And Roberta was saving every penny she could. Which is why it kind of surprised me that she went to buy new gloves. It's so hot out she could have done without. It's not like she's going to meet the queen anytime soon."

"Maybe she didn't go shopping," Inspector Hunter said. "Maybe she met someone."

"And that someone just took her away? You don't know my sister, Mr. Hunter. She'd scream her head off if anybody messed with her."

Not if she had reason to trust the person. Or plead her case for approval of her marriage. But surely all the Moretons must have been occupied at the funeral reception.

Addie needed to talk to Rupert.

Chapter Twenty-Four

It was agreed that Dev would be the one to stop Stephen Moreton from getting himself in deeper hot water. Of the four of them in Lady Adelaide's drawing room, he was probably the least objectionable to go to Maddox Street, so off he went.

It seemed all of London was out this Friday evening, on the way to one amusement or another. Taxis were impossible to come by, but he was close enough to walk from Mount Street to the duke's house. The night air was overly warm, and a bead of sweat escaped from the brim of his hat down his temple. It didn't slow Dev's pace; his single-mindedness was visible to anyone who chanced across his path.

His entrée was in his pocket—the check from her lawyers' office that Lady Broughton had approved so Stephen could spy on his own family. Despite the late hour, he was confident Stephen would see him and welcome him to boot.

If he hadn't already strangled his father.

Alistair probably deserved strangling, particularly if he was responsible for the disappearance of his new daughter-in-law. Both Jones sisters struck Dev as capable and intelligent young women, and he doubted Roberta would have gone off with a stranger.

Something had happened. Did it relate to Edmund's death?

The last thing Dev needed was an additional mission, especially if it involved combing through Oxford Street shops in search of the missing girl. He was sorry now that Lady Cecilia had been sent to the country. The shopping district was her natural habitat, and she could have helped with inquiries. But half the Empire passed through the popular stores—would anyone have noticed Roberta? The clerks were bound to be even busier on Saturday, making the job of asking them more difficult tomorrow. Walt Carter pledged that the band members would help once they woke up; they were all fond of the Jones sisters and looked upon them as the daughters and nieces they'd left behind.

Dev knew his own police force would not take Roberta's disappearance seriously. She was a jazz singer. A foreigner. Worse, a woman of color. He could hear the disparagement now. She would be automatically characterized as undependable and unworthy of their precious manpower.

But if they knew she was a marchioness, that might make a difference.

That would mean Stephen would have to defy his family and announce his marriage. Public opinion might even be in his favor. Dev imagined even Lombard could write a sympathetic story of the truly star-crossed lovers that would tug at heartstrings. Everyone liked a Cinderella story.

But there would be no happy ending until Roberta was found.

Dev checked his watch as he passed under a streetlamp. Ordinarily, he'd be in bed reading at this time of night. The books he'd ignored all week could wait. Sometimes he thought he was a hopeless case, trying to educate himself in subjects that only classics professors cared about. Dead writers, dead ideas, deader languages. But his books were an escape from the all-too-present vagaries of twentieth-century life, and reminded him of the bigger picture.

There *had* to be a bigger picture. If not, he supposed he was in for an unpleasant surprise.

He made the slight left from Grosvenor Street to Maddox Street and squinted at the illuminated numbers. The duke's mansion was in a row of identical Georgian flat-fronted buildings with recessed arched doorways and matching arched first-floor windows. Scrims of light were visible behind the drawn curtains of all four floors, so at least Dev wouldn't wake everyone up.

He considered going down the steps to the tradesmen's entrance, but decided to take his chances at street level. He twisted the brass bell pull and waited.

A tall, rosy-faced young footman appeared within a minute. Dev almost wished for his formal evening clothes of last night; this was a peer's residence, after all, and he was receiving a decidedly suspicious look.

"Yes?"

Should he produce his warrant card? He wasn't strictly working, and doing so might get him in trouble.

"Good evening. I have urgent business with the Marquess of Vere."

"He's not in. If you'll leave your card—"

A splintering crash came from above, followed by another. A woman screamed, and Dev pushed past the servant to run up the stairs.

"Hey! You have no right!"

The young fellow was tenacious, Dev would give him that. He shook the boy from clawing at his jacket. Pain sliced through his torso; he'd dispensed with the sling tonight. His injuries were proving to be very inconvenient.

"I'm a police inspector. If you don't want to be party to another murder in the family, I suggest you let me go up." He left the footman staring at him in disbelief and mounted the rest of the staircase wondering if any of the Moretons had aspirin.

Dev followed the noise. At the end of the hall, dark wooden double doors were open to an even darker wood-paneled study. Two men were writhing on the floor amidst a shattered glass lampshade. Papers had been swept off the desk, and a chair tipped onto the figured carpet. A woman stood against a wall of books, shouting ineffectually.

Dev could have used the footman's help. He hauled Stephen up by the collar and held firm as he windmilled in the air.

"Stop, my lord. This won't help." Dev spoke quietly. He'd learned long ago that a loud voice didn't necessarily make someone obey, particularly when that someone had lost all reason.

Stephen looked up at him in total surprise, and blinked those strange light eyes as if coming to from a dream. "You can let me go."

"Can I?" Dev asked, not quite trusting the storm was over.

"You're right. He'll only keep lying to me. As usual," he said under his breath.

The woman rushed to the duke, who still lay on the floor, his lip cut and bleeding. "Alistair, are you all right? I was so worried!" She tried to blot the blood from his chin with her black spangled shawl.

"Leave off, Penny, for God's sake. Get away from me," he snapped, struggling to sit up. His face was scarlet with rage. "Who the hell are you?"

"A friend of your son's. Devenand Hunter." Dev didn't bother to extend a hand.

"Then you can both get out of my house!"

"Not until you tell me what you've done with Roberta!"

"Done? *Done?* You stupid boy, do you think I've locked her in a closet or cellar? Perhaps I've tucked her under my bed. Feel free to inspect every inch of the place. I have no idea where she is, nor do I care." He pulled a handkerchief from his pocket and wiped his mouth.

"I don't believe you. If you've hurt her—"

"Stephen, dear, I know you're upset. I'm so sorry she's run away. But maybe it's for the best."

Dev studied Stephen's aunt. Her trembling hands picked at her scarf, and she looked as if she expected her nephew to yell at her, too.

"She wouldn't run away, Aunt Penny. *He's* done something with her." Stephen glared at his father.

"For once and for all, I do not know what you are talking about."

There was something in Alistair's tone that set Dev's senses on alert. "You might not have taken her, Your Grace. But it's very possible you arranged her disappearance. You have money and influence. Contacts."

"You bloody wog—how dare you come here and accuse me of a crime! Take my ignorant son back to your ridiculous nightclub. Let him live amongst the darkies and see how long he lasts. He'll not be getting a penny from me until he gets a divorce, so your little scheme has gone awry. You and that filthy, little whore you threw at his head—"

Alistair didn't get a chance to finish his tirade. Stephen shot across the room and punched his father in the face. The duke fell backward on the rug with a thunk.

Lady Penelope rushed to her brother's side. "Stephen! You've killed him!"

He rubbed his knuckles, his fair skin bruising already. "I hope so. He doesn't deserve to step into Grandfather's shoes. You know it as well as I do, Aunt Penny. He's disgusting."

Dev bent and put two fingers against the duke's throat. His pulse was strong, which was fortunate, as Stephen didn't need any more disasters in his young life. "He's too mean to die yet, Stephen. But perhaps we should go."

"He hasn't said where she is!"

"Perhaps he truly doesn't know. Lady Penelope, Stephen will be in touch once he's settled. I hope you are not too discomposed from the events this evening."

"Oh, no. I'm quite used to family skirmishes," the woman said with a nervous smile. "Stephen, I'm sure your father didn't mean to turn you out of the house. Perhaps when he regains consciousness—"

"I'm sure he did, Aunt. You know better than any of us what he's capable of. I bet he pulled the wings off butterflies when you were children." Lady Penelope flinched, which made Dev even more anxious to leave the house.

The duke apparently thought he was associated with the Southern Belle, so Dev had a quick word with the footman on the way out. The young man seemed to believe that he'd fibbed about being a policeman as an excuse to gain entry anyway. Dev did not need any of this to get back to the Yard.

Dev and Stephen headed out into the night. "Where will you go?" He was not going to offer his own sofa unless there was no other choice.

"To the Albert. Maybe…maybe Roberta's back." Stephen did not sound hopeful. "How did you know where I was?"

"Elizabeth came to Lady Adelaide's. She was worried, and I see she had a right to be."

Stephen stopped in the middle of the pavement. "He took her! I know it!"

"I think," Dev said carefully, "he might have planned something, or at least thought of planning something. But I don't believe he got the opportunity."

"Why do you say that?"

Dev shrugged. "It's just a hunch. I have them every now and again." And they sounded barking mad when he tried to explain. "Come, I'll walk you back to the hotel."

They set off towards Soho in silence. For all of Stephen's earlier bravado, he was chastened now at the enormity of what had transpired. To be disowned—at least he couldn't be disinherited, thanks to Britain's primogeniture laws. One day he would be the Duke of Rufford, although Alistair really did seem too mean to die.

Dev reached into his jacket pocket. "Lady Broughton has been kind enough to provide you with a check for your assistance. You won't be able to access the funds until Monday, I'm afraid. I can loan you some money to tide you over." How Stephen would gather information now that he'd been kicked out of his house was a question for another night.

Chapter Twenty-Five

Saturday

After a prolonged and ultimately pointless search for Roberta, Addie's feet hurt. She'd made an effort to wear sensible shoes, unlike what she usually wore in Town, to no avail. No matter how far she'd tromped up and down Oxford Street and its environs, no one she spoke to knew anything.

Stephen was bereft. The fight he'd had with his father resulted in a purpling eye and a determination to make someone pay for Roberta's disappearance. Mr. Hunter had taken charge of him as the ragtag group of musicians and waitresses from the Southern Belle had fanned out amongst the shops and restaurants of Oxford Street for several hours. They attracted considerable attention, but no information.

Stephen had booked his own room at the Albert, thanks to Addie's mother. It was truly ironic that her family was providing him financial and emotional support when his own had cut him off. He had the camaraderie of the musicians at least, who accepted him as one of their own because of his marriage. They were far kinder than his own flesh and blood.

Walt had talked Elizabeth into performing solo—half a pay-check, he reasoned, was better than none. Addie had promised to come see her this evening, although all she really wanted to do was bring a cup of tea and a book to her bed and shut the world away.

"Oh, poor you."

Addie had wondered where her dead husband was on the warm Saturday night. In life, he would have been whispering sweet nothings into the ear of one of their married friends, no doubt. "The situation is only getting worse, Rupert, not for me but my mother. It's been a whole week." She watched as Rupert arranged himself on her bed as though he had every right to be there. He had always been painstaking in getting the pillows just right.

He gazed up at the ceiling in innocence. "I've done my very best prying into paperwork and people. We know there were no financial irregularities, and old Edmund was the dullest stick imaginable with no skeletons in his closet. We also know most of the Moreton family are perfectly dreadful except for poor Penny and even poorer Stephen, so let's pick one and pin the deed on them. Manufacture evidence and plant some clues about." Rupert sat up and stretched.

Addie sighed as she unrolled her stocking. "You of all people know that's not how this works. Stop looking at my legs."

"There they are, my dear, right in front of me, but I'll avert my eyes if you wish." He winked and shut his eyes altogether.

"Wake up! Do you think Alistair is responsible for Roberta going missing?"

"He's capable of anything, but I doubt he'd get his own hands dirty. And as far as I know, he hasn't had any suspicious meetings with paid thugs in his free time—he's been too busy with lawyers, arranging the funeral, and lolling about with his mistress."

"I thought she was in France."

"Oh, that's Nancy. This one is called Phyllis."

"Could Phyllis have taken Roberta?" Addie asked. She might have been tricked to go with an unthreatening woman.

"Phyllis couldn't take a napkin off her own lap. She is not the brightest bulb, but quite dazzling nonetheless in certain areas, if you get my meaning."

"I do, and that's enough. Oh, Rupert, I really am in despair." Addie balled up her stockings and tossed them in the direction of the clothes hamper. She'd wash them herself; at least that was something positive she could accomplish.

"A night out will do you good. Will your inspector be escorting you?"

"He'll meet me there later. He is having dinner with his parents." Mr. Hunter had been somewhat evasive as to his plans. Addie suspected his mother had invited a young lady as well as her son, and tried to persuade herself she was not at all jealous. The man deserved happiness. One could not devote one's entire life to work, could one?

"How domestic. A devoted son. We should all have such devoted children. Rather too late in my case, but perhaps I can mentor some naughty cherubs when the time comes. Speaking of children, have you read Grace's diary yet? I suppose I ought to return it—adolescence is difficult enough without misplacing one's cherished personal possessions."

"The poor girl didn't misplace it, Rupert. You *stole* it."

"All for the cause. Let's not develop scruples now." He pulled open her nightstand drawer. "Here it is. Shall I read it aloud?" He thumbed through the little leather-bound book until his eyes lit. "Eureka!"

Addie walked to her closet and contemplated what to wear this evening. "I don't guess I could stop you." She would feel less guilty when the diary was delivered back to Maddox Street.

"*'Dear Diary,'*" Rupert began in a breathy, girlish voice. He'd always been fond of amateur theatricals and was wizard at cha-rades without uttering a word.

"'*What a day. You will never believe what has happened. My grandfather was shot at the RITZ HOTEL! And he is DEAD. As you can imagine, the whole household is in an uproar and the POLICE were here after we got home from church asking STUPID questions as if we had anything to do with it. It is a SCANDAL.*'"

He shook his head in disgust. "She's awfully fond of capitalizing random words, I'm afraid. Run-on sentences, too. Her governess must be eternally cross. At least the spelling is adequate."

"Go on, Mr. Schoolmaster."

"Mock if you will, but I do have grammatical standards. '*Mama says we will be laughed out of London, which will be fine with me. I HATE it here. I am stuck in the schoolroom all day with Miss Marsh and can only go to the BORING park with all the nursemaids and babies. It is nothing like home, where I can walk for MILES and still see the castle's tower. Grandpapa used to like to walk with me and Carola sometimes, but I don't want to think about him now or I will CRY. True, he was very STRICT and Gloria hated him but she is a WITCH as you know and I hope she elopes with Brendan and goes to live in IRELAND of all the beastly places.*'"

"She doesn't think much of her sister, does she? Or Ireland." Addie loved Cee to pieces, although did find her a touch trying at times.

"Evidently not. I've never been to Ireland myself, but I'm sure it's delightfully Irish. Shall I continue?"

Addie knew it was futile to try to stop him. He was enjoying himself far too much.

"'*Aunt Penny made me and Miss Marsh go to church with her this morning like she always does. She's a dreadful BULLY. You'd think you were going straight to H-E-L-L if you miss a Sunday according to her. She was in a STATE but then she often is. Mama says she is MAD at Uncle Franz and men in general and that I should never marry too young which I wouldn't do anyhow, even if V asked when we are older which he probably NEVER will now that our family name is BESMIRCHED. Carola and John refused to get up since they got in so late and Aunt Penny didn't even BOTHER to ask Gloria who needs to PRAY for her immortal soul after what she has got up to.*

"'*We went to St. George's and she was on her knees the WHOLE TIME. I do not see why one can't pray sitting down because it is much more comfortable and surely God does not mind.*'"

Rupert looked up, a frown between his brows. "Well, I suppose that remains to be seen, doesn't it? Old Testament or New? He strikes me as a much more reasonable fellow now. Mellow. I mean, if one wants to walk on hot coals or wear hair shirts or scourge oneself, that is one's own idea, not His. No more sacrificing sons and goats and whatever other animal is at hand. It must have been dreadfully messy for the Israelites in those days, what? Organs, entrails, etcetera."

This philosophical Rupert was unfamiliar, but Addie imagined he was doing what he could to get into His good graces.

"'*When we got home Aunt Penny FAINTED when she heard the news. If you ask me, she was PRETENDING to get attention. I think she is very silly sometimes. I have never fainted but must learn how to according to Miss Marsh.*'"

Addie remembered numerous lessons with her own governess in attempting to achieve a graceful yet bruiseless body. Ladylike behavior was not for the faint of heart. She smiled at her own pun.

Rupert turned a page, and modulated his voice. "There is one more entry, where Grace complains of being shut away upstairs while all the interesting things are happening downstairs. I could tell her they weren't all that interesting."

"And then you stole it. You must take the diary back. What

are you doing tonight?" Rupert claimed to have some sort of odd social life...um, social death.

"I thought I'd tag along with you."

Addie couldn't think straight in company with Rupert lurking. "No, thank you. I'm sure Stephen will be there in hopes of hearing from Roberta."

"He won't be any fun."

"And neither will you." Addie said firmly.

"Spoilsport. All right. I'll venture to Maddox Street, return the diary, and see if I can pick up any signals. It would be too much to expect to find a *useful* diary with a written confession lying about."

"Quite." Nor was Rupert apt to hear an oral confession any time soon. Addie shivered thinking of what she'd witnessed only a week ago today. There really had been no time to contemplate what happened at the Fernalds' house party, and perhaps that was for the best. She hadn't had a decent night's sleep since then as it was.

Rupert vanished with a wave, and she returned to examine the contents of her closet. It didn't matter what she wore—she wasn't going to seduce anyone. She grabbed her favorite "too green" dress and its matching shoes and laid them on a chair. A hot bath was in order, a good long soak for her tired feet and tired spirits. She tossed up a quick, vague prayer to the Fellow Upstairs, promising to be more specific tomorrow when she went to church.

She'd put in a good word for Rupert, too, even if he was something of a thief.

Chapter Twenty-Six

Saturday night was every bit as busy at the Southern Belle as one would expect. The band seemed to be making up for Roberta's absence with fervor—one sweet, wild song after the other, with barely a stop in between to breathe. The dance floor was packed, and the waitresses edged around it in their ridiculous hoop skirts, hoping to carry their trays to safety.

Addie nursed a club soda. She sat alone in a darkened corner table waiting for Elizabeth's performance. The singers usually appeared twice, and from Addie's check of her watch by candle-light, "Bettie" was a bit later than usual. The mistress of ceremonies had yet to announce the change in program.

Addie had expected to see Stephen, but so far had not. She doubted he'd be reveling with the other patrons. Perhaps he was backstage or in a dressing room. She was nearly relieved to be spared his presence—the young marquess was understandably miserable and anxious, and no well-meaning pabulum she might offer would lift his spirits.

The flush of young love—had she ever truly experienced it? Rupert was pretty impressive back then, but it was difficult to remember. She'd lost so many of her male friends that her social circle was decimated. A handsome hero flying into her orbit towards the end of hostilities was pretty irresistible. And Rupert had been charm personified what with all those years of exuberant, exhaustive practice. He'd been a success with ladies since he was in short pants.

It took Addie a while after their marriage to realize he was still exerting that boyish charm on just about any female, young or old. He simply couldn't help himself. Now he was being punished for all those successes, and, inadvertently, so was she. Addie prayed he would soon fly away on angel wings so her life could get back to whatever passed for normal.

She wondered how impetuous, impulsive Rupert ever thought he could settle down to give "normal," i.e., monogamy, a try. After the horror and uncertainty of war, perhaps he'd seen his friends newly domesticated, and envied them a little. He'd inherited the country estate from his grandmother; all he needed was an accommodating wife. Addie had tried to be one, for all the good it did. If they'd had children, would it have made a difference?

She mustn't allow herself to think along these lines—in fact, it was almost impossible to think anyway. The band was so loud she wished she had a pair of earmuffs, although it was much too warm for them. Although her dress was sleeveless, the fabric was heavy with intricate beading, and consequently rather hot. She might be more comfortable if she stepped outside for some fresh air, if any could be found in London.

Leaving her gloves and wrap but taking her bag, she pushed her way through the crowd and descended the steps to the street. The pavement was packed as well, with people smoking and fanning themselves with handkerchiefs. The air was nearly as heavy outside as in, and relief was not forthcoming.

Addie attracted the attention of several people, who stared without any attempt to conceal their curiosity. Did they know who she was, or was it because she was an unaccompanied female? She turned to go back inside, but was waylaid by the very last person she wished to see.

Perhaps not the *very* last. Addie was rapidly developing a long list of persons she'd like to avoid for the foreseeable future. But Joe Lombard was pretty near the top. He was dressed in ill-fitting evening clothes which did not seem to subdue his brashness.

"What ho, if it isn't Lady Adelaide Compton!" he boomed. If she'd gone unrecognized before, that advantage was now lost. "Lose your boyfriend?" He grinned as Addie imagined how a wolf might grin when it spotted an especially tasty sheep.

She was no innocent lamb. Her spine stiffened, and she managed to look down her nose upon him, even though he was several inches taller. "You mistake yourself, sir."

He laughed. "Oh, don't go all frosty on me. It won't get you anywhere—I've got a thick skin and your disapproval is almost fun, to be honest. You can la-di-da lady-of-the-manor me all you want and it won't hurt my feelings one iota. Having a night on the tiles?"

She was not having much fun. "Not exactly."

"I heard one of the Jones sisters has gone missing." Lombard offered her a cigarette, which she declined.

"I've heard that, too."

He blew a couple of smoke rings with ridiculous pride. "There's something havey-cavey about those girls. I spoke to them the other night, offering them a feature write-up, but they said no. You'd think they'd want me to make them famous."

"I believe they had an agreement with another reporter."

Lombard's eyes narrowed. "Say, you know a lot about them. Big jazz aficionado, are you?"

Not really. But if she wasn't, then why was Addie here? "I must have heard something somewhere."

"I'd better watch out—you'll steal my job. You never know what you might catch if your ears are open," he said. "Eyes, too. I bumped into your policeman friend the other day. He tell you?"

Addie really needed to discourage this familiarity, but for once she was at a complete social loss. The American refused to pick up her cues that he was definitely not wanted. Or, more likely, he picked them up and was tossing them right back at her with perverse glee.

To make matters worse, Stephen was coming down the sidewalk towards her. She coughed and shook her head violently. Thank heavens he noticed and understood, brushing by her and up the stairs into the club.

"Are you okay?"

"Bug," Addie said. "A big one." She waved her hand around her face for emphasis.

"Pshaw. You Brits haven't seen bugs until you come to America. We've got mosquitoes as big as dinner plates. And roaches the size of kittens."

"How nice for you. I'm afraid I have to go back inside now."

"I'll come with you. I'm not a member, but Miss Baptiste and I have an understanding."

Addie's heart sank. How on earth was she going to get rid of him?

"Don't worry. I won't be a fifth wheel. I don't expect to sit with you," Lombard said cheerfully. "Might ask you to dance, though. Why not? All you can say is no."

Which she would.

How could she talk to Stephen with Lombard's eyes on her? It would be odd indeed to see her civilly conversing with the grandson of the man her mother was alleged to have murdered. But at least Lombard wouldn't connect Stephen with Roberta's disappearance. The marriage was still a secret.

However, he would take note when Inspector Hunter joined her. Addie hadn't missed the annoying "boyfriend" reference.

Lombard ground his cigarette into the pavement and extended an elbow. "Shall we?"

"I've changed my mind. You know. A woman's prerogative. I'm not quite ready to go inside," Addie said, trying to smile. "It's awfully hot in there."

"It's awfully hot out here," Lombard replied. "I thought you Brits had to wear wool all year round."

"Some of us do, despite the temperature." She really couldn't believe she was chatting about the weather.

"Well, I'll take my chances inside. At least I can get a cold drink. That's if I ask for ice cubes. You'd think they were gold nuggets the way they're hoarded." He touched a finger to his temple and gave her a salute. "See you around, Lady Adelaide."

It was, she supposed, inevitable. The man was like a barnacle. Addie leaned up against the black railing and took a calming breath. She was tempted to go in, grab her things, and go home. Elizabeth wouldn't notice if she were not in the audience—all of London's Bright Young People were present. Addie was tired, and, if she was honest, depressed.

"Good evening."

She hadn't noticed Mr. Hunter come up behind her. Tonight the jeweled elephant pin was absent, but he was still as handsome in his evening clothes.

Another reason to be depressed. Oh, time to stop wallowing and whining. Addie looked up and smiled. "Good evening to you. How was dinner with your parents?"

Mr. Hunter patted his midsection. "I questioned whether I could stand upright long enough to come out. Frankly, I was very tempted to go back to my flat and lie down."

"Lying down does have its appeal." Her face grew warmer.

"I mean, I'm tired. As soon as Elizabeth finishes her first set, I want to leave."

"You haven't been sleeping well."

"How can I? When I think of my mother in that awful place—" To Addie's dismay, her eyes welled. Before she could fumble into her bag for a handkerchief, Mr. Hunter pulled his from his pocket. She took her glasses off and blotted her tears. "Sorry. Now I know I'm too tired when I can't contain my emotions."

"Why should you? You're only human. Even before this business with your mother, you've had a rough time. Think where we were a week ago. You must admit we've had no time off for good behavior."

Addie folded the handkerchief into a neat square. "Maybe we're being punished for something we did in a past life." Although what her mother could have done to deserve incarceration was a mystery for the ages.

Mr. Hunter gave her a crooked grin. "Karma. Have you been sneaking a look at my books?"

"I wish I *could* read; my mind isn't still enough to concentrate. Of course, if I did filch one of your books, I probably wouldn't understand a word."

"Don't sell yourself short."

"You should interview my governesses and teachers if you're so confident in my academic abilities—they'd disabuse you of that notion. I don't think I ever fully devoted myself to my schoolwork." Addie certainly hadn't planned on a career, and knew she'd marry at some point. She was a marquess's daughter, with every advantage that entailed.

"Plenty of time to make up for that. The rest of your life, in fact. That's what I'm doing, page by page."

Addie envied his discipline and drive. "I don't think I could get through the simplest paragraph at the moment. Should we go in? Stephen's already inside. Oh! I must warn you. Mr. Lombard is here rootling about."

"Is he? Are you sure you want to go in with me?"

Addie took his arm. "What's the worst that could happen?"

Chapter Twenty-Seven

The fairy lights pierced the lavender clouds on the ceiling and twinkled around the leaves and branches of the artificial tree in the center of the dance floor. Votives flickered on the tables. Dev still couldn't see a bloody thing.

His eyes were tired. *All* of him was tired. He'd not been joking about staying home. But he didn't want to let Lady Adelaide down.

Besides feeling full, he was feeling guilty, though it wasn't his fault his mother had invited her friend for dinner. And her friend's daughter. Neha was a perfectly lovely girl, with emphasis on girl. She could not have been much over seventeen. Dev was twice her age, and had no wish to be Pygmalion, shaping her to his will.

He was surprised his mother had miscalculated so badly—it was not like her to think he'd want a shy and submissive child bride. Chandani Hunter was never one herself, and had kept his father on his toes from the first day they met in Jhansi Province. Harry Hunter would not have it any other way. He was fond of saying he waited until forty to marry since it took that long to find someone as stubborn as he was.

Dev's parents' partnership was a good one. Something to emulate. Something, really, to envy. Dev doubted he'd ever be so fortunate.

Lady Adelaide had excused herself to go to the loo. Dev continued to squint in the dark looking for Stephen. Thus far, Lombard had not made a beeline for him. Dev spotted him at the bar talking to the hostess, Miss Baptiste, when they first came in. He hoped she wasn't revealing the relationship between Roberta and Stephen. That would complicate the attention the family was already receiving.

He took a small sip of his whisky and soda. It wasn't enough to ease the tension he felt, nearly a sense of foreboding. Dev never discounted the odd feelings he had. While they made no rational sense, they'd saved his hide a time or two.

"You're Mr. Hunter, aye?"

Dev looked up to see a pretty waitress in a picture hat and massive skirt. Surely she wasn't about to shoot him. It had only been a week since the last time someone decided to put a period to his existence. "Yes?"

"Miss Baptiste told me to give you this. It was on the bar." The girl handed him a damp folded envelope. Written in smeary blue ink were the words *Mr. Hunter. Important.*

"For me? Are you sure?"

"It's got your name on it right there, sugar," she said in a faux Southern accent.

Who on earth would leave a message for him here? This was just his second time visiting the club, and he wasn't and never would be a member. Dev lifted the flap of the envelope with care and angled the slip of paper it contained close to the sputtering candle.

To Mr. Hunter,

Roberta is safe. Tell Stephen not to worry.

A friend

"Can you ask Miss Baptiste to come over?"

The girl shrugged. "I can, but she's awfully busy. It's Saturday night, you know. She has to announce the Jones Sisters soon, too. I mean one of 'em anyhow. Bobbie's scarpered."

Dev knew the day of the week as well as anyone. "It's important. And can you find Lord Vere for me?"

"Stevie? What do you want him for?"

The note could be a fraud. He didn't want to get anyone's hopes up. "I just do."

The girl shrugged again and left. Dev studied the thin paper. No watermark, and the cheap envelope was just as ordinary as it could be, with no helpful embossed address. There would be no point visiting stationers.

Lady Adelaide slid into her seat next to him. She'd repaired her lipstick, and smiled brightly. "I just spoke to Elizabeth. She's going on after the band's fifteen-minute break, and then we can leave straightaway."

"I don't think so. Look at this."

Lady Adelaide held the paper out at arm's length. "Oh! Oh, my! Who brought this?"

"One of the girls. It was found tossed on the bar, apparently. It's a miracle it wasn't swept away into the rubbish."

"We must tell Stephen!" She swiveled her head, looking for him in the crowd.

"We will. I've asked the waitress to locate him, and want a word with the hostess as well. Perhaps she saw who left it."

"This must be a good sign, don't you think?"

Dev wasn't sure. There had been no request for ransom money, so perhaps a kidnapping could be ruled out.

But maybe that demand would come in a second missive.

"Too soon to tell. It might not be…truthful."

Lady Adelaide looked alarmed. "I pray Roberta isn't in danger! She hasn't done anything!"

Except to marry into one of Britain's grand old families. Dev covered her gloved hand with his in an attempt to reassure her. "We shan't borrow trouble."

"Beckett always says that, but it's hard not to."

They waited in silence while the band played one last song. The ceiling lights brightened, and dancers returned to their tables. The Belles swooped in to take drink orders, but there was still no sign of Stephen.

"Are you sure Vere is here?" Dev asked.

"He walked right by me when I was buttonholed outside by Mr. Lombard."

"I'm surprised he hasn't made himself a nuisance yet. Just what we need." Dev had no desire to read about himself in the society pages, although his mother might get a kick out of it. "Ah! Here's someone I do want to see."

Dorothée Baptiste undulated her way between the tables. She was not wearing a hoop skirt, but a black velvet evening gown with tight sleeves. Red camellias were affixed to one shoulder. Dev thought she must be roasting in the heat of the room until she turned to chat to a customer, revealing the dress had no back at all.

Dev tamped back his impatience. Finally disengaging, she sauntered over to them. "Good evening, *cher*. Agnes said you wanted me?"

"Yes." He showed her the envelope. "What do you know about this?"

"*Moi?* Why, not a cotton-pickin' thing." She patted her sleek black bob and glanced around the room, ever alert for mischief.

Dev found her Southern-fried attempt to conceal her Cockney origins somewhat ridiculous. He bet the name on her birth certificate was Dorothy, too.

"Who left it for me?"

Miss Baptiste shrugged. "Damned if I know. It's Saturday night, guv. The place is a madhouse in case y'all haven't noticed. It just turned up, and the barman knew who you were—he used to work at the Thieves' Den and says you're some famous detective. Gonna lock me up in a little cell?" She held out slender white wrists. Her nail varnish was blood-red and somewhat terrifying.

"Not tonight."

"What a pity. You look like you'd be a barrel of fun in tight quarters, if you know what I mean."

Dev almost smiled when he saw Lady Adelaide's grim reaction to this conversation. He cleared his throat. "The barman also didn't see who left it?"

"What do you think? The guy is run off his feet. Tony called in sick, and poor Johnny is all by his lonesome. It's so hard to get good help." She sighed. "Even one of the Jones girls ran off, so if you were wanting to see a duo later, you'll be disappointed."

"We know," said Lady Adelaide. "We spent the morning looking for her. Where were *you*?"

"Getting my beauty sleep, dearie. Which, to be frank, you need a little more of, if you don't mind me saying so." She turned back to Dev. "Here's what I don't get, Mr. Hunter—there's no reason for you to be ferreting around our humble club in a professional capacity. Not like that dump the Thieves' Den. You've met Freddy."

"I have," Dev acknowledged. And didn't much want to meet him again, although it probably was ordained. The club was aptly named.

Miss Baptiste shook a crimson-tipped finger at him. "Mark my words, Freddy Rinaldi's gonna wind up in gaol again if you ask me, even if he didn't kill all those kids. Why would anyone send you a note *here* and not over there or some other dodgy joint? You're not a member, and we're all aboveboard at the Belle. Clean as a whistle."

She posed a very good question. Was he being followed? As far as Dev knew, only Lombard was stumbling around after him.

Could the *reporter* have something to do with Roberta's disappearance?

Dev reached into his pocket for a card and penciled in his home telephone number. "Please call me if you or Johnny find any more notes for me or remember anything else. It's important."

Miss Baptiste tucked it up her sleeve. "Sure."

"You can call me, too," Lady Adelaide said. Dev handed her his pencil, and she wrote her number on an engraved ecru calling card. "In case you can't reach Mr. Hunter. We're working together."

"Lucky you. That must be nice and cozy," the hostess drawled.

Lady Adelaide's face flushed, but she said nothing. Dev felt duty-bound to rescue her. "You spoke of the Thieves' Den murders earlier. Lady Adelaide's sister was almost a victim, and she took an interest in my case. She was instrumental in capturing the criminal, at great risk to her personal safety." And his, too, but Dev didn't hold a grudge.

Miss Baptiste's thin black eyebrows raised. "Was she really? Well done then. I'm glad I didn't have to give that crazy person a membership application. We're more discriminating who we accept here—Freddy will take money from anybody with any. I don't suppose you're gonna close them down soon—they're still our stiffest competition. There's just no accounting for taste."

"I haven't heard anything along those lines." Though he knew a few young men who were there almost every night undercover. Freddy Rinaldi's days of freedom were probably limited.

The hostess checked her wristwatch. "Well, I'll keep an eye out for you, and tell Johnny and Tony, too, if he ever shows up. Gotta ankle. It's time for Bettie to go on solo."

She swished away, and Dev had to admit it was a formidable

swish. Miss Baptiste was a bit hard-edged for him, but she had her appeal.

"She was completely unhelpful," Lady Adelaide grumbled.

"Was she? I asked myself the same question when I got the note—why would it be delivered here of all places?"

Lady Adelaide blinked. "Do you think someone saw you this morning searching with the band and thought you had a connection to the club?"

"Why not send it to Walt or one of the other musicians? Or even Miss Baptiste. Someone thinks I work here, and I bet I know who."

"Don't keep me in suspense!"

"You won't believe me. I find it difficult to believe myself."

"Dev! I mean, Mr. Hunter. Spit it out."

"The Duke of Rufford."

Chapter Twenty-Eight

Addie was prevented from saying a word, as the room darkened and the spotlight fell on the flowered arch. Miss Baptiste stood at its center, smiling serenely. She apologized for Roberta's absence—"a triflin' tickle in her golden throat that a hot toddy will cure in a jiffy"—and introduced Elizabeth.

The girl's eyes were wide and frightened, and her first few notes were tentative. But as the band supported her, she gathered courage and her performance prospered.

Her voice was pure and powerful. Even opera buffs would be impressed at her range. Despite Addie's desire to sink deep into her bed and dream for about four days, she and Mr. Hunter stayed through the whole set for the sheer pleasure of it.

There was still no sign of Stephen—perhaps he'd decided to leave. Addie thought it was probably a good thing. Until they could determine the writer of the note, it was best not to have him going off half-cocked. Mr. Hunter had already intervened in a Moreton family fistfight once. If Stephen thought his father was holding Roberta somewhere, he would be unable to think straight.

They left the club and, after failing to find any taxis, decided to walk back to Addie's flat. The night was sultry, and their pace was slow. Addie's fancy dancing shoes were not meant for ambles through Soho and Mayfair, and Mr. Hunter seemed worn out. He'd dispensed with his sling, and prodded his shoulder every now and again.

"Are you in much pain?" she asked after observing this several times.

"Just sore. I'm fine."

Addie didn't press him. This past week had been a challenge for both of them, and the fact they'd survived it as well as they had was remarkable. "Do you really think Alistair has Roberta stashed away somewhere?"

He stopped and leaned against a shuttered shop, reaching into his pocket for his cigarette case. "You don't mind, do you? If I wait any longer, today's gasper will wind up being tomorrow's."

Addie knew he limited himself to one cigarette a day, and marveled at his restraint. Several people of her acquaintance were veritable chimneys, indulging in one cigarette after another. It couldn't be healthy.

But she didn't mind the pause on the pavement, and wished she could kick off her shoes. "Not at all." The matchlight flared across the planes of his face, and she saw the tension ease as he exhaled.

"Stashed? Where? It would be much easier to pay her off, although she didn't strike me as any sort of adventuress. And if Alistair sent that note, it makes no sense. The whole point would be to separate them. Make Stephen think she'd left him. Make him give her up and agree to seek a divorce, if the marriage is deemed legal. Why would his father try to reassure him and give him hope?"

"Do you think she did? Leave him, I mean?"

"You've seen them together. What's your opinion?"

Addie thought of them holding hands on her couch. "They're

awfully young—I cannot even remember being so young. But they do seem sincerely attached."

Mr. Hunter nodded. "They do. When we were marching up and down Oxford Street this morning, I tried to distract the boy. Keep his spirits up and remember happier days. I asked him how they'd met."

"How did they?" Addie said.

"Stephen and his sister accompanied their mother to Paris. It was a shopping trip for the ladies, but he was so bored up in Northumberland he jumped at the chance to tag along. Edmund didn't approve, which made it all the more enjoyable for the three of them to flout his authority."

"*Vive la révolution*," Addie said, shaking her fist in a mock salute.

"Exactly. I confess my experience in France was less romantic than Stephen's, but according to him, April in Paris is a magical time. All the trees are in bloom and whatnot. Roberta and her sister were singing at a little club in Montmartre, and one night Stephen wandered in. The rest you can imagine."

"A *coup de foudre*," Addie murmured. She didn't believe in love at first sight, although Rupert had certainly made a very good first impression in his uniform, medals gleaming.

"'For fools rush in where angels fear to tread,' to quote Pope," Mr. Hunter said with half a smile. "Somehow he persuaded her to meet him in Scotland right before she was contracted to begin at the Southern Belle and they married."

"They really *are* newlyweds," Addie said.

"Just a matter of weeks. I daresay we know each other better than they do."

Addie wondered if that was true. Some aspects of Mr. Hunter's life that were a mystery. For example, however had *he* avoided matrimony?

Perhaps it wasn't a good time to ask.

"I wonder where Stephen went. I thought for sure he'd come find us in the club."

"Maybe he received a message, too." Mr. Hunter crushed his cigarette into the cement. "Oh, God, I hope he hasn't gone to murder his father. I'm too fagged to stop it tonight."

"So you think it unlikely that the note came from his father?"

"I do. Very unlikely." He extended his good arm, and Addie took it. They'd taken but a few steps when he stopped.

"Wait just a minute! I'm an idiot!"

"Of course you're not. What's made you say that?"

"Last night—lord, was it only last night?—when I rescued Stephen—Rufford thought I had something to do with the Southern Belle, and I did nothing to convince him otherwise. I certainly didn't want him to know my connection to the Yard, so I let his remarks slide. But his sister was there, too. Lady Penelope."

Addie didn't know the woman, only what Rupert had told her, so she was careful with her words. "I've heard she's softhearted. Do you suppose she wrote the note so her nephew wouldn't worry?"

"Would she lie to him to make him feel better? That's almost cruel, when you consider something awful really might have happened to Roberta." He started walking again, and Addie tried to keep up.

"Maybe she knows where Roberta is," she said.

He stopped short again and frowned. "Good grief. Do you think Lady Penelope had her kidnapped? I thought she was fond of Stephen and he of her. He thinks she's his only decent relative, apart from his little sister."

Where was Rupert when she needed him? He was the Penelope expert. "I've never met her. What was she like Friday night?"

Mr. Hunter was quiet, presumably thinking as they resumed walking. After they crossed the road, he said, "She's—she's a bit of a blur, to be frank. As if she doesn't want to be noticed. Physically, she's rather pasty, with those odd pale eyes. She struck me as nervous. Cowed by her brother and his temper, I'm afraid. She's not a happy woman."

Probably not, when she was estranged from her handsome husband for whatever reason. "Did she say anything about Roberta?"

"Something about how it was better that she'd run away. As if the girl had a good reason to hide."

"Maybe she knew Alistair had plans to do something. I'd put nothing past him if he couldn't badger Stephen into submission."

"I thought the same thing myself. But I don't think he had a chance to do anything. He's spent the week meeting with solicitors and arranging the funeral. He acted surprised that Roberta was missing, and was quite convincing."

Irrational or not, Addie still wished to convict Alistair of patricide. Kidnapping was minor in comparison, and she'd happily accuse him of that, too.

But what if he'd murdered Roberta? Or had some lackey do it. She really didn't like him, which was prejudicing her thought process.

"So you're saying Stephen's aunt was under the same misapprehension—that you work at the Southern Belle?"

"Aye. I don't think I could do as good a job as Miss Baptiste, to be honest."

Addie was sure if he wanted to, Devenand Hunter would be a success at anything he tried his hand at. "I did not like her."

"She's a tough cookie. She has to be. All those private clubs are jockeying for the brightest of bright young people. What's popular one week is tiresome the next."

Addie didn't want to waste one more word on the woman who'd told her she was not looking her best, even if it was true.

"So you think it's conceivable that Lady Penelope has something to do with Roberta's disappearance. Or at least knows something."

Perhaps Rupert had picked up some vibration when he went to Maddox Street to return the diary. The diary. What had Grace said? That her aunt always went to church, no matter what.

"It's one of the few explanations I can think of."

"She attends St. George's eleven o'clock service religiously. And I don't mean that as a joke," Addie said.

"How on earth do you know that?"

How *would* she know that? Addie had already said she'd never met Penelope. "It stands to reason. It's the neighborhood church, after all, and where her father's service was. I—I've heard she takes her faith very seriously. Someone must have mentioned it—perhaps Mama."

"Maybe we can catch her after the service," Mr. Hunter said. "Accidentally bump into her on purpose and see how she reacts when she sees me."

"Why, Mr. Hunter, are you inviting me to accompany you to church?" It wasn't exactly a date, but Addie would take what she could.

Chapter Twenty-Nine

Sunday morning

Addie had been to St. George's scores of times. It was London society's church for weddings and funerals, and while it was not her own parish, she felt comfortable. Or as comfortable as one could be, when she was recognized by acquaintances and given the cut direct.

Their cruelty only made her more determined to clear her mother's name. But if she couldn't, then what?

No. Addie absolutely refused to let her mind wander to such a dark place. Someone else would eventually be the talk of the town, and the Merrill women could lick their wounds in private in the country. Addie had no wish to make a splash in London anyway. Those days were behind her, if they ever even were in front of her to begin with. The war had soon cured her of her girlish dreams. Bandage rolling and dull charity luncheons had soon replaced debutante balls.

She stood on the broad steps waiting for Mr. Hunter, a pillar providing shade for the already-hot June Sunday. Dozens of well-dressed congregants filed past her, the women wearing some enviable, and no doubt expensive, hats. Addie might be depressed, but she could still appreciate a fashionable chapeau, and was wearing one herself, a smart black straw cloche with a floppy, red silk rose. Her cream charmeuse dress was banded in black at the collar, sleeves, and hem, and she hoped she looked cooler than she felt.

She had no idea if Lady Penelope von Mayr had already walked by. For once she wished Rupert was there to point out the woman, but he seemed to be avoiding her, not paying her a midnight visit after Inspector Hunter walked her home. She hoped he'd been successful returning Grace's diary. If he'd learned anything else last night, he was negligent in informing her.

"Better late than never. Sorry, my dear. I got hung up. You know how it is in the Afterlife."

No, she really didn't, and didn't want to for years and years. Speak—or think—of the devil. Rupert once said she could summon him, and so she had, quite inadvertently. "Shh!" Addie hissed.

"Why? No one can hear me but you." Rupert pirouetted around a column like a demented ballet dancer, nearly bumping into an elderly gentleman who was trying to balance himself up the steps with a flimsy Malacca walking stick.

"I don't have anything interesting to report, however, and not for lack of trying," he said, after completing the circle. "I spent far too long in Maddox Street last night waiting for something to happen. The house was deader than I am."

Addie pulled a compact from her black alligator purse and held it over her mouth, briefly admiring her vibrant crimson lip rouge. Her mother would not approve of such grooming attempts in public—or the color—but people really did not need to see her talking to herself.

"Couldn't you read anyone's minds?"

"You do bear me a grudge, don't you? Listening in to a Moreton mind is rather like diving into a sewage-infested pool with the odd piranha floating about, but I did jump in for the cause. Alistair was scheming in his den with a very large bottle of cognac—only the best, no expense spared now that his papa is not paying the bills. His thoughts were so disordered they gave me a headache, but nothing like what he's experiencing this morning, I'll wager."

"He was drunk?"

"As the proverbial skunk. He's furious with Stephen, but I did not detect any direct culpability in Roberta's vanishing. If anything, he regrets he was unable to have a hand in it, as he'd have more supervision. I gather he was in the preliminary stages of arranging to have someone speak to her, and by speak, I do not mean a nice, convivial chat accompanied by biscuits and oolong. Threats, bribery, and who knows what other depths he or his minions would have sunk to."

Addie gulped. "He intended to hurt her?"

"Indubitably, if milder measures were rebuffed. I told you he wasn't a pleasant fellow. He has a legal team working on dissolving the marriage, and an illegal team if the first one fails."

"Do you suppose the family knows his intentions? His sister, for example?"

"Penny? She wouldn't approve of anything violent, although I can't see her standing up to him in any meaningful way. She's let people walk all over her all her life, poor dear."

"Was she home last night when you were there?"

"She wasn't, which came as a surprise, to be frank. It's not like her to be kicking up her heels and painting the town red when she's in mourning. I expected to find her knitting a lumpy black tea cozy or something."

He took his perfectly pressed handkerchief out of his pocket and mopped his brow. It *was* warm, but Addie was surprised to see him react to the heat. But then, so much of Rupert's behavior was surprising of late.

"Actually," he continued, "there was no one of interest at Maddox Street save old Alistair. And Grace, of course, who's too young yet to go anywhere on her own. Her other relatives were amusing themselves elsewhere. So much for proper family feeling—Edmund might as well never have existed for all the respect they're showing him. I hope you weren't so heartless when I kicked the bucket."

Addie had been in too much shock then to walk to the village post office for a stamp. Facing the reality of Rupert's mistresses at the funeral had taken whatever tenuous wind there was right out of her sails. It had required months for her to emerge from isolation, and when she did, she was cursed with Rupert's ghost and several dead bodies.

The bells above began to peal, which prevented her retort. Where was Inspector Hunter? She couldn't stand out here with her mirror much longer.

"I'd better go in," Addie said over the noise.

"Perhaps I should go in, too. Get a little extra credit with the Fellow Upstairs."

She was not in the mood to share a hymnal with Rupert. "Why don't you go back to Maddox Street? It might be livelier this morning."

"I doubt it—they're probably all still under the blankets trying to recover from too much giggle water. Young people today are such fools. At their age I was strafing convoys and shooting Junkers out of the sky."

And had all the shiny medals to prove it, Addie thought. They were in the safe at Compton Chase, along with Rupert's watch collection.

"Look!" she said with relief, snapping her compact shut. "Here comes Mr. Hunter now. We can catch up later."

"I know when I'm not wanted," Rupert sniffed. "You'll miss me when I'm gone. I know you'll always be fond of me. I represent all the sins you've never had the courage to commit."

"Courage!" That would not be the precise word Addie would choose, but there was no time to argue—Mr. Hunter was crossing the street and in seconds he would be by her side. He did not need to hear a one-sided row with her dead husband.

Addie bit her tongue, and Rupert danced down the steps on his way to annoy someone else, pitching far too close to the policeman. She stopped herself from yelling out a warning, and he turned with a grin and a two-fingered salute. That was Rupert, always too close to the flames for comfort.

Courage indeed.

"Sorry I'm late," Mr. Hunter said, slightly out of breath. "I couldn't get my father's Morris started. I thought a car might come in handy today, but the old girl had other ideas. My father hasn't taken her out of the garage in quite some time, and the engine seized."

Rupert could probably have fixed it, Addie thought. To give him credit where credit was due, he'd been a wiz with his automobiles, and was in anguish over her treatment of the Rolls. "Hold still." Addie took her lacy handkerchief out of her purse and wiped an oily smudge from Mr. Hunter's chiseled cheekbone. "There. You're presentable now." There was very little that could diminish Mr. Hunter's appeal, unless he was sporting a paper bag over his head.

"Now I really *am* sorry. I wouldn't want to ruin your reputation by being seen with such a ruffian."

"Oh, it's already ruined. I lost count of the people who ignored me while I waited. It was rather sobering to realize how swiftly one can fall from grace."

"Through no fault of your own!" Mr. Hunter said, a martial light in his eye.

"Through no fault of Mama's, either. I hope we can find out

something useful today, either about Roberta or the duke's death. Time is running out."

"I still have a week's leave, Lady Adelaide."

"I know. I don't mean to place more stress upon you. This business with Roberta is an added complication. Oh, bother! Is that Mr. Lombard?"

Mr. Hunter took her elbow and quickly steered her into the church. Since it was the end of June, many of its parishioners had decamped to their country estates, so there was plenty of room. They settled into a pew to the rear in a darkish corner. Mr. Hunter shielded his face with his hat, and Addie ducked behind the Book of Common Prayer as the reporter entered. If they were lucky, he hadn't noticed them outside, and would walk right by them now.

Addie held her breath as the organ music surged. Mr. Lombard headed towards the front of the church and climbed clumsily over several worshippers as the rector and his altar boys entered. She rose and sang and knelt and sat by rote, only half-listening to the particulars of the service. She noted Mr. Hunter had a pitch-perfect baritone, which was one more thing to admire him for.

"Is she here?" she whispered, earning a glare from a man in front of her.

"I can't tell. Too many hats."

He had a point. Unless the woman turned around, identifying her would be difficult. "Why is Mr. Lombard here?" The reporter did not strike her as being overly religious.

"Maybe he's following me. I was in such a hurry I didn't pay attention."

"Maybe he's following *me*."

"Shh!" the man said, now wagging a finger. He looked far too grumpy to get into heaven with ease. Addie refrained from sticking her tongue out at him.

"He keeps turning up everywhere we are," Addie complained.

"Like a bad penny. But he could be onto something. Maybe he's keeping our quarry under surveillance, too."

That would be extremely inconvenient.

Chapter Thirty

"There she is."

Addie stood on tiptoe to see around the throng of people leaving the church. "Which one is she?"

"The lady with the black hat. Come on. Let's go!"

As far as she could tell, nearly every woman was wearing a black hat, herself included. They broke protocol, exiting the pew before those in front of them. Addie struggled to keep up with the inspector as he dodged around those waiting to greet the officiant and his assistant at the open church doors. She apologized as she stepped on a few toes, earning more scornful looks. Addie definitely was not winning any popularity points today.

She lost Mr. Hunter in the crowd milling about the vestibule, and flattened herself to squeeze by a bosomy dowager and her equally bosomy husband. Once outside, she scanned the steps and pavement below. A piercing whistle drew her attention. Mr. Hunter was waving rather wildly, standing next to an idling taxi.

Addie clattered down the stairs, and was fairly shoved into the vehicle. "Follow that car I pointed out, driver. There's an extra fiver in it for you." He turned to Addie. "Lady Penelope hailed a cab before I could get to her."

"Did she recognize you?" Addie asked, pulling down her hem in an attempt to protect her modesty.

"I don't think so—she seemed like she was in a rush, and it's clear she's not going home. We've just passed Rufford House."

They had already turned left onto Maddox Street from St. George Street. One didn't need anything but shank's pony to go to church from the duke's residence.

Since it was Sunday, traffic was light on Regent Street. Mr. Hunter bent over the seat, encouraging the taxi driver to keep at it. Lady Penelope was at least three cars ahead of them, and Addie prayed nothing would cause them to stop.

The fine afternoon had attracted numerous pedestrians, and once they got to Trafalgar Square, at least a hundred people had gathered around Nelson's column. Addie checked her watch. Fifteen minutes had elapsed, and her stomach rumbled. A roast lunch would not go amiss—maybe that's where Lady Penelope was headed.

The car slowed on the Strand, and finally lost its luck. The light turned red.

"Let's get out. I have a feeling I know where she's going, and it's not that far," Addie said, opening up her purse.

"I've got it," Mr. Hunter said, pulling money from his pocket. Thanking the driver, he got out of the car, then held out his hand to help her to slide out. "I hope you're right," he said. "I don't fancy walking to Bloomsbury."

"She's going to the Savoy to see her husband."

"Really? I thought they were separated."

Addie nodded. "They are. Have been for years. But I told you Franz von Mayr is eager to resume the marriage. Now that Edmund is no longer in the way, maybe they can reconcile."

What advice would Addie give Penelope about a straying husband? It was none of her business, she reminded herself. People could change, couldn't they? Perhaps not Rupert, but Graf von Mayr appeared to be sincere in his desire to reunite his family. Would he give up his Liesls and Rosies when he was back in his Tyrolean *schloss*? It could happen.

They hurried down the Strand until they came to the exclusive hostelry. Built by the legendary theater producer Richard D'Oyly Carte over thirty-five years ago, it was the first hotel in London intentionally built to attract the crème de la crème of society. Nothing was deemed too luxurious or lavish, and the venue had only improved with age.

Entering the lobby, Addie blushed remembering the last time she was here. If he was working on a Sunday, she would avoid Mr. Reeves-Smith if she could help it. Several black-hatted women were sitting in plush chairs in the brilliantly lit space. The checkerboard floor shone beneath their feet.

"Do you see her?"

"No."

"Drat. She's gone upstairs already."

"*If* she's here," Mr. Hunter said.

"She is—I can sense it. You have those odd premonitions, too, don't you?"

"On occasion. I have to admit I'm drawing a complete blank today. The only things I feel are hot and irritable." He took his hat off and smoothed his dark hair back.

"What should we do?" Addie asked.

"Wait for her to come down, I suppose."

What if Lady Penelope and Franz had a heart-to-heart that took all afternoon? Or something even more intimate? Her blushes returned.

"I'm going to ask reception to ring him up." She wouldn't be Maeve Rose Beckett this time.

"What if von Mayr refuses to see us?"

"I know his suite number. We can sneak up there somehow."

Mr. Hunter grinned. "You in a maid's uniform, with a feather duster? No, I think it's time I brush the dust off my warrant card. I may be on leave, but I'm obligated to act if I believe laws have been broken. Lady Penelope has been acting suspiciously."

"By going to church, then taking a taxi to visit her husband?"

"By sending me that anonymous note in reference to a missing person. It has to have been her."

"All right. Nothing ventured, nothing gained. I hope you don't get into trouble with your superiors," Addie said. She hated to put Inspector Hunter in even more peril. On leave or not, she was quite sure Scotland Yard would frown upon the private arrangement he had with her mother.

They walked up to the front desk. Several clerks were already assisting people, and Addie tamped down her impatience as they waited in line. When it was their turn, she took a calling card out of her purse and placed it on the polished counter. A sleek young man, as shiny as the counter, picked it up and examined it between two manicured fingers.

"Good morning," she said with a smile. "No, it's afternoon now, isn't it? Silly me. Would you be so kind as to let Graf von Mayr that we're here? He's in Room 348."

"Certainly, Lady Adelaide." His gaze flicked to Mr. Hunter. "And your companion?"

Wordlessly, Mr. Hunter reached into his pocket and produced his identification. The desk clerk paled, as though he might be guilty of something himself.

"J-just a moment." He picked up the phone and turned his back, but the words "Scotland Yard" were audible. Addie heard the graf curse *auf Deutsch*—her limited schoolgirl vocabulary proved insufficiently broad to translate. She'd had several years of French as well, but was not much better in that language. There was more shouting in both German and English, and at last the young man set the receiver down, looking extremely uncomfortable. "The graf asks if you can wait five minutes before you go up."

"I think not," Mr. Hunter said, taking Addie's elbow. "Let's go."

They hurried to a waiting lift. "Third floor, please," Addie said to the operator. "Do you think he'll still be there?"

"I suppose I should have used the stairs to head him off if he's inclined to bolt, but I don't want to send you up alone if he isn't. We'll take our chances."

The ride up felt like years. Once the door was opened, Addie led the way over the carpeted hall to the graf's suite. Mr. Hunter knocked with one hand, his warrant card in the other.

More years followed.

"Has he done a bunk?"

"If he has, he'll be sorry," Mr. Hunter growled.

Just then, they heard the turn of tumblers and the door opened a fraction. One bright blue eye glared out.

"You!"

"Yes, it is I again," Addie said.

"You are not my wife's friend!"

"I don't believe I ever said I was," Addie replied, racking her brain for any lies she might have told. She'd certainly never claimed to be a masseuse.

"It's your wife we've come to see, Mr. von Mayr."

"Graf von Mayr, und sie ist meine Gräfin!"

Titles were really a ridiculous construct when you thought about it. Addie was often very tired of being "Lady Adelaide" and all the expectations that came with it. "May we come in, please?" Addie asked. "It's very important."

"She isn't here."

"But I am!" came a loud shout from within. "Lady Adelaide, is that you?"

Chapter Thirty-One

In his line of work, hardly anything surprised Dev anymore. He'd pretty much seen and heard it all, and then some. And then some more. But he admitted he was somewhat stupefied now. The Marchioness of Vere was hugging Lady Adelaide Compton on von Mayr's jacquard satin sofa, both of them weeping and laughing into each other's shoulders.

"I've got to tell Stevie I'm all right. He must be worried sick," Roberta said after blowing her nose in Dev's handkerchief.

"And you will. We can place a call to the Albert Hotel in just a minute. I'm sure the graf will have no objections to us using his phone." Lady Adelaide gave the man a radiant smile to make up for shoving him aside at the door.

Dev studied the Austrian. His face was as red as the apples that sat on a sterling silver bowl on the marble console table. "But first, I'd like to hear what happened."

"You can't really blame Franzi here," Roberta said, hiccupping a little. "He thought he was being a knight in shining armor."

"How so?"

"Penny—my wife—told me the poor girl's life was in danger. That I should protect her until it was safe for her to peep out of the nest. Just for a day or two. I of course complied. I would do anything to win back the trust of *meine Frau*." He held a hand over his heart for emphasis.

"He's not such a bad guy. We had a few laughs once we got used to each other. He tried to teach me a few words in German, and I taught him how to play gin rummy. He owes me almost forty pounds," Roberta added. "*Viertzig*, right?"

A considerable sum. The graf must be unlucky in love *and* cards.

"And I shall meet my obligations," von Mayr said gruffly. "Even if I suspect you cheat."

"So you weren't kidnapped?" Lady Adelaide asked, as she straightened her very flattering hat. Dev would probably have to work three or four months to pay for one like it, although he was hardly an expert on women's fashions.

"Not really. Aunt Penny—she told me to call her that—sent me a note at the club. She asked to meet me after rehearsal Friday. I felt guilty not saying anything to Elizabeth, but Aunt Penny said it was vital I keep it secret. She even snuck out of her own father's funeral reception to meet me!"

"And was it so important?" Dev asked.

"I'll say. She explained her brother was going to sic some goons on me. To rough me up…or worse. She'd overheard him talking on the telephone, you see, and put two and two together. She told me time was of the essence, that she had a hideout for me, and I couldn't tell anyone where I was—not even my husband— because the goons were sure to find out somehow. The Savoy!" She grinned, looking around von Mayr's elegant sitting room. "Not such a bad place to hang out, though I was awfully worried about Stevie. Did he go nuts?"

"Not entirely," Dev said dryly. "He did suspect his father was responsible for your disappearance, and I guess he was not far off."

"Thank God you're all right." Lady Adelaide returned her damp handkerchief to her bag.

"Aunt Penny thought of everything. She had a suitcase full of clothes for me. Not quite to my taste," Roberta said, looking down at the grim brown dress she wore, "but it's not like Franzi and I were going downstairs to dance last night." The hotel's band, the Savoy Orpheans, were broadcast live every Saturday night by the BBC, and the program was popular throughout the country with those who owned a wireless.

"Where is Lady Penelope now?" Dev asked the graf.

"When she heard the police were on their way up, she panicked. I could not stop her from leaving."

Dev bet the man didn't try very hard, either. He and Lady Adelaide must have been going up in one lift while Lady Penelope was coming down.

"Did you come to arrest her? She has done nothing but try to be kind. That poor woman—all her life she has been at the mercy of her wretched family. First her father, now her brother. I saved her all those years ago! I! She was too young, perhaps, but we had a good life until the war. You cannot take her away from me again! I won't have it!"

Lady Adelaide gasped. The graf was now holding a small but lethal-looking pistol, pointed directly at Dev's heart. Dev restrained himself from groaning. This was getting to be habitual, both boring and petrifying at once.

"Hey, Franzi, *Liebchen*," Roberta said in her honeyed alto, "I don't think a peashooter's necessary."

"Neither do I," Lady Adelaide pointed a trembling finger at him. "Please put the gun down. Back. Away." She seemed to be searching for the right word, not that there was one.

"Graf von Mayr, if you don't put that gun down, back, or away, I'm afraid it's you that will be under arrest," Dev said with what he hoped was a firm yet reasonable tone. "Threatening the life of a Metropolitan Police officer comes with serious consequences. Not to mention you are upsetting these innocent young ladies. I'll overlook your temporary aberration, as you've been a good friend to Lady Vere. And I'm sure she'd like us all to live so she can collect her winnings. Please don't complicate the situation. I did not come here today to arrest your wife. I only wanted to talk to her."

The gun held steady. "What about?"

"Why, Lady Vere, actually. I had a hunch your wife knew where she was, and I was right. Lady Penelope led us right here to the Savoy."

"You followed her?"

"We saw her at church," Lady Adelaide said. "She's very devout, isn't she? What would she think of her husband m-murdering someone?" Dev sincerely hoped it wouldn't come to that.

The man shrugged. "I have killed before. Lots of *Engländers*. Too many to count. She knows this."

"But that was wartime," Dev said. "We have peace between our nations." How long it would last was anyone's guess.

Von Mayr waved the gun in the air towards the ceiling medallion, but Dev's anxiety did not subside. The dueling scar on the man's cheek gleamed, and his blue eyes flashed with anger, and something else. He appeared to be a man who was on the edge and had nothing more to lose.

It was imperative to get Lady Adelaide and Roberta to safety. But how? The graf was between the door and the sofa, an imposing figure. He was taller and broader than Dev himself, but that wasn't a deterrent—Dev had gone up against veritable giants and come out on top.

The element of surprise generally worked. He could drop to the floor and roll across the carpet, kicking up with both feet if he didn't get shot first. Would Lady Adelaide obey his order to run? Doubtful. His shoulder twinged, reminding Dev he was not quite as fit as he needed to be for that particular maneuver.

Or he could charge at von Mayr like a hornless bull and hope to knock him backwards on his bottom. There would be a struggle for the weapon, and Dev imagined Lady Adelaide hovering above, accidentally clobbering both of them with her alligator bag. And if the gun misfired—

Well, there were no perfect solutions in life. Dev had to take a gamble, maybe throw that brass lamp that was on the end table. The cut-crystal ashtray. Possibly the table itself. He'd been a pretty good bowler in cricket. The Savoy management was sure to understand if Dev destroyed hotel property as he aimed for von Mayr's head.

Most unexpectedly, the graf solved Dev's problem, sliding the gun back into his jacket pocket. His shoulders slumped. "I want you to leave. All of you. Find a way to protect Roberta yourselves. I am finished with the English. With…with my wife. I wait and I wait and still is not enough. I beg the old man for months and he laughs in my face. And Alistair—bah!" The graf looked as if the very name left a foul taste in his mouth. "They are devils, these Ruffords…Moretons, or whatever they call themselves. Go arrest the rotten brother of Penny. I wonder if your young Stephen will turn out as bad. I pity you, Roberta. You are a nice girl for an American. To get mixed up with such people will bring nothing but heartbreak. I am living proof of that. Get! *Raus!*" he said without much belligerence.

Dev didn't need to be asked twice. He nearly felt sorry for the fellow but had the good sense to hustle the women out of the suite before the graf changed his mind. Roberta protested that her purse and original clothes were still inside in the second bedroom, but Lady Adelaide offered to replace them, so anxious was she to get away.

"Do you think he killed Edmund after all?" she asked breathlessly. They hadn't waited for the lift, but instead clambered down three flights of stairs as if an armed Franz was on their heels.

"He's probably quite capable of it. His nerves do seem to be stretched," Dev replied. He'd left his hat behind, too, but was not going to ask Lady Adelaide for a new one.

"He was a perfect gentleman the whole time I was there," Roberta said. "Though he doesn't have a head for cards. Can we call Stevie when we get downstairs? Maybe he can figure out a place for us to go."

"You can stay with me. Both of you. Alistair would not expect to find you with me, of all places."

Lady Adelaide was her usual generous self. Dev did not like the idea at all. If the duke was dispatching thugs to hurt Roberta, they could just as easily hurt her, too, if they discovered where his daughter-in-law was staying. "I think it's time I paid a visit to Maddox Street and put Alistair's machinations to an end." If the duke believed the police were on to him, surely he would drop his malevolent intentions.

"I want to meet Penny. I'm coming with you," Lady Adelaide said.

"No, you're not. You'll have to get Roberta settled."

"Pish posh. I'll give her my house keys and write Mike the day porter a note."

"Can y'all stop arguing for one second and give me money for the public telephone?" Roberta interrupted.

Dev reached into his pocket and brought out a handful of coins. He had a fair idea that he was going to lose this round and should be used to it by now.

Chapter Thirty-Two

It was a beautiful sunny afternoon, if too hot. They had arranged to wait for Stephen in the Victoria Embankment Gardens, a little away from the scrutiny in the Savoy lobby. Mr. Hunter stood guard while Addie and Roberta sat on a bench admiring the profusion of blooms in the well-tended beds. No one especially suspicious-looking wandered by, and Mr. Lombard was nowhere in sight.

Despite Roberta's bubbling joy, Addie was unable to relax. Being held at gunpoint tended to unnerve one, and it had occurred far too frequently lately for comfort. The gun had been trained on the inspector, and Addie could feel the invisible bullet whizz through the air.

She couldn't bear it if something happened to him.

He was in the wrong line of work for guaranteed safety, and her presence only seemed to make matters worse. She was a curse to him, putting him in unnecessary danger time after time. Once her mother was free, Addie would put her feelings back into the box she'd built over the years and turn the key. It was a thing of beauty—smooth, constructed of the rarest wood, lined in figured satin. Rather like a coffin, she supposed, holding and hiding her hopes and regrets. Life would go on in its limited fashion, and she would do what had always been expected of her.

She sat in the sun, letting Roberta's artless chatter wash over her. Addie was firmly over Young Love. But Stephen's arrival brought a tear to her eye, or at least she told herself that was the reason. The affectionate reunion attracted attention from passersby, and Addie quickly dispatched them to her flat with instructions and keys. They could sort out the practicalities later. Stephen was so happy to see his wife he didn't even ask to accompany them to confront his father. That, too, could be sorted.

Addie checked her watch. "Lady Penelope must be home by now." And full of Sunday lunch. Addie could do with a bite herself, but the sooner they went to Maddox Street, the better. She wondered if Franz von Mayr had informed his wife about the change of plans. Perhaps not. He had been bitter.

Desolate.

Addie understood.

They hailed a taxi at the park gates and settled in for the short drive.

"I wish you weren't coming with me," Mr. Hunter said, "but I know better than to argue with you. I have never met a more stubborn woman."

"You don't get out enough."

"Guilty as charged. I've allowed my work to take over my life. Perhaps that's been a mistake."

"You're good at it."

"Am I? Lately I feel as if my instincts are failing me. I never expected von Mayr to be armed, for example."

Addie patted his arm. "Why would you? Normal people don't go running around with guns." He gave her *that* look. "Well, all right, my mother did, and I did just that one time, but it's not as if I made a habit of it." Addie's pistol was now and forever locked away.

"I must be grateful for small mercies then. But you'd be surprised. There are a lot of service revolvers floating around causing no end of mischief. War unleashes incivility, I'm afraid. It's awfully hard to put the genie back in the bottle and return to normal, whatever normal is or ever was."

He was right. Addie gazed out the window at the crowded street. Who knew what was in the hearts of all the people they passed, dressed in their camouflaging Sunday best? They had survived war, the influenza pandemic, and loss of not only many lives but the *way* of life.

"That's why you study, to try to understand…them." She waved her hand towards the pavement.

Mr. Hunter smiled. "And myself. For all the good it does. Human nature defeats me on a regular basis."

Addie was quiet for the rest of the ride, contemplating the changes she'd experienced over the past year. She would turn thirty-two in a few weeks. It would be a rotten birthday if her mother was still in gaol.

At least the mystery of Roberta's disappearance had been solved. Addie was anxious to meet the woman who engineered it to protect the girl. She must be someone clever and special if she could bring her handsome Austrian husband to his knees.

The taxi wound through the light Sunday traffic, and they arrived in good time at the duke's house. Addie reached into her bag for her card case while Mr. Hunter paid the fare; it was remarkable what a simple rectangle of engraved paper could accomplish.

"I don't think you need to present your police identification," she told Mr. Hunter. "Alistair strikes me as someone who would make trouble for you."

"You're probably right. But he needs to know he can't go around threatening his daughter-in-law, no matter who he is."

Or who *she* is, Addie thought. No doubt Alistair might have wished for a conventional English rose bride for his son, but Stephen had other ideas.

"I agree. Perhaps I can make him see reason." She still had some social cachet, did she not? Though it was just as likely he would refuse to see her. The sting of his rudeness last week was still palpable.

Of course, he believed her mother killed his father. On the grander scale, rudeness was nothing compared to murder.

"We'll ask to see Lady Penelope first," Addie said. "We might have better luck getting in."

"Good idea." He turned the bell.

The door was opened promptly by a fresh-faced footman who raised both eyebrows. "Sir?"

"Yes, it is I again. Lady Adelaide, won't you present your calling card to this young man? We are here to see Lady Penelope von Mayr. Is she in?" Mr. Hunter spoke with confidence, daring the boy to turn them away.

The footman squinted at her card. "Um. I'll just go see. Would you care to wait in the Pink Room?" Addie didn't care what color it was, as long as there was a chair to collapse in. Suddenly, she was very nervous.

He led them to a small, uncarpeted chamber off the hall, which had a collection of plain wooden furniture and an alarmingly fuchsia-tiled fireplace, which as far as Addie could see was the only pink thing in it. Some dusty dried hydrangeas were stuffed into the back hearth, and a fair number of petals had escaped and were scattered across the floor. She stopped herself from bending over to tidy them up.

"My knees are knocking," Addie said.

"Sit down then. What do you suppose this room is used for?"

"Unwanted company. Belligerent tradesmen. Lectures to dis-appointing children. There's a room quite like it at Broughton

Place, just off the entry hall, only ours is much nicer." The furniture was upholstered at least. Addie's bottom could have done with a cushion or two at the moment. Arts and Crafts furniture may have been painstakingly hand-constructed, but it was painful to sit on.

"And were you lectured often?" Mr. Hunter asked with a grin.

"Often enough. My mother was much stricter than my father, but he would carry out the punishments. Sometimes I don't think his heart was in it, but he felt he had a duty. I got into more trouble in the country than in Town, and spent a good deal of time in the butler's pantry, polishing silver as penance. And alas, never up to Forbes's exacting standards." His opprobrium made her quite forgiving of Beckett's faults; it was hell to believe one could never measure up.

What would her father make of his beloved wife's current situation? Addie was glad he'd never know. Or would he? If he was watching over her, it didn't seem particularly peaceful to be up in Heaven and see the ones you left behind struggle below.

Addie was in no hurry to find out the Afterlife's arrangements for herself.

"I can't imagine running two households."

"Oh, there's a hunting box in Scotland, too, and a few other minor properties that are let. I'll tell you something—wherever you are, you've left what you want at one of the other houses. I try to keep the proper provisions in Mount Street, but inevitably the book or the dress or the jar of jam I want is in Gloucestershire."

He waggled a dark brow. "Such dreadful problems."

"I know it sounds ridiculous, and I'm not complaining! I'm completely aware how fortunate I am. *Too* fortunate. In fact, I'm thinking of selling my flat. It was Rupert who enjoyed London life. Actually, he enjoyed himself everywhere. Every day—and night—was a party." Most of the time, she was not invited.

Was Rupert still here lurking about? It was *her* detective work that found Roberta, even if it was a trifle accidental. At least he wasn't across the room rummaging through the hydrangeas. She hoped.

The minutes ticked by. Mr. Hunter paced the bare floor, stopping now and again to examine the three undistinguished line drawings on the walls. By the time the footman opened the door, he must have committed them to memory.

The young man was very pale. "She—uh—she can't see you right now."

Addie rose. "Is she well?"

"I—I don't know. I daren't go in."

"Why not?" Mr. Hunter asked.

"She and the marquess—I mean the duke—are having an argument. I listened at the door after my knocks were ignored. There was some shouting."

The footman was obviously frightened. A chill washed over Addie's body. "We need to go up, Dev! She's in danger!"

"You won't stay here and wait, will you." Mr. Hunter sounded resigned. It wasn't even a question.

"Of course not. Please, let's hurry." Addie turned to the footman. "What's your name?"

"W-William."

"You'll take us upstairs, won't you?"

William swallowed. "I shouldn't. I'll lose my position, for sure."

"Don't worry about that," Addie said briskly. "I have lots of friends who would hire you in a second." He was a good-looking fellow, and if she was exaggerating her influence, what was the harm? She'd make sure he'd get a job somewhere, even if she had to take him back with her to Compton Chase.

"It's Mr. Stanhope's afternoon off. He's the butler, and I can hear him telling me right now to turn you two out onto the street."

"But he's not here, William," Mr. Hunter said. "And I'm sure he wouldn't like any harm coming to Lady Penelope, would he?"

"No, sir. He's right fond of her. We all are."

"Well then, what are we waiting for?"

Chapter Thirty-Three

The gunshot came as a surprise. Mr. Hunter turned to her on the landing, looking like thunder. "You must stay here!" His voice was low, but firm, and definitely audible.

It was the sensible thing to do. Poor William looked perfectly ready to keep her company. He was employed as a servant, not a soldier, and frankly looked too young for either job.

"No! She may need me," Addie said. She pretended not to hear the expletive-filled oath Mr. Hunter expressed.

"Are they in the study?" he asked William. He'd been here before, rescuing Stephen from a charge of attempted patricide.

"Aye. Th-that was a gun, wasn't it? The, uh, bang. Um, don't you think we should fetch the police?" William was white as a ghost, obviously not eager to climb the stairs any higher.

"No need for that. You might gather up the family and servants and get them out of the house, or at least keep them in one place out of harm's way."

"Y-yes, sir. All the ladies are already out, even little Lady Grace. The late duke's sister invited them to lunch in Grosvenor Square. I don't know where Mr. John is."

"Good. Tell everyone it will be all right."

Would it? Addie wondered. A relieved William jogged down the stairs while she followed Mr. Hunter up and then along a paneled hallway. He stopped outside a double door and put his finger to his lips.

There had not been a second shot, and she heard muffled voices inside, a man's and a woman's. Which must mean that no one was dead yet, mustn't it?

"Right on time."

Addie kept herself from squealing. Rupert lounged against the wall, grinning like Alice's Cheshire cat.

"What's happening?" Addie whispered, hoping either Mr. Hunter or her late husband would tell her.

"Sh!" Mr. Hunter replied, rather sharply. He held his ear to the door, his eyes shut in concentration.

"Bossy, isn't he?"

Addie bit her tongue so she wouldn't "sh" herself. She glared at Rupert.

"All right, all right. Enough with the Stare of Death—it's quite frightening, even if I'm already dead. I just got here myself. You know as much as I do. If you weren't so stubborn, you'd leave us men to handle this."

Addie imagined shooting Rupert, and the satisfaction it would give her. It wouldn't even do any real harm—his bespoke suit would probably mend the bullet holes all by itself in some miraculous way. But the only person with a weapon was behind the doors.

From where she was standing, she couldn't distinguish any of the words within. Addie eased next to the inspector, and leaned against the other door.

"For God's sake, Penny! Who cares about the little trollop? Why are you making such a fuss?"

"She's a human being! Stephen loves her!"

There was a snort. "What does the stupid boy know about love? He's a babe in the woods. Just like you were when that Kraut von Mayr kidnapped you. An innocent. And see how that turned out. Twenty years of misery and mountains of Wiener schnitzel that ruined your figure. I'm only looking after my son's best interests."

"As if you cared anything about anyone except yourself."

"Of course I care about myself!" Alistair snapped. "I'm head of the family now. Everything you lot do reflects upon me and the Rufford dukedom. I'm beginning to see our dear papa's point of view after all these years. The family is in absolute shambles. And here you are, Penny, taking potshots at me when I'm only trying to do the right thing for all of us. Don't be such a fool."

Addie met Mr. Hunter's startled eyes.

"I hope she aims better next time," Rupert said genially from behind her.

"You never took me seriously, did you, Alistair? Even from the time we were children."

There were footsteps behind them, and Addie's heart contracted. Two uninvited guests, caught in the act of eavesdropping, and bound to get tossed onto the pavement. But when she turned, she was shocked to see William holding a cricket bat between his white-gloved hands. "It's the best I can do," he whispered. "The gun cabinet is locked."

Addie would have taken the cricket bat to the gun cabinet, but each to his own. Mr. Hunter took it with a grim smile. "Where is everybody?"

"I told them to stay in the kitchen. They were there anyway having lunch."

"Good lad. Do you want to go back down to be with them?"

"N-no, sir. If I can help, I will." He was still pale, but determined.

Addie thought of all the boys William's age who went off to

war ten years ago and never came back. "Thank you," she said, squeezing his arm.

"Oh, now you've done it! The poor boy has fallen head over heels in love with you," Rupert teased. Addie made a concerted effort not to pay any attention to him, but it was difficult.

"Is there another way into the room?" Mr. Hunter asked.

William shook his head.

"I think we need to go in before someone gets hurt. William, are you agreeable to that?"

"What about me?" Addie did not want to be left out at this stage.

Mr. Hunter looked pained. "*Please.* Just this once, do as I ask. Think of *my* safety. If I'm worrying about you, I might not be able to prevent a tragedy."

He believed he knew best, but his words chafed nonetheless. "All right," she said, trying not to feel mutinous.

"Very wise. That's a good girl," Rupert said, infuriating her all the more.

"My first priority is to disarm Lady Penelope, and then have a little chat with the duke. Stay behind me. On the count of three, William, I'm going to throw open the doors. Are you game?"

"Yes, sir."

"One...two...three." He put his good shoulder to the door and turned the handle.

It didn't budge.

"It's locked. Is there a key?"

"Mr. Stanhope has them all," William said, deflated. He'd been ready to charge.

"Go away!" Alistair boomed from inside. One would have imagined he'd like being rescued, or at least interrupted.

"It—it's important, Your Grace," William said, his voice faltering. "A m-matter of life and death."

Possibly his, Addie thought.

"What nonsense! Damn it, Penny, put that thing away before someone gets hurt. Let me find out what the bloody idiot wants."

William flushed, but remained by the door. When the duke, appearing beyond irritated, flung it open, William pushed his way through, quickly followed by Mr. Hunter. The inspector promptly shut the door in Addie's face.

"Attaboy," Rupert cheered, clapping his hands.

And then Lady Penelope fired again.

Addie saw stars, but Rupert was instantly by her side, holding her up. "Now, now, love. No time to faint. I'll just go in and see if everything's all right, what? You behave and stay right here." He disappeared, as only he was capable of doing.

Addie nodded, but had no intention of remaining in the hall. She turned the door handle. There had been no time to lock it, and one of the doors swung open.

"Christ. It's like Piccadilly Circus in here," Alistair said. He was sitting cross-legged on the floor, holding his shoulder, blood oozing between his fingers. "What in hell do you want, Lady Adelaide? Come to kill me off, too? You'll have to get in line— apparently my sister has first dibs."

"Shut up, Alistair!" Lady Penelope von Mayr was seated at the duke's desk leaning forward on her elbows, both hands gripping a small pistol. It had been trained on her brother, but before Addie could say a word, it was pointed at her. Mr. Hunter muttered something in what Addie presumed was Hindi, but she imagined she could translate it with some degree of accuracy. He shot her a look and stepped in front of William, who bravely stepped next to him instead.

"Good afternoon, Lady Penelope. We haven't met before, and I'm most sorry for the present circumstances. I'm Adelaide Compton. I think you were very brave trying to help Roberta. She's a lovely young woman."

"Your mother..." Lady Penelope trailed off.

"Yes. But she's innocent. Inspector Hunter here has been helping me try to prove it and find the real killer."

"Inspector Hunter? What is this nonsense? This man works at that ridiculous club," Alistair sneered from the floor.

"Actually, I work at Scotland Yard. Detective Inspector Devenand Hunter at your service. Lady Penelope, I would strongly advise you to put down that gun. I'm sure whatever quarrel you have with your brother can be settled without further bloodshed." He took a step forward, and she turned the gun on him. Addie was unable to feel any relief at all.

"Do you? Then you don't know my brother." Her hands shook, but she didn't put the gun away. "It was you at the Savoy. You saw my husband?"

"Yes. And he seems sincerely attached to you. What would he think if he saw you now?" Mr. Hunter asked gently.

"It doesn't matter. Nothing matters anymore. But if I am to die, *he* can go first." And with that, Lady Penelope fired on her brother for the third time.

Chapter Thirty-Four

Three shots. That left three in the chamber. A bullet each for Addie and William and himself. Dev considered his chances of getting across the room to the desk to disarm her. Hadn't he just calculated such a thing in von Mayr's hotel drawing room? The day was getting worse by the second.

Alistair Moreton, sixth Duke of Rufford, lay sprawled out on the Indian rug, his pale eyes open yet sightless, blood pooling beneath his head. The man may have been abhorrent, but no one deserved such a death. Just seconds ago he'd been sitting on the floor, but even from that position had exuded contemptuous authority. And now...

Dev regretted that he hadn't asked William to call the police—he'd badly underestimated the situation. Where were his fabled instincts? If there was a God or an Allah or a Yahweh, the remaining servants or the neighbors would be dialing them up this minute. It was hard to ignore so many gunshots on a Sunday afternoon in Mayfair.

"I don't understand, Lady Penelope. Why do you think you will die?"

She was not a pretty woman and had not made the best of her

looks, with a choppy haircut and too much rouge, badly dressed in an overly ornate black frock. Lady Penelope rolled her silvery eyes, as if he was the most clueless individual in London, which wasn't far from the truth.

"You came to arrest me, didn't you? Would it help to tell you that I didn't intend to? I...I lost my head when he mocked me, laughed at me, and there was that little gun in the open handbag, just sitting on the floor at my feet. I reached for it just to show him I was serious. That I was tired of being treated like a...like a *nobody*. Like the stupid schoolgirl I once was. I'm a grown woman! I have two children, you know. Twins. Not everyone can manage twins, but I did."

She took a breath and smiled, and Dev's blood chilled. "He told me where he was staying. I was the only one in the family he trusted. In case I needed anything while we were in Town, I should come see him, day or night, and he'd take care of it. What he really meant—he'd run my life for me. Imagine, a secret love nest at his age, the randy old goat!"

The woman looked over at Lady Adelaide, who was as still as a statue. "No offense meant. Anyway, I went there before break-fast to tell him I was taking the children and finally going back to Austria with Franz, even after all the things he did to try to ruin my marriage. The women...the photographs...he set it all up to discredit my husband. Franz loves me. He told me so."

The truth was dawning on Dev in a most unexpected twist. "You killed your father?"

Lady Penelope didn't meet his eyes. "Something happened, and the gun went off. It didn't even make much noise. As I said, I didn't mean to shoot him. It was an accident."

But she had certainly meant to kill her brother, so determined there had been no chance to stop her. The cricket bat was heavy but useless in Dev's hand.

"How did you get up there without anyone seeing you?"

"Ah. That was a piece of luck. I know my father's habits—he rises before six and reads the newspaper from the first page to the last. I thought I'd catch him alone, or hoped to anyway. When I arrived outside the Ritz, some very merry Americans were getting out of two other taxis. They'd been out all night and much the worse for wear, shouting and laughing and stumbling about on the pavement. The concierge was anxious they'd lower the exalted tone of the lobby, and had them whisked right up in the elevator. Corralled them just like naughty sheep, with a promise of a champagne breakfast to be delivered to their rooms. Very efficient. I just kept quiet and rode along. No one noticed me. No one does."

"And when you left?"

"I used the stairs. It didn't seem wise to summon the lift operator."

"You could have stayed and explained to the police," Lady Adelaide said. After seeing a murder committed before her very eyes, her face was as white as her dress, but her voice was steady, almost friendly. Dev wished she'd be quiet and not attract any attention to herself, much preferred the quivering pistol to be pointing at him again.

Lady Penelope's lips twisted. "Really? Alistair would have been sure to see me hang. Papa always liked me better. Even as a little boy, Alistair was loathsome, and my father knew it, trying to keep him out of trouble, one restriction after another. Alistair hated him for it. But he interfered in my life as well, for no good reason. He always, always thought he knew best. It became...tiresome."

Perhaps the elder duke's death was not such an accident after all. Lady Penelope may not have planned to kill her father when she went to see him, but after years of provocation, she'd simply snapped.

"Parents mean well, but sometimes they are overbearing,"

Lady Adelaide replied. "My mother always had high expectations for me that have been hard to live up to. Sometimes impossible."

"Exactly!" Lady Penelope nodded, taking one hand from the gun and tucking her shingled hair behind her ears. "I am sorry about your mother. I didn't even know who she was, and it never occurred to me she'd get arrested."

"Well, she is in gaol. But she's bearing up. She's quite a remarkable woman."

Dev kept his mouth from dropping open at this relatively pleasant chitchat between the two women. He'd never felt so at sea.

Lady Penelope's eyes flicked down to the desk briefly, then stared back at Dev. "I suppose they'll let her out now."

Three people heard her confession, but only William was an impartial witness. It was vital Dev get the weapon away from her.

"That depends, Lady Penelope. Won't you please give me the gun? I'm sure we can discuss this like civilized people."

"Discuss my guilt, you mean. You'll make me sign something and lock me up. I'll never see Franz or my children again."

"My mother has excellent legal representation. I'm sure if I spoke to them they'd do their utmost to help you," Lady Adelaide offered.

"Like they've helped your mother. Where is she again?" Lady Penelope's expression was grim. "No thank you."

"What can we do to make this easier for you, Lady Penelope?" Dev asked.

"Easier? Can you go back in time? And not just a week. My God, it was only last Sunday, wasn't it?"

A long, exhausting week for Dev, following an equally hellish previous week in the Cotswolds. He was ready for a *real* leave, away from madwomen and madmen and secrets and lies.

"A difficult week, but you did a good thing protecting your nephew's wife. That shouldn't be discounted."

"Oh, I'm a devoted aunt. A better parent to those three children these past six years than their own. But it won't absolve me of murder, will it?" She patted the gun as if it was an old friend.

Would it matter if Lady Penelope shot him? He'd like to think he'd be missed by someone other than his parents. But it was imperative she didn't hurt Lady Adelaide or poor William, who stood stoically beside him throughout this bizarre interview. Dev's mind raced, estimating how much time he'd have to charge forward across the room or toss the bat before she pulled the trigger. The space was not large, but Alistair's body was inconveniently in the way.

He'd try to keep her talking instead.

"We can call your husband if you'd like us to." But would he come? The graf said he was finished with the lot of them, including his wife.

"Poor Franz. He doesn't deserve to get mixed up in this. Although I don't think he'd really mind that Alistair is dead. Even Elaine won't care much. That's my sister-in-law. Do you know her, Lady Adelaide?"

"I'm afraid not. I—I've lived rather quietly in the country since my husband died." She was not exactly telling the truth, but Lady Penelope was not apt to find out about her recent dubious adventures.

"I bumped into Rupert here and there. He was such a charmer. Everyone loved him. Did you?"

Lady Adelaide didn't speak for at least a minute. "I did. But he wasn't faithful." Dev could hear the pain in her words.

"So we have something in common. But *your* father didn't sabotage your marriage."

"No, Rupert did that all by himself. But Graf von Mayr loves you, as you said. I think it's an excellent idea to call him."

A telephone sat on the corner of the desk, just inches from

Lady Penelope's hands. If she could be persuaded to ring up her husband, she'd need both of them to do so.

"No. I don't want him to see me like this."

"You look just fine," Lady Adelaide said encouragingly.

"Really? You need new eyeglasses. I know what you think. What everybody thinks. When Franz and I eloped, no one could understand what he saw in me. I was only sixteen. Awkward. And he's so handsome, don't you agree? I almost couldn't believe it myself." She stared off into the corner, remembering better days. Dev felt a little of the stress in his spine release, until her gaze—and gun—turned back on Lady Adelaide.

"I had no confidence, you see," she continued. "How could I, with my father and Alistair constantly criticizing everything I did? Even my fancy French governess was a bitch *extraordinaire*. Franz was such a relief. He didn't care about the fortune my grandmother left me—he had money of his own, and a *schloss* and a grand city apartment in the *Schubertring*. We were so happy until the war came. But when it was over, he was…different. Short-tempered, and not always very nice. I thought if I came home for a visit with the children, it would do us both good. I was wrong."

For many, even after so many years, the war continued. Wounded veterans begged on streets. Many men could not sleep through the night. Wealth had been lost, dynasties derailed. Dev imagined German soldiers and their society were equally affected, if not more so. The economic depression and unemployment on the Continent were formidable.

"All of us have changed. That doesn't mean you should make a bad situation worse," Dev said, willing her to train the gun on him again.

Lady Penelope grimaced. "A bad situation? How you sugar-coat things, Inspector. There's my brother, dead on the floor. Quite a 'situation,' wouldn't you agree? I can't say I'm sorry at the moment. Perhaps I'll be overcome with guilt later. But perhaps not. I expect I've rather done the world a favor. Ironic, isn't it? That girl's a duchess now. How angry Alistair would be." She gave an unpleasant laugh.

The murders superseded any scandal Alistair had anticipated for the family. Poor Stephen. What a way to advance. Dev hoped the lad would last longer as a duke than his father had. One whole week—it must be some sort of demented Debrett's record.

"Lady Penelope, I implore you. Please put the gun down before someone else gets hurt." If she didn't relent soon, Dev was prepared to act. He simply didn't trust the woman, and the conversation was going nowhere. If he could somehow get Lady Adelaide to safety—

She stood a few steps away from the double doors, one of which was slightly ajar. If only she'd turn tail and run, he'd feel one thousand percent better.

And then, he could feel nothing at all. Loud footsteps and shouts came from the hallway, and Lady Penelope fired her gun.

Chapter Thirty-Five

"Get off me!" Addie whispered. Rupert had hurled himself on top of her, pinning her down on the carpet. Alistair's body was altogether too close, and Addie shut her eyes. There seemed to be a great deal of activity going on around her, shrieking, yelling, and the clunking of many booted feet, but she couldn't see over Rupert's pinstriped shoulder.

"Shh! You might thank me. I think you'll find the bullet embedded in the door, right where your pretty little head was before I saved you, once again. You didn't want a hole in that charming hat, did you?"

Addie's hat had flown from her head when Rupert tackled her. She wasn't sure she wanted it back if it was anywhere near the corpse.

"I was ducking down anyway. My reflexes are excellent," Addie grumbled. She'd seen the mad light in Lady Penelope's eye when she heard the disturbance outside the doors. Addie preferred to think she wasn't the true target.

"If this doesn't do it, I have a bone to pick with the Fellow Upstairs. Lie still! I'm not a plaster saint, you know."

"What's happening?" she hissed.

"The cavalry has arrived. Your inspector fairly flew at Penny and batted the gun right out of her hands. It's a wonder her arms are still attached. He's, uh, under the desk sitting on her now, and none too comfortable. She's writhing and spitting and scratching like a scalded cat. One thinks one knows one's friends, but alas, I never suspected the poor dear of homicidal tendencies."

More than tendencies. Addie had watched the poor dear kill her own brother.

"The room is crawling with constables and servants, and the French chef is stomping about wielding a lethal-looking kitchen knife."

"You've really got to let me up. Dev probably thinks I'm dead."

"Dev, eh? Oh, very well. Give us a quick kiss then. I really think this might be The End, my girl. The happily-ever-after, at least for me. Smell those apricots? Hallelujah!" He gave her a brilliant smile that reminded her of the Rupert she'd loved with all her heart so many years ago. Addie didn't smell anything except the dust from the ancient rug she lay on, and a somewhat distressing whiff emanating from Alistair.

"You'll have to sort the rest out without my help. I'm sure you can do it. You are the most extraordinary woman I've ever known, and I've known quite a few, to my everlasting regret. I was a complete, total, and consummate idiot. It wasn't ever you. It was I." His cold lips brushed hers briefly before he vanished.

Rupert was gone.

Was he gone for good?

Addie struggled to sit up, still a little out of breath from her ignominious toss to the floor. The study was crammed with people tripping over each other. It was a wonder she hadn't been stepped on. She spotted her hat under a chair and reached for it.

"Not so fast! Who are you?" A burly uniformed policeman stood above her, glowering.

"I am Lady Adelaide Compton," Addie said crisply, not bothering to try to charm. After today, she wasn't sure if she had any charm left.

"Do you have a weapon?"

"Not even a hatpin, which you will see if you let me retrieve my hat."

"Addie?"

Hearing Dev speak her name brought tears to her eyes. She hadn't realized how very frightened she had been, even with Rupert winking and twinkling since she walked into the study. Despite his reassuring presence, anything could have gone wrong.

"Yes, it's I."

"Are you all right? I thought…" His voice thickened.

"Perfectly. I'll be better once this gentleman allows me to get up off the floor."

"Thank God. Staples, handcuff this woman. Lady Penelope von Mayr, you are under arrest for the murder of Edmund Moreton, the fifth Duke of Rufford, Alistair Moreton, the sixth Duke of Rufford, and the attempted murder of Lady Adelaide Compton."

Addie heard some rather blue language denying that any harm had been intended for her. While she more or less agreed, now was not the time to stick up for the double murderess. Chastened, the constable extended a hand and Addie was on her feet again, more or less.

"Here, madam. You look a mite poorly. Sit down on that chair. I'll fetch your hat."

Addie obliged, and hoped the room would stop spinning. While she was well-versed in fainting in a ladylike fashion, there was not much room to do so with so many people milling around.

Dev emerged from beneath the desk, his tie askew. Fingernail scratches marred his weary face. "You really are all right?" he asked, his voice husky.

"I will be. Dev—I mean, Inspector Hunter, we have to get Mama out of gaol."

"We will. *I* will. I'll see to it this afternoon, even if it's Sunday. I'll find a judge somewhere. William, are you prepared to sign a statement that you heard Lady Penelope confess to the murder of her father?"

"Yes, sir."

"Good. Then come to the Yard with me. Whoever called in the police, thank you. We probably owe our lives to you."

"C'est moi," the chef said, still brandishing the knife. "One can ignore a gunshot or two even in the best of houses, but three is *de trop.*"

Addie shrank back as two policeman steered Lady Penelope from the room. Her hysteria over, she exuded calm, her posture erect. The woman stared straight ahead, as though being in restraints escorted by policemen was an everyday occurrence. At this moment, she never looked more like a duke's daughter, and Addie wondered if she was fully cognizant of what she had done.

Was Lady Penelope evil? Insane? Addie would like Mr. Hunter's philosophical opinion.

"Say, what's going on? This house is like Grand Central Station at rush hour. I could barely make my way up the stairs. Why are the coppers taking Rufford's sister out all trussed up?"

Unbelievable! Joe Lombard stood in the doorway, his camera at the ready.

"Put that bloody thing down! How did you get in here?" Inspector Hunter growled.

"The front door was wide open. There's a little crowd in the street, too. It's a wonder more haven't come in to see the action for themselves. You solve the case?"

"None of your business. You are impeding a police investigation. Get lost!"

"Looks like you got your man already, or should I say woman? Holy cow, who's on the floor? Is that Rufford? Is he bleeding? Is he *dead*?" Lombard raised the camera and Mr. Hunter wrestled it out of his hands.

"Have you no decency? You can't go around taking pictures of dead people!"

Addie knew some grisly Victorians were very fond of immortalizing their dead relatives in posed photographs, but kept her own counsel.

"All right, all right. Calm down. You can't blame a guy for dedication to his job. Here we both are on a Sunday afternoon when we should be relaxing with a pint and having a roast dinner somewhere. Beef, lamb, or pork? I'm not particular myself. You Brits do a bang-up job, no matter what. Beats my ma's roast chicken any day of the week."

Addie had completely lost her appetite and found this conversation too strange for words. She reshaped the rose petals on her hat and put it back on. Somehow it seemed important to cling to convention and appear unremarkably proper.

"How ya doin', Lady Adelaide? I didn't think I'd find *you* here."

Addie decided it was best to ignore him. He'd be getting his byline on the front page soon enough without any help from her. "Mr. Hunter, I won't be needed, will I? I'd like to go home and prepare the spare room for my m—" She closed her lips, noting the interest on Lombard's face.

"Certainly. You've had a terrible shock. I'll get one of the men to take you home. I'm just sorry I can't do it myself."

For all her hard-earned independence, Addie wouldn't refuse the company. "That's fine." She held out her gloved hand. "Thank you for all you've done, Inspector Hunter. My family will be eternally grateful."

His face flushed, and he took her hand, giving it the gentlest of squeezes before he released it. "It was nothing. It was…it was an honor to spend another week with you."

Addie turned away before she said or did something she'd be sorry for, especially in front of Mr. Lombard. With any luck, when her name next appeared in a newspaper, she'd be dead and unable to read it.

Duke's Daughter Declared Deranged

By Joseph Lombard
Exclusive to *The Daily Star*
July 31, 1925

When you're a star, they let you do it. You can do anything.

It sure pays to have friends in high places and grow up in a high castle. Notorious Lady Penelope von Mayr, *née* Moreton, who committed both patricide *and* fratricide, will not be standing trial for the deaths of her father, Edmund Moreton, the 5th Duke of Rufford, and her brother Alistair Moreton, the 6th Duke of Rufford. Her nephew, Stephen Moreton, the 7th Duke of Rufford, is safe for the time being as his auntie is currently residing in Broadmoor Criminal Lunatic Asylum.

Faithful readers on both sides of the pond will know "Stevie" as the husband of singing sensation Bobbie Jones of the Jazzy Jones Sisters. The American Negro lass captured his and the nation's heart with the duo's recent recording of the old favorite "Farewell Blues." The songbird duchess has no plans to retire, and has the full support of her husband to continue her musical career with her sister Bettie. "It would be a real crime to deprive the world of their talents," the young duke stated to this reporter.

And if anyone knows crime, it's a Moreton. Rumor has it the duke's sister, Lady Gloria Moreton, seemingly inspired by the girl gang the Forty Dollies, attempted to walk out of Asprey (established in 1781, right about the time Cornwallis surrendered to Washington) with a diamond bracelet, a gold cigarette case, and two cabochon ruby rings tucked into her French knickers. Claiming the thefts were "accidental" and an "oversight," she was forced to pay for the items in full, and has decamped to the Republic of Ireland until the gossip dies down.

Getting back to Penny, as she is known to her acquaintances and cellmates, she began her life of scandal when she eloped with an Austrian Count (they call it graf over there) when she was just sixteen years of age. Her loyal husband, Franz von Mayr, and their two adult children, Carola and Johannes, are remaining in London to lend their moral support.

It was von Mayr's tearful testimony to authorities which ensured that the double murderess would not hang. Citing the years of torment and mistreatment she had endured at the hands of her domineering father and, most especially, her abusive brother, he prevailed in convincing Judge Claudius Archibald that she is not a further danger to society and has in many ways already suffered for her sins. He even enlisted the famous Viennese doctor Sigmund Freud to examine Countess von Mayr, who corroborated his account. It is hoped after some time of rehabilitation under the Crown's supervision, Penny can return with her family to Austria and put the past behind her. If I were old Franz, I'd lock up my guns anyway.

Scotland Yard Detective Inspector Devenand Hunter was responsible for Countess von Mayr's arrest after an exhaustive investigation. He has received a commendation to add to the ones he's previously racked up, but refused to comment for this article.

The Epilogues
EPILOGUE NUMBER ONE: MAEVE

Christmas Eve, 1925
Compton Chase, Compton-Under-Wood, Gloucestershire

Maeve would *make* him.

Oh, who was she kidding? She'd never met anyone more stubborn than the Scotsman, and she was Irish on both sides. Jack Robertson had his priorities. And she, apparently, wasn't one of them, even though she had a good job and handsome wages. Lady A was generous to a fault, and not at all draconian. So Maeve had a pretty penny saved up, even after she sent money home to her old mam and spent a little too much on lip rouge and cinema tickets.

Jack had come to be head gardener at Compton Chase the summer before last, as handsome as one of the movie stars Maeve watched on the flickering screen. He might have left a leg behind in France, but he was a hard worker, and had the greenest fingers. The flower beds had flourished under his care, and he'd been rewarded accordingly. He had a sweet little cottage on the estate, perfect as a honeymoon house.

If only Jack would ask Maeve to marry him.

They'd pussyfooted around the idea for more than a year. Maeve knew Lady A had no objections—she wanted everybody around her to be happy, since she herself wasn't. But Jack was old-fashioned—he wouldn't touch Maeve's nest egg. Wanted everything to be "proper." What he meant by that, Maeve wasn't sure, but he'd not once tried to take her into his ground-floor bedroom in that sweet little cottage to test out his bed.

Oh, he'd kissed her—*how* he'd kissed her—until her head spun and her heart beat right out of her modest chest. Rudolph Valentino himself couldn't have done it better, and Maeve had seen him kiss for years in the dark, never imagining she'd be lucky enough to fall in love herself.

Was Jack afraid what she'd think when his prosthetic leg came off? She didn't care about that a bit. She knew he'd had a lot of trouble after the war getting used to his disability—foolishly brave, he'd gone when he was still underage, and got unfairly punished for it. If he'd only stayed home—

Well, if he had, Maeve would probably never have met him, and wouldn't that be a terrible shame?

So, tonight was the night. Maeve was going to propose to *him*, and make him say yes. And why not? Life was too short to be old-fashioned and "proper." Put things off until everything was just right, like that Goldilocks story. Not use the good dishes or wear the fancy knickers. Look at all those poor dead people stopped in their tracks that Lady A had mixed herself up with. Murder! Maeve might be a maid but was not going to die in her sleep an *old* maid. Just in case someone tried to put a period to *her* existence, she was going to have some fun beforehand.

Lady A was off to the midnight Christmas Eve service at Compton St. Cuthbert's in her Lagonda, and had told her not to wait up. So Maeve took off her uniform and climbed into her own tub. A dozen stars twinkled outside the window, and she thought about the brightest star all those years ago. If a baby born in a stable could grow up to be the King, anything was possible.

Warm and clean, she put on her best dress, a plain, pleated navy jersey, and ruffled up her dark bobbed hair. She had plenty of cosmetics, but decided to go to Jack as she was, a little pale, freckled, and very determined.

Coat, boots, scarf, torch. The house was quiet, the tree in the front hall shimmering under the bright electric sconces left on for Lady A. Maeve slipped out the door, her feet crunching on the frozen grass. The path through the garden was familiar, even as the torch revealed odd and ominous shadows. But she wasn't afraid, not of bare bushes anyway.

Jack's cottage was not far past the formal plantings, and stood alone surrounded by a grove of trees. Lady A had fixed it up for him, and a work crew from the village had knocked down the two neighboring cottages that were past saving. So Maeve wasn't worried about anyone snooping. She was just worried that Jack wouldn't let her in so he could protect her unwanted virtue.

What if he was asleep? It was late, and he'd been busy the past few days. He'd brought the giant Yule log in single-handedly, and the tree and greenery and mistletoe to decorate the house as well. Everything looked beautiful indoors, thanks to him.

Light spilled from a window into the inky night. She balled up her small fist and knocked, while her booted feet were poised for flight. A minute passed, then two.

Perhaps she was being ridiculous coming here.

The door opened. Jack was fully dressed in his good suit, right down to the new necktie that she'd given him for Christmas—he'd opened his present early. His brown hair was slicked back neatly, and he smelled of Blenheim Bouquet.

"What...what are you doing here?"

Was he going out? With someone else? Not if she had anything to say about it. Maeve dropped to one knee, no easy feat on the cold stone step. She angled the torch at his face and he blinked. "I've come to ask you to marry me."

"You can't! I mean, I was about to come to you! Toss pebbles at your window." He shook his coat pocket, and Maeve heard rattling. "Lure you out under the stars. Be, uh, romantic. Get up, Maeve. Please." He extended a work-roughened hand.

"You haven't answered my question."

"It wasn't a question, was it? Besides, *I'm* doing the asking— I'm the man. I can't get down on one knee, though. You don't mind, do you?" He pulled her to her feet as if she were made of feathers.

"No." She still had to look up at him. "Go ahead."

"Maeve Rose Beckett, will you be my wife?" He reached into the pebble-pocket and drew out a small box. Inside was a silver ring made to look like a band of roses. "F-for your name. It's not much, but Lady A said—"

Maeve didn't care what their employer said. She stood on tiptoes and kissed her answer in a very improper way, leaving no doubt that he might be the man, but she was definitely the woman.

EPILOGUE NUMBER TWO: CEE

Christmas morning, 1925
St. Mary's Church, Broughton Magna, Gloucestershire

The procession marched by, and Mama scurried after it to talk to friends in the churchyard. Her sister closed her hymnbook and tucked it back between the oak slats. "Shall I invite Ian to breakfast at the Dower House?"

Cee wrinkled her nose. "No."

"Why not?" Addie asked.

As if she would finally accept the same answer Cee had given a thousand times already. Lady Cecilia Merrill was not romantically interested in Ian, Marquess of Broughton, even if everyone in the county thought she should be, expected it, counted on it. Had already made a wager on the most likely date of their wedding, as they used to do in the betting books of Regency gentlemen's clubs.

She did not wish to have breakfast, lunch, or dinner with him. Not a cocktail or a canape.

She pulled down her cloche and pulled up her fox fur collar, as the old stone church was invariably freezing, no matter what time of the year. She could see her breath, for heaven's sake! Cee wished she was wearing long woolen underwear and boots, but as a Bright Young Person, fashion was everything, so silk stockings and smart suede pumps it was.

"You know why. If he comes to breakfast, Ian is going to ask me to marry him when he finishes his kippers. I can feel it in my bones."

"So what if he does? A Christmas engagement is most suitable. You can be a June bride. And your bones are twenty-six. It's time you got settled."

Addie had driven over from Compton Chase to accompany Cee and their mother to Christmas-morning worship in her childhood parish. She must be feeling extra holy, as she'd attended her own church's midnight service just a few hours ago. It didn't make her any less irritating, though.

Addie always thought she knew best. Six years older than Cee, she'd been married and widowed and had briefly been something of a crime-solver, which would be fatal if the news ever reached the upper echelons of society. The Merrill sisters were daughters of the late Marquess of Broughton. Daughters of a marquess did not generally mess about with murder. Far too many deaths had occurred for anyone's comfort. Why, Cee's own life had once been threatened!

"Don't you dare leave me!" Cee whispered as her sister sprinted from the pew before Cee finished putting on her kid gloves. Addie was soon lost in the exiting crowd, and Cee bit back a curse.

She was in church, after all.

She sat back down and blew her nose into a monogrammed handkerchief, wondering if she'd wind up with pneumonia for following the family's Christmas tradition in this ancient, arctic church.

Ian had adapted to family traditions remarkably well. He was a distant-enough half-cousin who had inherited the marquessate when Cee's father died. There was nothing wrong with him per se. Papa had liked him and thought him a worthy successor. Mama liked him. Addie liked him. Even Addie's terrier, Fitz, liked him, but that meant nothing—the dog liked anyone who had the potential to provide a rasher of streaky bacon or a pair of good leather shoes to chew on.

Everyone Cee knew liked Ian. And deep down, she did, too. He'd been invaluable recently, standing up for them all in the face of family scandal when he could have shrugged and walked away.

But Cee didn't want to be *pushed*. And right now, she felt poked on all sides, even if she was last person to leave the church. The match was practically predestined, and, as her sister said, very suitable indeed. Cee would return to the house she grew up in, have a lovely batch of fair-haired children, and lead local society, just as her mother had.

Where was the excitement in *that*?

"Good morning, Cecilia. Happy Christmas."

Cee turned, and there was Ian, looking straight out of an Arrow Shirt advertisement, golden curls, blue eyes, square jaw. Any girl's dream, really.

She rose. "Hullo." She sounded surly even to herself.

"Your mother and sister are stopping at the Vincents on the way home with a basket and asked me to take you back."

No wonder Addie was in such a rush, the fiend.

"They invited me to breakfast, too. I hope that's all right." He touched her elbow, guiding her down the slate aisle.

Just as he'd do when they were married.

"Why wouldn't it be?" Cee snapped. "One has to eat."

Ian greeted the still-lingering vicar and shook his hand. Cee followed suit.

"My lord, Lady Cecilia, it warms my old heart to see you two young people in church together. You make a handsome couple."

"We're not a couple!" Cee and Ian spoke at the exact same time, Ian quite forcefully, it should be noted.

The vicar's fluffy, white brows knit. "You're not? I was under the impression—oh, well, never mind. At my advanced age, I get muddled, or so my wife is only too pleased to tell me at every opportunity. She's always after me to close the cupboard doors or turn off the hob. You'll know who to blame when I turn up with a black eye or the rectory burns down, ha ha ha. Go on home and enjoy some figgy pudding. Separately, of course."

They walked down the gravel path through the lych-gate. "You didn't drive?" Cee asked with some regret, since her pretty new strapped shoes pinched a little.

"No. I walked over from Broughton Park. It's a glorious day, isn't it? Look at the color of the sky! I've never seen such a blue."

With her luck, if Cee looked up to admire the allegedly perfect firmament, she might slip on a patch of ice. So she minded her steps, reluctantly holding onto Ian's arm. He was very quiet. Too quiet. Cee was tempted to chatter with nerves, but she held her tongue. The silence became almost…comfortable.

They took the shortcut, a hedgerowed lane that eventually led to Broughton Park's back fields. Cee had been this way hundreds of times, but could still admire the jewel-like berries in the frost-tipped bushes.

"You're right. It is a lovely day," she said. "Chilly, though." My word, she was discussing the *weather*. Ian would think she was a flat tire.

"Yes. I wonder if I'll miss the cold."

"I beg your pardon?"

"Don't you know? I'm off to Australia at the first of the year. It's high summer there. My friend Matthew and his sister Abigail manage a sheep station in Queensland. I hope to pick up a few tips for my Cotswold flock, but I should be back before spring planting."

Cee had briefly toyed with vegetarianism last year, but she

did like a good lamb chop with mint sauce. She couldn't imagine personally shearing—or worse, butchering—a living creature, however. "A woman sheep farmer?"

"Oh, Abby's a great girl. You'd like her." Ian sounded far too enthusiastic.

"I suppose she's some Amazon."

"Oh, no. She's about your height. Pretty as a picture and smart as a whip, too."

What rot. They emerged from the tunnel of trees to the fenced open field. Cee allowed Ian to help her over the stile and stayed a little too long in his arms. She looked up into his smiling face. His eyes were as blue as the sky above.

"You won't forget me while you're out there, will you?"

His smile vanished. "No. I could never forget you. Wouldn't want to."

"You'd better not," Cee said. She lifted her chin, which had frequently been called stubborn. "I haven't any mistletoe handy, but I would not be averse to a kiss before we get home. To…to celebrate the season. It's Christmas, you know. Of course you know. We've just been to Christmas service. There was a creche and everything. Carols." Goodness, she was a babbling idiot.

"Really? You're quite sure?"

"Quite." Cee closed her eyes and waited.

His gloved hands cupped her face, his lips brushed hers. He was far too gentle—she wasn't a glass ornament to be hung high on the Christmas tree to prevent breakage. Cee rectified the situation by tugging down on the velvet collar of his Chesterfield coat and was well-rewarded. Her toes curled inside her new shoes and she shivered under her fur coat.

Who knew Ian was such a capable kisser? More than capable. If he continued in this extremely satisfactory manner much longer, they'd be late for breakfast.

Kippers be damned.

He broke the kiss too soon and dropped down on one knee. "Cee, will you—"

"Yes. Yes, I will. Get up, please. You'll ruin your trousers in the mud and snow."

Sighing with relief, Ian obliged and held her close. "You are the very best Christmas present a man could ask for. An angel."

Cee was very sure that wasn't true, but she'd much rather kiss him again than confess to her many faults. He'd find out soon enough. June didn't leave much time for her to turn *completely* angelic, but she'd give it a try. Miracles happened at other times of the year besides Christmas, didn't they?

EPILOGUE NUMBER THREE: ADDIE

Boxing Day, 1925
The Dower House grounds, Broughton Park,
Broughton Magna, Gloucestershire

Cee and Mama had gone to Broughton Park for lunch, probably to measure for new drapes afterward. Her sister was positively giddy with the Broughton betrothal ring sparkling on her finger, and Mama was not far behind. To have her younger daughter accede to her dearest wish had nearly erased the heartache the family had gone through this year, and even Addie's spirits raised a notch.

She had been invited to join them, but declined. Fitz was not feeling well, the result of eating an entire plum pudding yesterday that her mother's cook carelessly left too close to the edge of the pine kitchen table. At least it had not been flaming.

So, Addie was walking him—or he was walking her—dragging, actually—in hopes that his constitution would soon return to normal. She let him off his lead before he pulled her arm out of its socket, and he tore off down the disused driveway to the Dower House. The dog didn't mind the potholes and icy, uneven surfaces, but Addie had no intention of breaking an ankle for the new year, so she minced along like an elderly dowager.

Not that she had any special plans for 1926—tomorrow she would go back to Compton Chase and resume her life of good works, reading the occasional mystery novel, and running Rupert's estate the best way she knew how.

A perfectly unexceptional life.

No dead bodies, thank God.

But no detectives, either.

Addie sat on the dry-stone wall to catch her breath, grateful for the heavy tweed of her trousers. Mama did not approve of such attire, but her mother's dictates had lost some of their ferocity after she spent a week in gaol. Each of the Merrill women were forging new lives, and things would never be the same.

It was a crisp, cold day, the sky bright, the sun making every effort to pretend it was not December 26. To her left, the crenellated roof of Broughton Park was visible through the leafless trees. She really was delighted that Cee would be its mistress. Addie had a happy childhood there, and so would her sister's progeny. With luck, she'd soon be an aunt, and she'd spoil the next generation rotten with the utmost pleasure.

Fitz bounded back with a stick in his mouth, looking hopeful. She knew he didn't play fair; once she tossed it, he would not bring it back for love or money. But Addie obliged him, and he raced off barking happily. He took it into the privacy of the tall brown grass where he could gnaw it in peace, and Addie prayed he wouldn't swallow too much of it. Splinters could not possibly be beneficial to his impaired digestive system.

She lifted her face to the sun, wondering if she should take a break from the winter in a tropical climate. With a smile, she recalled she'd sent her imaginary friend Lady Grimes on a Caribbean cruise some months ago, never to return. Perhaps

Addie should join her to indulge in rum punches and rambling walks along the beach, warm pink sand between her toes.

She'd come back, though. People depended on her.

Addie heard the rumble of the engine before she saw the car, and hopped down from the wall. A Morris was coming up slowly from the auxiliary gate, bumping along the ruts. No one who knew better used this entry to the Dower House in the winter, so it must be a stranger.

No. She knew that Morris.

Fitz abandoned his stick and ran yapping towards the car, and for one terrible moment Addie thought he'd be run over. The driver stopped in plenty of time. Fitz jumped against the car door, wiggling with excitement.

He knew that Morris, too.

Dev. No, Inspector Hunter. Formality must be observed. They had parted as friends, but it had been final.

Why was he here?

He climbed out of the car, thinner than she remembered, and a bit careworn. He wasn't wearing one of his usual sharply creased suits, but a thick gray jumper and loose corduroys. His windblown dark hair showed a few strands of silver glinting in the sun.

It had only been six months, but he had changed. Had she?

Addie tucked a curl under her silk scarf and started walking. Her brogues crunched against the frozen grass, sounding to her like the crack of a gunshot with every step.

At least no one was shooting at them today, which made for a refreshing change.

"Hello, Lady Adelaide." He smiled, and she stumbled over a rock. She had missed that smile quite dreadfully.

He was at her side in an instant. "I didn't mean to startle you."

"I'm—I'm just surprised," she said when she found her voice. "What are you doing here?"

"I called at Compton Chase first. Beckett told me where you were. I take it she and Jack are getting married."

Addie nodded. "Yes. It's been an eventful Christmas. Cee is marrying Ian when he gets back from Australia, too. Romance is in the air."

He looked down at her, his dark eyes assessing. "I do hope so."

She tried to be playful. "Are you marrying someone, too?"

Was that why he was here, to break it to her gently that he'd found a suitable young woman? Addie really didn't want to hear anything remotely like that. It wasn't any of her business anyhow.

"Not yet, but a man can dream. You know I've left Scotland Yard?"

No, she knew nothing, had wanted to know nothing about his exploits at all, refusing to read the newspapers in the event his name turned up. Once her mother's case was closed—and his part in it—she'd taken a pledge to ignore current criminal events completely. Ignorance might not be bliss, but it suited her.

"I turned down your mother's reward money, but she is a devious woman, you know. She pulled some strings for me to sit for the entrance exam at Oxford. And then she arranged for a scholarship when I showed some promise. I couldn't say no to that. It's a dream come true."

"You're in *school*?" Addie was stunned. Her mother had said absolutely nothing about any of this.

"Oldest student on campus. A veritable graybeard. The boys are afraid to tease me too much, though—they all know I used to be a copper. I've even befriended some Indian princelings who've been sent over to study. You should see me in my robe cycling through town. It's good exercise, but I'll never win any races." He grinned. "A bad shoulder, and creaky old knees."

"Wh-what are you reading?"

"Philosophy and religion. Fancy being a vicar's wife?"

Addie's mouth flew open and stayed that way.

Mr. Hunter laughed. "No, no. Don't worry. That's not a proper proposal, and I'm leaning more towards teaching one day anyway. That's a few years off even if I burn all the midnight oil there is, and I'd never expect you to wait until I got my degree."

"I would," Addie said, trembling and not from the cold.

He stood very, very still for the longest time, then took some steps so she could count every eyelash. "Do you mean it? Don't be hasty. You know I can't give you the life you have, Addie."

"Maybe I don't want the life I have."

He took her mittened hands in his. "I tried to be honorable. To stay away. To forget you. It didn't work." He gave her a rueful smile.

Fitz was between them, looking interested. Mr. Hunter— Dev—was always good for a bit of fun or a smidgeon of crust, but nothing was forthcoming. Giving up, the terrier trotted away after his stick, and Addie moved even closer and rested her head on Dev's shoulder.

"I tried, too. It didn't work for me, either."

Dev cleared his throat. "I write to your mother regularly to keep her up to date on her investment. She's not supporting me financially—I tutor and tend bar and have some savings, so I can keep body and soul together, just. She didn't discourage me from approaching you, although I don't think she entirely approves."

"I don't care."

He set her back a little so she could see his face. "You might. Apart from being a poor schoolmaster's wife, there is the fact that our backgrounds are…different. You have seen firsthand what racial prejudice does. Will my love be enough? I do love you, you know."

The magic words. She hadn't heard them in a very long time. "More than enough. Do you suppose you could kiss me again so I can be sure? It was only that one time last April, and I've forgotten," she lied.

"I haven't." And he did as she asked.

Up above on his apricot-infused cloud, Rupert looked down like an indulgent uncle. He was now right where he supposed to be. Finally. He'd pulled a few strings, too, a whisper here, an encouraging word there, late at night when hearts were listening.

It wouldn't be much of a heaven if he was forced to see all the strife on earth, but his brief foggy glimpse into the future revealed it wouldn't be all cakes and ale for either of them, but they'd persevere. And drat, Addie was going to make an investment of her own and sell Compton Chase—and all his beautiful cars—to his bloody second cousin Alfie, who was entirely undeserving of the honor. The man couldn't figure out how a toaster worked without burning the bread. What was he going to do with real machines?

Well, probably not crash into a Cotswold stone wall, so perhaps Alfie did have an advantage. After that Fernald business, the Rolls was a lost cause anyway, so it was only six cars for the fool to tootle around in, slavishly following the speed limit. Alfie never took a risk greater than putting an extra dollop of jam on his muffins, which usually dripped in an awkward spot onto his plus fours. The man was a constant challenge to his valet, and rotten at golf to boot.

Rupert squinted ahead, seeing a newly established progressive school down a long Cotswold country lane, with expansive playing fields, modern dormitories, and a comfortable headmaster's house full of spotted students coming and going. These boys and girls had not been born with silver spoons or forks or any sort of shiny implement. Rather, they had potential and a thirst for knowledge, and were sponsored by a network of charities established by their headmaster's wife.

Being intelligent, most of them were half in love with Addie or Dev, and then fully besotted with their daughter, Amara, who arrived so late that her parents had given up any expectations. The child would grow up to be a singular beauty, and make her Auntie Maeve proud when she starred in a spate of Hollywood-produced Biblical epics in the fifties.

The screenwriters would get the Fellow Upstairs all wrong of course, but that's as it should be. Life and the Afterlife were supposed to be mysteries, worth much more than the price of a cinema ticket.

THE END

READ ON FOR AN EXCERPT FROM

NOBODY'S SWEETHEART NOW,
THE FIRST LADY ADELAIDE MYSTERY

Chapter One

Compton Chase, Compton-Under-Wood,
Gloucestershire, a Saturday in late August 1924

Once upon a time, Lady Adelaide Mary Merrill, daughter of the Marquess of Broughton, was married to Major Rupert Charles Cressleigh Compton, hero of the Somme. It was not a happy union, and there was no one in Britain more relieved than Addie when Rupert smashed up his Hispano-Suiza on a quiet Cotswold country road with Mademoiselle Claudette Labelle in the passenger seat. If one could scream with a French accent, it was Claudette, and it was said her terrified shrieks as they hit the stone wall were still heard on occasion by superstitious farmers and their livestock near midnight when the moon was full.

Addie was just getting used to her widowhood when Rupert inconveniently turned up six months after she had him sealed in the Compton family vault in the village churchyard. The unentailed house was hers to do as she pleased, and she had decided to open it up to her family and a few convivial friends for the weekend now that she'd made some much-needed improvements. Rupert had always been stingy with her money, and with him gone on to his doubtful reward, she had employed most of the district's laborers in an attempt to bring Compton Chase into the twentieth century.

True, it was early in her mourning period to entertain, but she made the concession to wear black, even if there wasn't much of it in yardage, thank God, because it was so bloody hot. And her mother was there to chaperone.

When Rupert appeared, Addie was dressing for her house party, and dropped the diamond spray for her hair on the Aubusson.

"That dress is ridiculous, Addie," Rupert intoned from a dim corner. He was wearing the dark suit with the maroon foulard tie she'd had him laid out in, and apart from being rather pale, was still a handsome devil, emphasis on the devil. If he'd been in his uniform, she might even contemplate marrying him again.

Oh, she was going mad. Too much stressing over the seating arrangements in the dining room. Who was billeted next to who. Or was it whom? She'd tried to make it easy for those who wished to be naughty tonight to be successful. Then there was the bother over her sister turning vegetarian and ruining the menus at the last minute. Cook was cross and was apt to get crosser.

Addie was already sitting at her vanity table so she didn't collapse alongside the diamonds. She shut her eyes.

"I'll be here when you open them. And believe me, it's no picnic for me, either."

Addie did open them, and her mouth, but found herself incapable of uttering anything sensible.

"Yes, I'm back. But, one hopes, not to stay. Apparently, I have to perform a few good deeds before the Fellow Upstairs will let me into heaven. It will be a frightful bore for you, I'm sure."

She told the truth as she knew it, feeling absurd to even speak to someone who couldn't possibly be there. "You're *dead*."

"As a doornail. What does that mean, anyway? The expression dates from the fourteenth century. Langland, Shakespeare, and Dickens all used it. Dickens was of the opinion that a coffin nail is deader, but there you are."

Addie reached for her cup of cold tea and downed it in one gulp, wishing it was gin, brandy, anything to make Rupert go away. But if she were drunk, more Ruperts, like those fabled pink elephants, might actually appear. It was a conundrum.

"I'll try to stay out of your hair as much as possible. Speaking of which, thank God you haven't cut it into one of those awful shingles. I always did like your hair."

Addie's hand went up involuntarily to the golden roll she'd so recently pinned up without her maid's assistance. Beckett was seeing to Addie's impulsive sister Cecilia, who, apart from her sudden conversion to vegetarianism, *had* cut her hair into a bob that was more or less untamable because of the stubborn Merrill curls. Beckett had her work cut out for her. Cee resembled someone who had stuck their finger in the newly rewired sockets of Compton Chase and lived to tell the tale.

"What's wrong with my dress?" Addie asked, peeved. Though she knew he wasn't truly there—that he was *dead*—he still had the ability to irritate her, even in her imagination.

"It's far too flimsy and sheer and short. I can practically see your nipples if I squint hard enough. I admit you do have lovely legs, but everyone and his brother doesn't have to see them. Your father would not be pleased."

"My father is dead." Panicked, she looked around her bedroom. "My God, he's not going to turn up too, is he?"

"Only one ghost at a time, I believe. I'm still not entirely conversant with the rules. It's been a confusing few months."

"It's the very latest style," Addie said to herself—and *only* to herself—tugging down the beaded skirt. It really could have been much shorter. She'd had it sent over from Paris after a flurry of letters and telegrams back and forth from Charles Frederick Worth's grandson Jacques, who had recently taken over the famous fashion house. Addie had sketched the initial design herself, not that she had any pretensions to become a couturier. A marquess's daughter was supposed to be decorative, and possibly witty and wise, but never *work*.

"I don't like it, but then so little appeals to me nowadays. *Ennui* is my middle name, but I hope this little visit changes things up. Who have you put in my room? That bounder Waring?"

"I understand it takes one to know one. Lucas is not a bounder, as *you* must know. Why am I talking? You are not here."

Lucas was, in fact, assigned a bedroom across the hall. Addie didn't trust a mere connecting door to stay shut all night long, and in her well-run household, servants were apt to be scurrying down the corridor at any moment at a guest's whim, discouraging all attempts of Addie's to be naughty herself. She was not ready to be a merry widow anyway, despite Lucas' tentative blandishments. Rupert wasn't cold in his grave.

Apparently, Rupert wasn't *in* his grave.

Rupert smiled ruefully. Could an apparition be rueful? Or was Addie really unconscious, perhaps on her deathbed, suffering from heat stroke or a regular stroke or some kind of tea-induced hallucination? Cook could easily have put poisonous leaves in the pot in retaliation for the menu adjustments. She was set in her ways, and had been at Compton Chase since the dawn of time.

Addie had only just turned thirty-one, much too young to die in the usual course of things. However, the past few months had been more than difficult for her too, even apart from Rupert's death.

"I admit I bounded in my time. Poor Addie. I wasn't much of a husband, was I?"

"Please go away. I haven't time for this." In ten minutes, there would be a dozen houseguests downstairs in the Great Hall admiring its two-story, multi-paned window and having cocktails without her, and Lord knows, she needed one. Or three. She bent over, picked up the pin and stuck it behind an ear.

"Tut. Let me help you with that." Before she could say a word, she felt his hands in her hair. Cold hands. Really quite icy. He moved the diamonds over a few inches, and she began to see spots dance the tarantella before her eyes.

Good. She was going to faint and stop all this. Addie knew how to faint like a champion—her mother, the Dowager Marchioness of Broughton, a short but formidable woman, had indoctrinated both her daughters in all the ladylike accomplishments. She slid with ease off her slipper chair to the thick carpet and waited to black out, knowing her limbs to be in perfect order, and the hem of her dress where it should be, not riding up to show Rupert her French silk knickers.

Not that he'd care.

"Dash it, Addie! You have more spine than this! I recognize the situation is hardly ideal, but you're stuck with me for the foreseeable future, so buck up, my girl. I'll leave you alone for now, but look for me before bedtime for a little chat. No finky-diddling with that Waring chap, no matter how much he bats those baby-blues in your direction. I know what he's up to—you're a rich and attractive widow, ripe for the fuc—um, plucking. Don't fall for his innocent act."

"I've known Lucas since I was six years old. He *is* innocent," Addie said from the floor. You couldn't find a nicer man than Lucas, not that she'd tried. No, she'd allowed herself to be lured away by Major Rupert Charles Cressleigh Compton of Compton Chase, an ancient Jacobean pile in dire need of restoration. The house, not Rupert. Rupert had been unbearably handsome and fit and had shone with good health and bonhomie. If he could live through the horrors of the Great War, he should have lived forever, were it not for too many French 75 cocktails, unnecessary speed, and that Cotswold stone wall.

"That's what he wants you to believe. All men are the same, perfect hounds."

"You're giving dogs a bad name." Idly, she wondered where her terrier Fitz was. Would he be able to see Rupert, or would he be barking at the shadows? Fitz had never met Rupert; he was Cee's crackpot idea of a mourning present and arrived with a big black bow around his scrawny neck a week after the funeral. The fleas in her bed had been an unforeseen complication.

Fitz's neck was thicker now, the fleas a distant memory. Addie supposed that since she had no children, the dog was the next best thing to distract her from her lonely state.

She wasn't lonely now. There were far too many people in her house for comfort, starting with the man who was disappearing right in front of her. Going, going...

Absolutely gone.

She swallowed back a little cry and struggled to sit up, the room still spinning a bit. That afternoon nap hadn't helped. It had been a long day, perhaps way too hot to play tennis. Far too much sun had roasted her cheeks and brought out her freckles. She was rubbish at tennis anyhow, being too vain to wear the glasses Dr. Bergman had prescribed before he retired two years ago. Maybe if she put those glasses on—

Addie leaped up and rummaged through the dressing table drawer. Wrapped in an embroidered lace handkerchief, the dratted tortoise shell spectacles were still as ugly as ever. But they would help her see clearly, wouldn't they? To *not* see things or dead husbands that really weren't there. The mirror came into focus and she noticed at once that the diamond pin was dangling from a strand of loosened hair. She'd have to start again, this time with no assistance from the man who'd made their five-year marriage a living hell.

Ha. So he thought he'd eventually wind up in heaven? It would take more than "a few good deeds" to send him to the front of the queue. If he hadn't died six months ago, Addie might have been tempted to shoot him herself. Her father had done his bit and taught her and Cecilia all the *un*ladylike accomplishments, and when she wore her glasses, she was a very fair shot.

Addie had been vastly tired of the faux sympathy she received from her so-called friends as she tried to hold her head up and pretend Rupert was a faithful husband. Despite the potential scandal, the exhortations of her mother, and reservations of her sister, she'd been close to demanding a divorce from Rupert when he'd skidded off the slippery road with that French wh—hussy.

She pulled out all the pins with a certain amount of viciousness, her hair tumbling down her bare shoulders and catching on the jet and sequins and cobwebby lace. Picking up the silver-backed brush, she tried to smooth the curls and her life back into some semblance of control.

By God, she was going to need something more than a hairbrush.

ABOUT THE AUTHOR

Maggie Robinson is a former teacher, library clerk, and mother of four who woke up in the middle of the night absolutely compelled to create the perfect man and use as many adjectives and adverbs as possible doing so. A transplanted New Yorker, she lives with her not-quite-perfect husband in Maine, where the cold winters are ideal for staying indoors and writing.